LOVE NOTES

"Good morning," she whispered as the CD went into the next slower cut.

"Don't stop dancing," he murmured. "You're a work of art in motion."

She appraised the new dimension of his damp shorts and walked over to the CD player with a smile, and backed up the music to "Put Your Lights On." She then proceeded to show him the way she felt through slow, aching dance movements just beyond his reach.

Her father had been right—people talked too much and didn't listen. But she was sure from the way her husband swallowed hard as she lost her negligee to the middle of the floor as she danced that he heard her loud and clear. "La la la la . . ." Her voice blended with the music, the words meant nothing and everything, and his eyes said it all. As the next cut brought a fast flurry of Spanish words she didn't understand, she allowed her body to interpret them for him, giving him the naked truth of how she felt about him.

BOOK YOUR PLACE ON OUR WEBSITE AND MAKE THE ARABESQUE ROMANCE CONNECTION!

We've created a customized website just for our very special Arabesque readers, where you can get the inside scoop on everything that's going on with Arabesque romance novels.

When you come online, you'll have the exciting opportunity to:

- View covers of upcoming books

- Learn about our future publishing schedule (listed by publication month and author)

- Find out when your favorite authors will be visiting a city near you

- Search for and order backlist books

- Check out author bios and background information

- Send e-mail to your favorite authors

- Join us in weekly chats with authors, readers and other guests

- Get writing guidelines

- AND MUCH MORE!

Visit our website at
http://www.arabesquebooks.com

LOVE NOTES

Leslie Esdaile

BET Publications, LLC
www.bet.com
www.arabesquebooks.com

ARABESQUE BOOKS are published by

BET Publications, LLC
c/o BET BOOKS
One BET Plaza
1900 W Place NE
Washington, D.C. 20018-1211

All Kensington Titles, Imprints, and Distributed Lines are available at special quantity discounts for bulk purchases for sales promotions, premiums, fund raising, and educational or institutional use. Special book excerpts or customized printings can also be created to fit specific needs. For details, write or phone the office of the Kensington special sales manager: Kensington Publishing Corp., 850 Third Avenue, New York, NY 10022, attn: Special Sales Department, Phone: 1-800-221-2647

First Printing: February 2001

10 9 8 7 6 5 4 3 2 1
Printed in the United States of America

Some say love is the sweetest music . . . it hosts complex chords and melodies that range from the heights of ecstasy to the blues. Wide variances of sharps and flats and whole notes and half notes climb and fall down scales and octaves, often clashing, yet coming together to form a pattern amid the chaos. Perhaps that's why music is said to be the universal language, just as love is a universal language that binds all ages, races, and genders in a unique, interpretive human experience. And . . . jazz . . . the highly complex, original American music language, can be chaotic, smooth, undefined, with unparalleled definition, in its ageless format as it seeps into your bones—like love.

This book is dedicated to my family and friends, who understand that I often march to a different drummer, and have stood fast by me through my highs and lows, my sharps and flats, and discordant moments . . . always knowing that there was ultimately a melody of good intent and love to my song. Thank you for adding your percussion, horns, bass notes, and vocal scats to this highly complicated work in progress called life . . . and for loving me as we compose.

Special thanks go out to Karen Thomas, my editor, who had enough faith in me to take the risk on allowing me to try my hand at this again, and to Donna Hill, my fellow sister-writer, and Constance O'Day-Flannery, the Thelma to my Louise, who forced me to do a "comeback album"!

One

Nina Carpenter allowed her hands to work in broad, loose strokes as she focused her line of vision on the single-cell droplets of water that created tears against her in-home studio window. She loved April, especially early mornings in April. It was a time when the earth seemed to renew itself, but had to cry a river of tears before it could.

She understood that part of changing seasons all too well. They followed the patterns of life. Tears were always a part of major change. She'd been a witness to the rhythms of the cosmos. Indeed, she'd lived through her first awakenings in the mature, second spring of her youth, falling in and out of love while in college, and experiencing a deeper planting of commitment after graduate school—when she met Anthony Williams. It seemed then, she thought, putting down her pad and wiping the charcoal from her hands while she sat still to simply observe the rain, that summer would be eternal, and a season of harvest would grow from all they'd planted. But it never did.

She let the tears fall from her eyes in easy unison with the droplets that coursed down the window. Adjusting her legs beneath her on the window seat, she considered the differences between herself and her husband. She was light strokes . . . lean, airy shades of complex grays. He had always seemed to be thicker, intense strokes of black with few muted shades. Oddly, they had once also been the perfect complement to each other on this canvas they called a marriage.

She was tall and angular with light brown hair that matched her eyes and café-au-lait skin which she waxed religiously to ensure no hint of body hair befell it. He was a tall, muscular, richly hued, semisweet dark chocolate, with ebony eyes and a well-groomed beard. She'd always liked deeply intellectual men; he was a stark realist who shunned hypothetical discussions. She was a quiet Cancer, born in the summer, which accounted for her need to have a shell, her home, as a sanctuary during the high tides of life. She retreated into her home to find personal space.

Conversely, he was a gregarious Leo, also born in the summer, where his home was his castle too, but he needed exterior space in order to feel balanced enough to rule what seemed to be his empire. Initially, that was a complementary difference.

Anthony was what one could call self-made, and not formally educated, but had become fairly wealthy through the establishment and operation of his club, The Jazz Note. He was an entrepreneur. She was a professor, now . . . and had been a true artist once. His long nights at the club had initially fit her dawn-driven lifestyle, where she needed the prisms of light and aloneness to create. And, not unlike jazz, their conversations once had a syncopated rhythm of idealist thought posing sharps and flats to philosophical realism that always ended on a high note in bed. . . .

A new stream of tears overflowed as she thought of those good times of fall harvest, where love had been bundled and stored in the house they'd selected together.

The brownstone in Queens Village, where her paintings hung and art gathered from their courtship travels, had set the stage for his extensive collection of music. It was too empty now. There had been so much anticipation in the planting . . . a five-year, easy romance, a nonconventional wedding with self-created vows, and a synchronicity of body rhythms, timing, and fulfillment of mutual needs. Their home had once contained a palpable vibration—of their lovemaking, of their laughter, of their plans and discussions and dreams. But there was a critical sound that was missing. The cry of new life never filled the air, nor gave them a reason to come together for something greater than themselves.

Upon her mother's advice, Nina had finally agreed to take a job with the university to plan for the future, for winter. Anthony got wrapped up in expansion plans for the club, and they began passing like ships in the night.

Ironically, she mused, standing to stretch and to move the pain out of her soul, both families, as diametrically opposed to each other as they had been, had warned of their differences. His brother used to tease him about being with a citified, educated woman with petite breasts—unlike the options available to them at The Jazz Note. In fact, all his siblings had said what his religious parents declined to comment on. But his mother was the one who'd made the key observation that Nina was an only child, and her mother had had her late, which meant that Nina might not be able to have any babies of her own—if they allowed time to press on. Everything had its season, his mother had wisely said. By now, Nina was thirty-nine and Anthony was forty-one.

But her family had been no less judgmental. Her parents had practically gagged in disgust when they found out that Anthony Williams didn't have a degree, and that his parents had no lineage of note, and—worst of all according to their value system—he was running what they considered to be a bar. Nina chuckled sadly. Her mother had taken the news so hard that her father had almost run into the kitchen to get a spoon for the woman's tongue before she convulsed to death when Nina and Anthony had announced their engagement.

Unfortunately, the season of harvest had only brought them material things, while pushing them further apart spiritually, Nina noted.

Anthony worked at night; she worked during the day. He focused on money. She focused on developing the dreams and artistic discipline of her students. He paid for a woman to come in and clean, since no concessions on either side could be made. He ate when he got to the club. She fixed light meals for herself, which she ate alone, at home, in her third-floor studio. She'd refused to take his last name because she was an artist already known by her maiden name. He'd refused to accept her reasons, but ultimately had to let it rest. It was a discordant melody, but one with pauses and rests in places that kept the song from fracturing. It, too, was a form of jazz. However, it was not smooth, relaxing jazz any longer.

Her two-year marriage was in the deadliest winter she could have ever imagined. She needed a spring rain to thaw the earth and to open its arms and to push up vibrant new colors from the barren earth. . . . Perhaps that's why she'd returned to charcoal sketches. She couldn't see the colors in her mind anymore.

Nor could she feel the rhythms. It was something she had always taken for granted . . . their rhythms of speech, of intimate dialogue and pacing. They were out of sync. Nina moved to the chaise lounge and picked up her herbal tea from the low coffee table. Colors were to be felt, she mused, like music. Each had a distinctive vibration, a timbre and tone. They were not seen or heard, but felt. And that melodic consistency translated into touch, which too had a sound that was to be felt.

She closed her eyes as she allowed a lukewarm sip of honeyed tea to slide over her tongue, and she focused on the sweetness in her mouth before setting down her cup again on the side table. Her light silk lavender nightgown gently caressed her skin, and she became aware of the soft texture that brushed her nipples each time her chest rose and fell as she breathed. It had been four months, and she wondered if he'd even noticed.

He seemed too nonchalant, so cool about it all. He even refused to argue these days. At least that would have gotten everything out in the open, once and for all. She had adored his discipline about things, but had come to hate the seeming self-control he exerted. It was a crock of machismo ethics. A man thing, she supposed.

Nina slowed her breathing and tried to mentally sweep away the mounting feelings of desire mixed with anger and sadness. That was a lethal combination that had given rise to too many fights, she knew—to want him, and to be angry and hurt all at the same time. But she allowed her mind to delve into the question she needed answered most, the one that their physical hiatus had created. Did he need to touch himself as often as she did, to relieve the burning ache, just to make it through a day? It was a dangerous question, one almost too perilous to say aloud, because either response could create a permanent marital divide.

If she asked and he said yes, then why would he choose that option over compromise? It led to one answer. Pride. If he said no, then there were two unacceptable conclusions—either he no longer desired her or he had other alternatives. That's why she would not be weak this morning. She refused to be left wanting a person who didn't want her, who had betrayed her trust, or perhaps worse, was too stubborn to work out a compromise of their differences.

Again, she focused on her breathing. She could kill off

this feeling that tortured her if she could just keep the anger and sense of indignation mentally in front of her.

But, ironically, moisture began to collect in the swollen memory of his touch, and again she tried to sweep away those thoughts to meditate on calmness. This morning, she would not give in to the need to love her body alone. She wanted more—despite the fact that he'd not come home. She had to be stronger than this! How could she feel such desire for a man who'd been God knows where? It was shameful. She mentally chided herself, but her body argued in defiance.

It reminded her of the first few weeks of her celibacy, and how the change in household rhythms had nearly driven her out of her mind. However she debated within her mind, there were a lot of verbal fights. But her body continued to remind her about each night when she had slid into bed alone and wrapped her body in the deep warmth of it, smelling his scent, creating an ache that could only be relieved by her own touch. And what of the oppressive days that contained missed household responsibilities, the ones that were supposed to be mutual, and what about the promises? She asked her body hard questions, too, becoming peeved at the concept that she had to have sex.

She could resist the need to quell her thirst for touch this morning, if she thought about it all in context. Yes, what about the times when he said he'd come home for dinner, then gone back to the club, but would forget to even call? Or what about when he had promised to turn the evening over to his brother Cecil, then reneged? And how could one forget spending every holiday at the club . . . never having the time to get away like they once had, or even being able to share a companionable meal these days? There was even a time when they would cook together, laughing and playing in the kitchen at all hours of the night.

True . . . her body crooned back easily, trying to seduce her while dampening her ire. *And, what about the days when you couldn't get his touch out of your mind, and even rushed home from work to relieve the pain yourself* . . . *then stubbornly ignored what you both probably needed—by turning your back on him and refusing his attempts at an apology? And, what about after the first month,* her body softly whispered in discontent, *when your pillows became him and you satisfied me with fantasy? And, after the second month, when he'd spoon you in your sleep, and you'd dream about what you wanted him to do, waking up to your own gasps and movements, but refusing him haven out of spite? Or, after the third month, when you began taking long baths to soothe the part of you that was burning for him, lovingly touching me, alone, by wine and candlelight in the tub, while he was gone? Don't you wish he were here? So now, here we are,* her body sadly chuckled, *you have driven him from your bed, but not from my memory* . . . *and, there's a price for such petty indulgence.*

Gooseflesh rose and pebbled her arms as she railed against herself in vain, and the swollen, moist part of her began to throb in unison with her body's argument. She took in a deep, cleansing breath, but it had the effect of sending wisps of silk fabric from her nightgown across her nipples, drawing a shudder of want. Her hands cupped her breasts to stop the insistent stinging, and a reflexive murmur escaped her lips, forcing her to squeeze her thighs together hard. She would not be weak this morning, she told herself, even though her thighs had begun to press and release in a rhythmic pulse that quickened her breathing.

She lay there for what felt like a long time, her eyes closed, her fingertips gently caressing the distended pebbles at the ends of her breasts, while her body slightly rocked against the ever-dampening source of her pain. "Four months," she whispered, tears brimming and falling from the corners of her eyes as her hand slid down

to her belly, trembling where it rested. She was so
weak . . . why couldn't she just ignore this part of her
like other women did? Immediate warmth echoed back
into her palm, sending it down further to hunt for a
deeper core of heat. Finding it, her thighs parted of their
own volition—her fingers gently opening the angry, wet
folds that had begun the argument in earnest, moving
frenetically to a staccato beat now matched by her shallow
breaths . . . until there was rest. There was indeed a
price.

Anthony Williams loved his wife, but hated his marriage. He felt trapped, and he paced behind the bar,
counting liquor cases as he cleared his mind. It was simply
easier to spend the night in his office on the sofa than
to go home and launch a battle of wills at four o'clock
in the morning. It was also easier to sleep alone than to
wrap his arms around a luscious body that refused him
entry.

Hell, he couldn't even look at his wife anymore . . .
her soft skin; long, lean form; and hazel doe eyes wreaked
havoc with his concentration. It had been so long since
her full mouth had turned itself up to his for a kiss, or
even offered a smile. Just the sound of her light coos as
she slept, or the movements of her body, sent tremors of
desire through him that he knew would again go unanswered.

First, he'd begun turning his back to her as they'd
slept, he remembered, in an attempt to be strong against
the siren in his head nagging him to beg her. But after
four months, even that no longer worked. Just the way
she smelled . . . each night he'd slip into bed next to her
and feel her against him as her velvet rings of auburn
hair barely dusted against his nose, but enough to allow
her scent to waft through his nostrils. Dear God, it had

become more than he could bear . . . and, as his body engorged again at the thought, he tried to shake the memory from his mind.

Although he was alone in the club, shame washed over him as he straightened his back and paced toward the washroom. What was wrong with him? Midstep, he wondered about their future, trying to stop himself as he entered the bathroom, and then a stall, unable to stop—even at his own mental command.

He was stronger than this, and no woman was going to run him out of his mind, he internally argued, loosening his trousers to begin what had become his evening ritual before going to bed—and the only mercy to this nightmare he'd found to allow him to sleep.

It was adolescent, but necessary, he rationalized . . . in the wee hours of predawn, he'd lie there next to her, feeling her soft curls brush against a part of him she no longer desired, until he was forced to slip away from her to find quiet relief. And, in the afternoon, it would be the same, and just as necessary to find sanctuary and privacy within his memories of her, alone, before he went to work and she came home. How long could he keep going like this, he wondered, before something gave?

His hands slid against the angry skin that demanded an answer, drawing the first shudder, then rapidly sealing off the indignity to his soul, moving with defined purpose, eclipsing bad times with her whispers and his moan, until the first shudder merged with the last.

Defeat claimed his spirit as he regained his breath and cleared away all evidence of his mental lapse. He had work to do, damn it!

Anthony paced back to the bar and tried to concentrate on tabulating the new shipment against inventory. Fatigue pulled at him. Months had passed since they'd talked to each other, much less made love, and with each passing evening, a newer, harder-to-resist temptation presented it-

self to him. Yet a small voice within his brain countered
against the louder, more indignant one. It told him that
he'd watched his friends' and brothers' marriages and
relationships go out like that. You didn't run a club without being an astute judge of human behavior. And what
temptation could compare to all that Nina had once
given him?

She'd floated into his club with a group of her artist
friends more than seven years ago, standing five feet nine
inches tall in a filmy, royal purple, tie-dyed sheath, he
recalled begrudgingly, moving slower at his task as he remembered her. Her laugh was deep and quiet, and her
eyes caught the shimmer of candlelight at her table, re-
flecting an odd mixture of worldly innocence that had
drawn him to her. His place had been a lucrative dive
then, and she'd come in and regally graced it with her
easy presence, never looking afraid—despite the fact that
he'd never expected a woman like her to enter his place
in a million years. He'd worked hard to get close to her,
and wound up becoming her friend, while she'd become
his best friend and his pillow-talk advisor.

Tony looked around the room and let his breath out
in a heavy sigh. She'd turned The Jazz Note into one of
the area's hottest artist havens, with her touches of class
and upscale way of doing things. He had to give his wife
her due for that. She was indeed a queen, his queen, but
he could never allow her to know what types of seedy
things went on in the underbelly of the club scene. How
could he explain to her about payoff money, and sup-
porting politicians he didn't believe in, and slipping a
little somethin' somethin' to Licenses and Inspections
hacks? Or how he had to have *extra* security to keep from
getting robbed, or to ensure that a bogus police raid
didn't occur to drive away honest customers? She was
such an idealist . . . and she believed so much in him.
How could he allow her to know that he wanted out of

what they'd built together, this nightmare of a business—especially if they had children?

Her parents had been right. It was, under all the trappings of jazz and culture and art, still a bar. It required knowing undesirables, breaking bread with them upon occasion, and it was no place for a lady—much less kids. And the time . . . he'd always envisioned being able to throw a ball with his sons, and to be there for his daughters' recitals . . . but working like a slave every evening in the place that didn't sleep, every holiday and weekend, had a price. He couldn't share this life within the standard family timetable; it did not lend itself to the way his parents had raised all the Williams kids.

Besides, where was a forty-one-year-old man going to take his career, to be able to cover their now-expensive lifestyle, and to add children to the burden, when he didn't even have a degree? It was easier when they were both struggling . . . and in love, with lusty nights to cloud perspectives and the future. Again, her parents had been right—as much as he hated their observations. But were he in their shoes, would he have said it any less plain, were it his girl-child?

That's what he could not express, and what she'd never be able to understand . . . unlike the women who sat across the bar from him, or the ones that joined his back-room table, did. They were from this environment, and they were like vampires that shunned the day and waited for nightfall. He wondered how long it would be until one bit him, and he transformed himself—never able to come into Nina's light. That had always been his biggest fear.

Two

Nina twirled the end of a stray curl around her finger as she talked on the telephone. Somehow, explaining the details of her life with her best friend Vonetta always seemed to help her regain balance. It was a special brand of phone therapy, developed over the years, where confidences were strictly kept, and where laughter and self-directed, off-color humor were a significant part of the treatment.

"Gurl, I know you are lying!" Vonetta exclaimed through the receiver, almost rupturing Nina's eardrum.

Nina laughed, imagining her friend on the other end of the line. She could mentally picture Vonetta either pacing the floor with one hand on her curvaceous hip, or sitting with her shapely legs crossed, pecking her neck as she tapped an ash off the end of a Virginia Slims—using a business-length, perfectly French-manicured nail for the task. "You heard me," Nina said, chuckling sadly. "No, he did not come home last night after that last argument, and he didn't call."

"And you're arguing with me about going to the club tonight? Are you crazy!" Vonetta huffed, sounding so indignant that it made Nina shake her head in wonder.

"Now, think about it," Nina reasoned, her voice taking on the tone of psychiatric detachment. "If I go looking for him, then it just sends the signal that I'm insecure, don't trust him, and have issues."

"Well, first of all," Vonetta shot back, "you do have issues, and rightfully so. And second of all," she continued quickly, not allowing Nina to interrupt, "you're his wife. You don't have to play coy cat and mouse, like you were dating him or something. Get it in your head, you have the heavyweight championship belt called W. I. F. E., *wife*. Okaaaay? And let me tell you, if Anthony Williams were my husband, I'd blow through that joint so sharp, so fly . . . so fierce, and prop my big butt up on a bar stool in his face, with hair beat and nails done, and pull out all the stops that, if there was a challenger to my throne, she'd—"

"But, that's the point," Nina cut in. "It isn't about another woman being the threat. It's about him. I'm not in competition with other women for my man, and I shouldn't even have to deal with that. He should know where home is, and—"

"Says who? Where did you get that crock? Off a morning talk show? This is war, gurl! Do the stats yourself, since we're being clinical about this. Anthony is tall, fine, has his own business . . . and money, honey, and hasn't slept with you in four months."

Nina fell silent for a moment, her girlfriend's comments giving her serious pause. "And the core of this relationship and marriage has always been built on a foundation of trust. Without that, we have nothing. I'm not about to compete with other women, and turn my head inside out, worrying every time he's late, or says he has an errand to run, or—"

"All right, all right," Vonetta said in a weary voice, followed by the sound of her taking a long drag of her cigarette. "I can understand that. But you have to at least survey the terrain—to see if there's a potential threat to your situation, while it's in a vulnerable state. And, to remind him that if he goes there, you have options too."

"What are you talking about?" Nina was filled with confusion as she rummaged through the kitchen cabinets in search of more fresh, loose tea to fill her now diluted tea ball.

"Duh-uh," Vonetta sighed. "Look. You might be all metaphysical and reasonable right now, but his judgment may be impaired due to fights and lack of nookie, at present. I say, let's go by the club, since it's Friday night, and since you don't have to teach tomorrow. We'll have a few glasses of wine, listen to some jazz, survey the terrain, and you can harmlessly flirt with the men in the establishment that have always had their eyes on you— should the brother ever mess up. Trust me, men know when other men are appreciating their women from afar, and they send off pheromone gamma rays to one another, like, 'Yo, man, if you don't treat it right, I will,' you know what I'm saying?"

This time, Nina laughed out loud. "Vonetta Winston, you have been in the field too long as an insurance detective! I think all of that cloak-and-dagger stealth you deal with to uncover fraud on a daily basis has affected your reasoning. Girlfriend, the last thing I want to do is add any new issues to this impasse between us. Lord have mercy!"

"See, the problem with you is," Vonetta scoffed, pausing to take a drag, "that you're trying to handle an emotional situation, a hormonal situation, with academic rhetoric. I know how men function—work with them every day. Trust me, honey, there's a time to be rational and to take the observation tower approach. Then there's a time for hand-to-hand combat . . . and there's a time to nuke the bastards. Dig? I say we go in on a reconnaissance flight, do a site survey, build a tentative alliance with our agent—whose judgment may have been compro-

mised by enemy forces, then leave. It will be a demon-
strable show of force to let them all know that we, too,
have the bomb."

All Nina could do was to shake her head. Her long
pause enabled Vonetta to press her point.

"C'mon, gurl . . . what's the worst that could happen?" Vonetta argued. "If anything, you get to see that
he's alive, have a glass of wine, and listen to some jazz
while showing him that you have enough couth to be
civil in public, and are classy enough to make nice
around his brother and employees. You will simply be
acting as U.N. peacekeeping forces. Besides, if I drive
and leave you there, he'll have to bring you home—
where you guys can talk, if need be. But if it were me,
I'd have him bring me home, rock his world, then talk
in the morning . . . and leave him wishing that he
hadn't acted like a total fool for the past four months.
Now, that's a win-win strategy, if I ever heard one."

Nina took a slow sip of tea before she answered. As
insane as it sounded, and as much as it went against her
grain to give in to opening the dialogue first, she had to
admit that Vonetta might have a point.

"I'm not going up there to look for any evidence of
another woman," Nina said in a quiet voice. "I'll be going
up there to enjoy myself, and to relax, and to let him
know that we need to talk. In fact, I want him to know
that we can talk about this before it gets out of hand."

"Correct," Vonetta affirmed. "And you should be as
gorgeous as you can possibly be when you do so—just to
let him know what he's been missing, and that you are
still armed, but have just decided not to deploy the full
range of your nuclear capability."

"OK," Nina conceded. "But, I still think that he should
be the one making the overtures, expending the energy
on this, because I was not the one who stayed out all
night without a phone call. In fact, he owes me a double

apology—one for the fight we unnecessarily had about going to a fertility specialist, and the other about not even calling to say where he was."

"Point well taken," Vonetta agreed, her statement blowing into the receiver on a heavy exhale. "However, like you have so often told me, communication is a two-way street. Does it matter who starts the conversation, as long as the conversation occurs?"

A pause engulfed them, and Nina sat down heavily in a kitchen chair, trapped by her own logic.

"Did you not once tell me that ego was his biggest problem, and that as a Leo, it was the nemesis that made him stubborn to a flaw?"

"Yeah, I did," Nina admitted.

"Then how can you fight a flaw with a flaw? Don't you have to rise above his area of weakness to deal with him? Hmmm, oh Zen Master?"

Nina laughed, "OK, you win. Just like you always do. You get on my nerves. You'd better be glad I love you so much."

"How could you help yourself," Vonetta laughed as she made little kissing sounds into the receiver. "I am Yoda. So get dressed. I'll be by in two hours, and we'll fall in there like ninjas—they won't know what hit 'em."

"I feel like I'm going on a blind date," Nina conceded as Vonetta pulled into a reserved parking space adjacent to the club's back entrance. "This is crazy. I have butterflies in my stomach; my palms are getting all sweaty. Maybe we shouldn't do this?"

"You look like a million bucks," Vonetta soothed. "Just look at you! Hair all swept up, face beat, got his favorite perfume on—and that little black dress with no bra is a killer. Where did you get it? Honey, you'll be all right. Just act natural."

Nina kissed her girlfriend's cheek gently, trying not to smudge either of their makeup. "I love you, lady. But remember—behave yourself."

"Moi?" Vonetta chuckled as they exited the candy-apple red, two-seater BMW. "I'm always good. Just ask any man."

The high-pitched saxophone tore through Tony's concentration as he focused on the register tapes and tried to reconcile the books. For months, nothing had balanced. Liquor shipments didn't add up to the inventory stock, food purchases didn't match the client receipts, and the cover charges seemed way off, even though the place had been packed every night. The financial hemorrhage had eluded him for more than a full quarter, slowing his plans to expand the operation to the soon-to-be-vacant adjacent storefront when old man Weiss sold. Where could a five-thousand-dollar-a-month leak be coming from? And damn if quarterly taxes weren't gonna be due soon. How could he even claim the loss if he didn't know for sure it was theft—which would make him vulnerable to an IRS audit? More money, more money, more damned money out the door!

Without tangible evidence of employee theft, he couldn't just launch accusations against his loyal staff. And his brother, although irresponsible, was no thief. Cecil would never steal from the family business that supported them as well as his four sisters—two of whom were unmarried with little kids, while the other two were divorced with children and receiving a pittance of child support. That just didn't make sense. Plus, his brother's woman, Maxine, had been with them as the office manager since they'd opened. Actually, she was the only one who seemed to be able to keep Cecil's head in the business and away from the party.

Bass chords from the next room sent a connecting pulse through his vertebrae, rupturing his frayed nervous system with the blare of a horn.

"Hey, now. If it ain't my two favorite specimens of fine." Cecil laughed, clearing a space for Nina and Vonetta as they approached the bar. "Wow," he muttered appreciably, pouring Nina a glass of Chardonnay and beginning to mix a martini for Vonetta without being asked. "Long time no see in here, strangers."

Nina smiled and leaned over to kiss her brother-in-law's cheek, immediately feeling self-conscious about the low neckline she sported. "Hey, Cecil. How are you? Where's Maxine?"

He returned her quick peck, but his eyes never left Vonetta as he did so. "I can't complain. She'll probably blow through here tonight to sit on this side of the bar," he said, chuckling. "But, look what the west wind blew in. Where's my hello kiss, lady?"

Vonetta smiled and leaned across the bar to give Cecil a kiss, then laughed as he abruptly turned his cheek to make her kiss land on his lips.

"I see you haven't changed at all," she said in a sly, sultry tone, accepting the martini glass from him as he handed it to her with a wink.

"I mighta got better, baby." He laughed easily, filling orders and conducting business as he worked. "Looks like time ain't hurt you none, at all. Ummph, ummph, ummph."

"Well, you know, you know," Vonetta replied coolly, taking a decidedly sexy sip from her glass, then licking the rim before she set the glass down. "Time changes everything."

"But time can also heal a thing or two as well, baby." He lit her cigarette as she produced it, and slid a glass ashtray under it. "Sometimes you have to let bygones be bygones."

"Sometimes you do," Vonetta quipped, turning her attention to the jazz trio and giving Cecil her shoulder to consider.

Nina watched how Cecil's gaze slid over her girlfriend's collarbone and landed on the ample tops of her bosoms, which had been pushed up by a Wonderbra under the barely concealing red fabric of her dress. For a moment, she wished she were as well endowed and could draw the same appreciable gaze from her own husband.

"Why you treat old Cecil so bad, girl?" her brother-in-law lamented, his eyes never leaving Vonetta's skin.

"Because," Vonetta chuckled, not making eye contact with him, "old Cecil's a dog, and he has a new master, or should I say an old one named Maxine Richards. Let me know when you don't have her tags anymore, then we can talk about the past."

"Your girlfriend is rough, Nina." He laughed, moving away to fill another patron's order. "Just as mean as she is fine, and I love it!"

His good-natured tone made both women smile, and as soon as Cecil moved toward a waiting customer, Vonetta turned back to face the bar and to whisper in Nina's direction.

"I noticed you didn't ask him where his brother was . . . and he didn't volunteer."

Nina took a casual sip of wine from her glass. "And I'm not going to. I shouldn't have to." She canvassed the crowded establishment.

Trying to stave off anxiety, she admired the odd-shaped tables that she and Anthony picked out years ago, remembering how much they'd both put into redecorating each one with small circles, triangles, and squares of brass and wood to seat up to four guests. Her art graced the walls, along with the work of other local artists, each having its own soft light to show off the piece. She liked that, and it gave the entire place a cozy, cultural feel. The sanded light wood floors, matching exposed wood beams that played against bare brick walls, with small white candles set amid royal blue miniature water bottles and wildflowers at each table, cast stained-glass prisms of light, which fused with the starlights that rimmed the high ceilings to give everything an open, loft-like atmosphere. She and Anthony had built this place together. From choosing napkins and brass flatware, developing a chic gourmet menu of light cuisine, finding the right chefs, employing the right people . . . As much of her had gone into the revitalization of this establishment as had gone into their home. Damn straight, she had a right to be here!

"Hey, sister-in-law!" Vicki squealed, approaching Nina so fast that she almost dropped her tray.

Nina hugged Vicki back, and they giggled as Vicki set down the small round platter she carried that was laden with several dirty wineglasses and dessert-size plates.

"When did you do this?" Nina laughed, admiring her sister-in-law's new natural twists, while Vonetta hugged the young woman too. "And you're a blonde!"

"You know I needed a dramatic change after I finally left Donnell's stupid ass," Nina's sister-in-law quipped, giving Vonetta a high five. "Plus, having to go back home to live with Mom and Dad for the last two months . . . with my two, and Darla in there with her three wild kids, and Rhonda and her twins . . . gurl! One day, I came in here on my hands and knees, begged Tony to let me work—just to get away from them. I told your husband, and my brother, I'd work for free, since he was having financial problems, then twisted my hinny out the door and got my 'do bleached. You like it?"

Vonetta exchanged a look of concern with Nina, but spoke as though nothing was wrong. "Like it, gurl? I love it! It works for you."

"How are Mom and Dad, and all the tribe?" Nina asked calmly, still feeling shell-shocked from her sister-in-law's implication of potential financial turmoil at the club.

"Oh, you know, everybody is fine over in Jersey, thank God. Dad's still chasing Mom around the kitchen when he thinks we ain't lookin', and he still goes in the basement for a nip when he thinks Mom won't catch him. Complaining all the time about wanting us all to leave— but spoiling every child rotten in the process. But all the little birds are fine. They have the best of both worlds— Grandmom and Pop Pop. Me, Darla, and Rhonda are fine, but the only one getting any decent child support after her divorce, though, is Pebbles. That's why she didn't have to move back home. In fact, if she wasn't so particular about things, I think I would have moved in with her since this is only temporary. Good thing we've all got Tony."

"Speakin' of which, you seen Tony?" Vonetta said easily between sips of martini while glancing at the jazz combo. "Club looks like it's doing well tonight. Every table filled, people laughing. It's all good. He should be proud."

Her delivery was so smooth and so effective that even Nina had to give it to her. Vonetta was definitely a master. She was so glad that her girlfriend had asked the pivotal question that she couldn't seem to phrase.

"You know Anthony is back there in the office, poring over the books and trying to find out why tapes ain't matching up. I told him that things would work out, but you know my brother is totally anal about this business."

"Well, Maxine can help him," Vonetta commented as she lit another cigarette. "I mean, that is her job."

Vicki sucked her teeth and leaned in toward both Nina and Vonetta, then began speaking in a conspiratorial tone. "She was in here when I got here this afternoon. I came early to set up, and she was in the back with my brother, all up in his face talking yang, like she always is.

I don't know why Cecil allows it, or why Tony keeps her around—but she is good with money. I'll give her that."

Nina blanched inwardly and took a deep sip of her wine, placing her empty glass on the bar without responding. Vonetta had obviously read the unspoken distress signal, and went in for the professional kill.

"Yeah, I can't stand the hussy myself. But she is a solid businesswoman—respect where respect is due," Vonetta murmured in a low tone, turning the glass by its stem between her manicured talons. "But I've noticed, she has been letting herself go lately."

"True that!" Vicki huffed, slapping Vonetta's palm with her own. "That's why she isn't here now. Claimed to be up all night, needed her rest, so she'd come by here later. Miss Queen Bee Prima Donna that she is, couldn't be here to open tonight, like my brother, Tony, had to—after being up all night too. Like I said. She gets on my nerves. Will probably sashay in here around eleven, all dolled up—and tryin' to act like she didn't look like something the dog dragged in this morning."

Nina instantly saw red, and this was not how she'd envisioned the return of colors entering her mind. She could literally hear her own heartbeat in her ears. "Where was Cecil?" she asked in a low rumble. "Why couldn't he open up so Tony could get some rest?" She ignored the warning glare that Vonetta cast in her direction. She knew she was an amateur at such delicately orchestrated interrogations, and could blow it by a single wrong word, incorrect tone of voice, or by appearing too eager for a shred of information to be revealed. But her nuclear button had been detonated. Now she was looking for a target. All the formerly pleasing effects of her Chardonnay had worn off.

"Where his trifling butt normally is, at home, asleep, after drinking half the bar away, and talking too much bull to every woman who comes in here. Tony always opens if Maxine isn't here, and insists that it's too dangerous for any woman to be in here to close up shop alone at night. Cecil could definitely take some of that weight off Tony, if he would act right." Vicki waved her hand with a flip of disgust and placed it on her hip. "Look at me, just hoggin' the conversation, and lettin' my tables go. You both look like life is treating you well, though."

"You know me, gurl," Vonetta chuckled to dismiss a reverse interrogation.

"I do know you." Vicki laughed back, giving her a good-bye peck on the cheek. "And, my sister-in-law here looks like married life is treating her real good."

"Yeah," Nina said with a weak smile. "It's treating me just fine."

Three

Tony hesitated in the short hall by the interior glass-paned door leading into the club as he surveyed the seating area, then the bar. It was force of habit, instinct, to assess the establishment before walking blindly into it. If there was a problem, he needed to be close to one of the pump shotguns, and to know and address danger promptly, before any intruder did. Damn, his back hurt . . . he'd have to rethink sleeping on the office sofa versus his own bed. Age was whippin' his ass.

His gaze made two clean sweeps, then stopped as Nina came into view. Although his guard was up, and senses keened, the sight of her, there, temporarily took over his intent to make another security round within the club.

He'd never seen that dress before . . . it was a short, sheer black, with a deep scoop neckline and spaghetti straps—just low enough in the front to show the very beginning of the well between her breasts. The light was perfect for her—she was a work of art. The way it danced off her eyes and reflected off the glints of natural gold and reds in her hair . . . No, he definitely would have remembered her in that little black getup, especially the way the scatter of jet beads and sequins barely hid her nipples while letting one know that they were unencumbered by anything else.

He watched his Nina watching the trio with her best

friend, Vonetta, and he appreciated the understated class that his wife's outfit presented in contrast. It was sexier, he thought as his imagination took hold of him. There was a certain level of exposure, but only a hint of it—everything wasn't all hanging out, or pushed up in one's face. The fabric didn't cling, but gave the airy illusion of softness, as though a caress on the woman's skin. It made him want to touch her, to know what that felt like again before exploring what was beneath it. He'd always loved Nina's long, shapely legs—the edges of her dress brushed them midthigh in a way he longed to now. God she was beautiful.

When she smiled and laughed, he felt a smile begin to reflexively form on his own face. She could be such a nut; a funny, zany, sexy lady, he thought as he watched Nina cover her mouth and laugh at something her outrageous girlfriend Vonetta must have said to her. What was he thinking when he'd stormed out of the house that afternoon? Whatever it was, he'd squash it for sure, because tonight he was not going to be so stupid. Once he'd made his rounds, he'd go attend to his household business.

"Hey, baby," Anthony murmured, approaching the bar and kissing Nina on the cheek—to first test the waters. Nina's scent filled his nostrils like the slow, lazy notes of the sax that floated over the crowd. Damn, he missed his wife. "Vonetta, how you doing, lady?"

He watched Nina's eyes intently for a reading on where she was emotionally. She simply greeted him with a difficult-to-gauge half smile.

"I'm good," Vonetta said with a wide grin, sliding from her stool. "Keep my seat warm while I make a trip to the ladies' room."

Anthony nodded, and the two exchanged a knowing

glance. Nina had not spoken, but she also had not stiffened against his kiss.

"I never see you on this side of the bar." Cecil laughed, breaking the silent communication between Nina and Anthony. "You drinking tonight, man?"

"Maybe I'll have a long-overdue glass of wine with my wife," Anthony said quietly, hailing a few guests as people briefly approached and chatted, then took their drinks to join others. She had been right. They didn't have enough one-on-one space anymore. This place drew steady regulars, which was good, but it was also like being at a constant family reunion, where they could not have a private conversation without interruption.

"Want to go sit at a table? I think Cecil can keep a seat open for Vonetta, and I'm sure he'll keep her entertained when she gets back." Again, he hesitated, because Nina had not said a word since he'd sat down.

"I suppose so," she murmured, handing him her glass to carry for her as she stood and waited for him to lead the way.

It was like a slow dance, he noted, as a long-forgotten sense of nervous anticipation swept through him. There was only one thing to do—fall on his sword immediately, apologize, and squash the argument. He could feel her walking behind him as he guided her to his reserved table at the back of the open space. Lord, how he wished he could watch her walk in front of him, but he made himself content with the fact that in a few moments he'd be able to look at her again.

She slid into the seat as he held out the chair, and sent another waft of her fragrance to surround his senses. The candle at their table sent a shimmer of light off her small silver and amethyst earrings, which bounced off her fragile necklace and kissed her shoulders.

"You look lovely tonight," he whispered, handing her back her glass as he sat down. Then he waited.

Her reply was a lowering of her eyes until her long lashes seemed to dust against each other before she took a sip of wine.

"I'm sorry," he began, not wanting to waste another moment. Her sad expression entered his soul and connected to his muscular system, sending his arm out to touch her face with his fingers. "I don't know what I was thinking. I should have called you."

"Yes, you should have," she said quietly. "I was worried."

This was not going to be easy. He'd overstepped his bounds and breached the fundamentals of marriage. Any brother knew that. Rule number one: Call your wife.

"I know. I should have called you."

She looked at him directly for a moment, then sent her gaze toward the small stage. "I know we had an argument, but I would have never put you through that kind of worry."

Aw, man . . . he'd really blown it this time.

"I know. It's just that things here at the club have been so crazy . . . and then we got into this hassle about me and you going to the doctor . . . and, baby, what I'm trying to say is, I'm sorry."

"I am, too," she whispered. "I'm sorry that we can't seem to talk without yelling at each other anymore, and that you can't tell me things."

He watched her sad expression, and the way the wine sparkled off the muted color that tinted her lush, full mouth. Then she blew him away by gathering a stray wisp of hair and tucking it behind her ear—her signature—then trailing a forefinger along her collarbone in search of her necklace to toy with. Heaviness filled his groin as he watched her finger trace her skin back and forth, then under the necklace, and back to the bone, which was so close to the valley between her breasts, while candlelight shimmered against the tiny beads strategically sewn to hide what was her most erogenous zone. Their fullness pulsed with the music's slow tempo and her deep, even breathing.

"I'll go to the doctor," he murmured, then took a deep drink of wine.

"It's not just about going to the doctor," she sighed. "It's so much more. I need you to talk to me."

Panic rushed the tempo between his legs, and shot confusion through his brain. The club noise, the music, her sultry voice and intoxicating presence made it hard for him to think, much less talk.

"Tell me what you want to talk about?" he whispered, leaning closer to her than was probably advisable given the circumstances. "I'll fix this, baby. I miss you."

She lowered her eyes again, and then looked up at him. "I miss you, too. But whatever problems we have can't be solved by one night in bed."

He felt like his heart was going to rip itself out of his chest. Being two inches from her face made it difficult for him to breathe. "It's a start," he murmured, on the verge of begging her to relent. Then he mentally reached deep for control, and sat back.

When she leaned back in her chair too, he immediately knew that he'd chosen the wrong course of action. If he'd just kissed her . . . just stayed two inches from her face. But he'd retreated like he always did. Therefore, she'd retrenched. His groin muscles tightened. Four months had been too long.

"Come with me for a minute," he whispered, extending his hand across the table for her to accept. When she did, he stood and came around to her side and helped her out of her chair. "This is not a conversation for the club. Let's go into the office."

This time he allowed her to lead. He watched her form gracefully negotiate its way through the small clusters of tables and guests, stopping occasionally to say hello to people she knew, and to nod at Vonetta and Cecil at the bar as they exited the main part of the establishment. Through the dim hall light, his gaze fixed on her saunter, and the way her dress brushed her firm buttocks beneath it, swelling then tapering to her thighs. His tension mounted as she turned the doorknob to the office. Everything had been so unpredictable between them lately. She might slap his face and launch into a yelling match, or might accept the deep kiss he wanted so very much to give her. That was the problem. He just couldn't be sure.

Anthony had closed the door slowly, she noted, and had turned the lock. This was new. He always kept the office door unlocked until he shut down for the night to count the register receipts. She watched him from the corner of her eye as he approached her, wondering what excuse he could come up with—and wondering why everyone but her seemed to know that there was something going wrong with the club books. She was, after all, his wife, and they had built this together. And why the hell was Maxine Richards at the club with him overnight? There were no words, regardless of how nice he smelled, or the fact that he looked good enough to eat. She appraised his Nile blue silk shirt and olive-toned chino pants and jacket, and leather slip-on loafers. Oh, so he was keeping a spare set of clothes down here now, too?

When he placed his hands on her shoulders, the warmth of them penetrated her skin, entered her bones, and started wearing away at her resolve to get her questions answered first. Then he lowered his mouth to hers, moving in closer to narrow the gap between their bodies, making hers drink in the heat of his, as it assessed the unmistakable want that rigidly caressed her thigh. She tried to force her mind to speak by breaking the seal of his mouth upon her own, but his tongue responded by finding hers and gently coaxing it to be silent. The deep moan that he released within her mouth sent a shock wave of desire through her system that shattered every question. Her hands found his back, and his trembled as they slid down to cup her backside and pull her hard against him.

"Let's talk the way we used to," he breathed. "Without too many words."

"All right, then," she conceded as his hands deftly traced her bottom. "What was Maxine doing here with you all night?"

"She wasn't here all night," he whispered, nipping her neck. "She came in this morning."

"Then where'd you sleep?"

"On the couch, and washed up in the sink."

"But why are you keeping clothes here?" she murmured, lolling her neck as he caressed it.

"I went to Boyds this afternoon," he whispered, "because I knew you'd be double mad, and I didn't want to fight today."

"I wouldn't have started a fight when you came home to change," she argued softly. "I just wanted to finish the conversation."

"But I didn't want to talk," he whispered against her ear, capturing her lobe between his teeth briefly, then letting it go, "I wanted to make love to you so badly that I thought I was gonna go blind, girl. Can you understand that?"

His voice had rushed against her senses in a harsh whisper that she could definitely comprehend. But when she felt herself beginning to fall against his desk, she broke the seal and chuckled. "Here? Now? Oh, my God, Tony . . . no! What if somebody comes in?"

She had not seen that look on her husband's face in a very long time. His eyes intensely gazed into her own, and then swept the room like a predator's. His jaw was set hard, and his expression was so serious that it made her stifle a smile. As he pushed aside a few items on his blotter, his nostrils flared with deep inhales and exhales before he answered her.

"The door's locked," he said on a short gulp of air. Then his gaze swept hers again briefly before his face nuzzled her neck.

The sensation of his close-cropped beard against her skin felt wondrous. It was like being stroked by velvet as he moved his jaw in one direction, then leaving her skin with a tingly sensation as he rubbed his cheek against her in the opposite direction. That delicious feeling was followed by deep, warm, moist kisses from his full mouth, which now edged along her collarbone. As his mouth captured a nipple through her dress, she felt her body sway and a rivulet form and spill between her thighs. He smelled so good.

"God, I've missed you so much," he said on a heavy breath as he found her earlobe and sent a shaft of heat into it, then began to move in a rhythmic pulse against her.

"I missed you, too," she whispered back on a short breath, finding his zipper and unfastening it slowly. "You have no idea how much. But we need to talk about the club, and us."

"I can't right now," he admitted, staring at her hard. "Baby, later . . . please."

She watched the unsteady rise and fall of his chest as she brought the zipper down one notch at a time, never losing the steady eye contact he demanded. "Promise?" He only nodded, and swallowed. But when she allowed her hand to slip under the fabric of his pants and connect with his searing skin, he shuddered, closed his eyes tightly, and let out a deep gasp that ran through her entire skeleton. Oh, yes, he was talking to her . . .

Feeling her own breathing become shallow, and the

river at her seam beginning to spill new liquid readiness for him, she covered his mouth with her own.

This time when he pushed her back, she yielded to the fall, trusting in his hands to catch and guide her. Her back arched with anticipation and her legs opened to accept him, while he nuzzled his face against her inner thighs and his hands worked on her hose and panties. The feeling of his broad palms, and the fact that he had yet to touch her where she needed him to so badly, made her shut her eyes and allow her head to fall back. God, yes, he was talking to her . . . it had been so long till it was sheer delirium—brought to levels of semiconsciousness as his mouth drank her in and gently tugged at the soft folds of her. She could feel tears of pleasure cresting against her closed lashes, but nothing could have prepared her senses for the sudden, forceful change in texture from his tongue to his body, and the taste of her on his lips as he found her mouth again.

The initial sound that traveled up from inside him as he entered her was so primal that it registered within her own cellular memory.

"Now you can talk to me, baby . . ." he whispered harshly as he bit her shoulder and trailed his tongue up her neck.

His intense shudder fused with her own, and they both clung to each other briefly without moving, reveling in the reconnection to each other's bodies, and trembling with four months of repressed need. She couldn't speak.

"Sometimes, there are just no words," he murmured in a deep rumble that came from inside his chest. "Am I right?"

She could barely string the words together to answer him. "Oh, yes . . ."

For a moment, the world faded. The exterior club noise evaporated as their private dance consummated upon the staccato chant of unison breaths, and bites against tender skin, and clothing clutched in fists, until each hard-driving stanza of their original music made them remember just how much they liked to talk while they danced together.

He laid against her, breathing hard and trembling, chuckling as she chuckled, gulping air and kissing his face, occasionally shuddering as another climax made her stop giggling, drawing another jerky thrust then sigh from him.

"Girl, see what you do to me?" he said, laughing, moving deeper within her as he found her mouth.

"I don't believe we just did this," she murmured as his mouth left hers, suddenly feeling the environment come alive around her again.

"I need some more ones," a male voice impatiently called from the other side of the door, which made them stop, look at each other, and burst out laughing.

"Give me a minute, Cecil," Anthony yelled, and then hurriedly withdrew from her.

Terror and reality hit Nina at the same time. This was bad. She immediately hopped off the desk, glanced around for her underwear and hose, snatched them up and hid them in a drawer, straightened her dress, then glanced at the large wet spot on the desk. "Do not open that door yet," she warned through her teeth, rushing around the office to find a tissue, giving up, then hiding the spot with a potted plant. "Oh my God, Tony, give me a minute, make up some excuse. We'll never live this down if Cecil knows . . . he'll be telling this at the Memorial Day reunion at your parents' house!"

"Can a brother get some change?" Cecil demanded, sounding more impatient as he banged on the door. "The bar is loaded, man, and me and the girls are clean out of small bills. You all can argue later—I need to handle the bar!"

"I'm comin', I'm comin'," Tony chuckled, giving Nina a sideways glance and a wink.

The double entendre just made her rush around more, and the fact that he found the situation amusing made her want to hide under the desk.

Tucking in his shirttail, Anthony zipped his pants and pulled his belt through the loops, heading quickly toward the door as he did so and talking through it to Cecil to stall for time. "I gotta count out a new drawer. Five minutes, tops," he yelled, cracking the door slightly and putting his head through it. "This isn't a good time, man."

"Man, we ain't got time for you to be counting every penny in a drawer like this is a supermarket," Cecil argued, barging in past his brother and going toward the safe. Collecting a large stack of ones, fives, and tens, he then stopped for a moment and appraised both Nina and Anthony. "Listen," he said in a serious voice while looking at Tony, "Nina is not the kind of woman to be hittin' on. I'm not getting in your bizness, man, but you can't just throw my sister-in-law around the office and be in the club fightin'. If you beat on her, me and Pop are gonna whip your ass."

Anthony opened and closed his mouth. Nina just stared at Cecil and blinked. Had things gotten so bad between them that even his own brother would think that he'd be capable of such a thing? The reality of just how much tension they must have exuded momentarily frightened her. And the fact that Anthony had recounted their woes to his brother was enough to make her recognize that the problem between them was possibly deeper than even she'd imagined. Then again, she had told her own confidante the most intimate facts as well. They both smiled as Cecil turned to her and put his arm lovingly around her shoulders.

"I'll take you home, baby. If he's put his hands on you, just let me know."

"No," she said with a smile, patting his arm, and escorting him to the door. "He didn't beat me . . . but I did bang my head."

Cecil's gaze went from one mistaken domestic combatant to the other, then surveyed the disarray on the office desk. When they both laughed, his expression went from awe to pure shock. Then he just shook his head.

"Let me go mind my business. Damn . . . who woulda thought Vonetta coulda called this one so right? I thought y'all was just in here talking."

Four

He could feel the sun coming through the window to warm his face, and with his eyes still closed, he stretched the ache of all-night lovemaking out of his limbs. This was how it was supposed to be, he thought, rolling over to the empty space beside him. Easy.

Pulling himself up slowly, he listened for Nina's movements in the house. He could hear her rustling around in the kitchen below as the smell of fresh-brewed coffee penetrated his senses. Oh, yeah . . . coffee. That was a good sign. She'd obviously gotten up earlier than he and had made him coffee. Normally, she only had tea, and it had become an unspoken trigger between them. If she was angry or in a bad mood, she didn't consider making him what he liked.

Anthony shuffled into the bathroom, still listening to the pleasant sounds within the house. She'd been right about them needing time alone. Maybe he'd take her down to Boathouse Row for a walk in the park before he had to start his Saturday. The fresh air and newfound peace between them might ensure another evening like they'd just shared. Maybe he'd even be able to coax her back to bed.

As he ran the water in the sink, the smell of bacon and eggs drifted lazily on the slight draft coming down the hall. He closed his eyes as he splashed water on his face.

Good Lord, it had been fantastic last night. Every muscle in his body felt the residual effects of a four-hour marathon that began as soon as they'd walked in the door. He'd even thrown the phone across the room and had disabled his beeper to ensure no interruptions. Then, he'd slept like a dead man.

"Good morning, baby," he mumbled with a kiss on her neck, pulling her to him from behind as she turned over a piece of turkey bacon at the stove. "Something sure smells good down here," he whispered into her ear, catching her tender lobe between his teeth and allowing his hands to travel down her belly against the silk fabric of her robe. "I think it's you."

When she stiffened, an alarm bell went off in his brain. She hadn't said good morning back to him, nor had she melted into his kiss. What the hell was it now?

"I made you an omelet, and there's coffee in the pot," she said monotonously. "The bacon will be ready in a minute. Toast is on the table."

She had not turned around and had barely acknowledged his presence, and she sounded like a diner waitress, not the lover she'd just been. His mind tore through his performance as he fixed himself a cup of coffee and sat down. Last night she'd seemed to enjoy herself. . . . From the staircase, up to the bed, in the shower, then again before they'd gone to sleep. She'd been the one to beg him to stop at one point. Her body had responded like it was on fire, and she'd cried out enough to potentially make the police show up at their door. So what was wrong?

"I've been thinking," she said, bringing two plates to the table.

He resisted the urge to groan at her comment. It was going to be a cold-light-of-day, woman-logic, morning-erection-killing discussion. He just looked at her as she sat down, sadly dismissing the way her deep purple silk robe hung loosely on her frame to expose her nude form beneath it.

"Even though last night was great, we still need to talk."

Again, he just stared at her. His body was tired, his mind was too relaxed to launch into a full-blown conversation, and severe hunger carved a hole in his gut. Why didn't women understand these things? It was basic. Let a man get his grub on first and wake up before launching into some deep discussion about the state of the union.

"OK," he mumbled between mouthfuls of bacon and eggs.

She just stared at him. Why were men so stupid? Granted, last night had curled her toes and made her call on Jesus, but why would he think that would eclipse the need to address their outstanding issues? And wouldn't it be the perfect time, in the morning, to start the day with a clear-the-air discussion, rather than wait until the pot simply boiled over again? She was incredulous. How could he just scarf down food like a yard dog while there was so much looming in front of them?

"Are you just going to eat?"

Anthony looked up from his plate. "Baby," he mumbled through a slurp of coffee, his jaws still working a combination of eggs, bacon, and toast. "I'm starved. Haven't slept good in months, and I'm just coming out of that coma you put me in last night."

Nina let her breath out slowly, and she took a sip of tea, then picked at her mushroom-and-cheese omelet. "Yeah, but I just want to keep things going as well as they were last night."

He peered at her over the rim of his mug. A sense of satisfaction swept over him. So it wasn't his performance. This was about before last night. As long as it wasn't some-

thing to do with the way they'd made love—anything but
that.

"Cool," he said cheerfully. "But last night took the
edge off anything I was dealing with. How about you?"

He watched a smile come out of hiding on her face,
and the sight of it renewed his confidence. "I missed you,
girl," he said in a tone designed to draw the conversation
to a close, so that his next hunger could be satisfied.
"Now that I've got a little fuel in the tank, wanna go for
another ride?"

She chuckled and stood up to pour herself some more
tea, encouraging him with her slow saunter to the stove
and back to the breakfast table.

"You want a warmup?" she asked easily, taking away
his empty plate.

New heaviness loaded against the muscles in his groin.
"Definitely," he murmured, his voice dropping an octave
on its own volition.

"I'm talking about a *coffee* warmup." She chuckled, taking his mug away and filling it, then bringing it back.

Sudden defeat claimed him. There was no use. They
had to talk.

"OK," he said with a sigh, straightening himself in the
chair to look her in the eyes. "Shoot."

"Why do you always say that? I mean, start a conversation with that phrase, as though you're going into some
kind of battle?"

He thought better of responding with the stark truth,
which would mean telling her that it was because that's
how it felt. Like he was staring down the barrel of a
loaded gun.

"I'm sorry. OK, where do we begin?" He was not up
for this conversation this morning. She looked too good,
his belly was full, and another hour of sleep after making
love would be the beginning of a perfect day. Why spoil

it with rhetoric? But if they didn't have the conversation, it could mean a return to solitary confinement.

"Thank you," she murmured between sips of tea. "I just want to know why you object so much to going to a fertility specialist."

Oh, damn . . . she'd pulled out heavy artillery and had him at point-blank range.

"The truth?" he muttered, standing to walk toward the sink for needed distance.

"Nothing else," she shot back casually, not breaking eye contact.

He was cornered.

"Because for one, I can't get it in my head that I have to sit in a waiting room where everybody knows that we're all there to pick out a *Playboy* magazine to jerk off. Nina, I just don't know if I can do that."

She laughed. "I'll go back there with you so you don't need a magazine, if it comes to that, but you haven't even gone to get tested. It might be that neither of us has anything wrong. It could be the timing. But if you don't go, how will we know?"

"What did the doctor tell you when you went to get checked out?"

"That everything appeared to be normal," she said calmly.

"Which means, if we're not making babies, then there's something wrong with me—"

"Not necessarily," she cut in.

"Well, maybe I'm not ready to find out what's wrong with my plumbing."

She stared at him. "You mean to tell me that your ego would get in the way of us starting a family?"

"No, that's not what I meant—"

"Put the shoe on the other foot, Tony. What if I said I didn't want to have babies because I didn't want to get stretch marks? You'd call me vain."

His morning peace was ebbing away from him, and the comment went right to his central nervous system. "See, that's just it," he shot back, his voice escalating a notch. "You haven't seen it from my point of view. You think I'm just being stubborn, and that I haven't thought about it. Well, I have."

"Then talk to me," she said again coolly. "Since I've misjudged you."

"All right," he began confidently while pacing. "Let's review the facts. One," he counted, ticking off his point on his finger. "We're both over thirty-five, which means that if you did get pregnant, you could be at risk." When she didn't speak, he continued. "Two, if you are at risk, then that means I'll have to make the club produce, because during the pregnancy, the household income could drop to your disability pay scale, which is eighty percent of what you make now. Then there's no telling what will happen after the baby is born."

"What are you talking about?" she demanded, pushing her chair back and folding her arms over her chest. "Is this whole thing about money, Anthony, or what?"

"Now, see, there you go," he exclaimed, defending himself. "You want to know what's in my head, but don't want to really hear it. Then you say, 'Baby, talk to me.' Well, I'm giving it to you from a man's perspective."

"Go ahead," she sarcastically shot back. "You have the floor."

"If—" he stammered. "If something is wrong with the baby, since we're starting so late, then that will mean you'll have to stay home, which also means we lose your salary. The club will be the sole source to cover all these bills, and there may be additional costs like special schools, treatments, or whatever, needed to care for this child—if it isn't 'normal'."

He watched tears form in her eyes then appear to burn

away with what he could only imagine to be rage and disappointment.

"First of all," she yelled, "why do you assume that *I* have to be the one to quit my job if there's something wrong with our child? Huh? Where is that written? And, second why are you so intent on looking at the worst-case scenario?"

He drew a breath to steady himself before responding to her. "Because I'm a businessman, and I have learned to weigh the best-case, worst-case scenario of any new venture before plunging into it. That's why." He decided to not answer the first part of her question about who should stay home. In his mind, it didn't require the dignity of an answer.

"So this is like a business deal to you?" She was aghast.

"No, not at all. But it is a lifestyle change, and that brings certain realities, Nina. Realities that cannot be wished away, ignored, or overlooked because you want to wear rose-colored glasses about the situation. That would be no different than these teenagers who get pregnant and hope for the best."

He could tell it was on, now. She was standing and walking in a circle near the sink. He sat down. This was not how this morning was supposed to go.

"So my judgment and planning skills are no better than a teenager's—in your mind, Mr. Entrepreneur? And my career has no place in this?"

"Nina," he coaxed, "let's try to be objective."

"OK," she spat back in a salty tone. "Tell me, from a business perspective, why now is the wrong time to seriously work on starting our family."

Again, he drew a breath and stared at the angry woman with her arms folded over her breasts across the room.

"Because," he started slowly, choosing each word with care, "there are household financial issues we need to cope with first. And, unlike the club, your career is transportable. You can do your art from any location, and can teach in a million places. The Jazz Note can't be picked up and moved, and it's a very fickle business—if you lose the crowd, then you're done. I'd have to start all over from scratch."

"And after being out of the loop, my art wouldn't suffer?"

"Yeah, it might, but you aren't dealing with the immediate financial realities—"

"Like?"

"Like the fact that the mortgage is fifteen hundred dollars a month, our utilities come to about four hundred, the car notes and insurance payments are almost the same as the mortgage, plus food and your credit cards, and incidentals, like the maid, bring the whopping total to approximately five thousand dollars a month. That does not include the studio supplies you need to continue your art. So let's just round the number up to six grand to cover everything comfortably. So, if my club stops—"

"*Your* club?"

There was something in her eyes that made him more uneasy than he'd ever been in any of their previous arguments.

"My club, your club, our club. The club," he stated firmly. "Let's not even go there."

"No, let's definitely go there. You said, 'my club,' Anthony."

"See, this is how things get blown out of proportion," he said, sighing. "One wrong word, and you're—"

"I'm hearing what you really meant. *Your* club. Not mine, not ours. That's the root of this thing. That's your baby, not a real baby!"

Her comment brought him to his feet. "Nina, it's the only thing that I have that makes me feel like I did something with my life," he argued back. "That's real!"

"Oh, and I suppose that my art is just some little hobby

that I can give up once I do my real job, which is be a stay-at-home wife and mother, huh? Oh, I don't have any dreams deferred? You have no respect for what I do, at all—"

"That's where you've got this script flipped. You have no idea what it took to start this venture!"

"I do so!" she screamed back. "How can I forget?"

"No, let's be sure we clear the air on this subject, once and for all," he stormed. "I put my life on the line and saved every dime I had in the service. After I came out of the military at twenty-five, I didn't have the luxury of Mommy and Daddy paying for my education!" he bellowed, losing his intent to remain calm. "Me and my brother went into that shell of a building, got it for a song, gutted the place at night while working day jobs. Some nights we'd fall asleep standing up, we were so tired. And, we caught liquid hell trying to get it up to code, getting the liquor and occupancy licenses, you name it, Nina. And you tell me where I'm going to restart my career at forty-one. Huh?

"Ever think about what I would do if I wasn't running the club, or how I could bring in more than four grand a month to add to the two you bring in here, to keep this household running? Damn straight I'd have to be the one to keep working! What you bring home from the university can't begin to cover what we spend around here. That's real. That's straight, without a chaser, baby. And until you can do the math for this uneducated brother, I can't even think about making babies. I don't know much, but I can count. And you tell me what you have ever put that much blood, sweat, and tears into in your life? Am I supposed to throw it all away, without a plan, and hope our asses won't end up on a grate? And, *I'm* the bad guy, I'm delusional, I'm your enemy, all because I want to plan for our future, and to ensure that my wife has the option—unlike all of her girlfriends and

my sisters—to stay home with our baby? What about this
don't I understand? Talk to me!"

His diatribe left them both staring at each other, the
silent tension curling around their marriage and strang-
ling it.

"So," she whispered, "it's a financial and career impasse. And nothing I've ever contributed to this union
matters . . . nothing I've contributed to turning the bar
into a hot area jazz club is to be considered? And I'm
foolish for wanting to feel a child of yours in my womb,
and to be like any other woman. And I'm stupid for wanting to also be an artist, because that hasn't turned the
same profit level as *your* club. I just want to be sure I'm
hearing you right."

He let his breath out in a rush and stared at the floor.
"That was not what I was saying at all. I know your work
is important. I just meant that I have to be able to support
my wife and children to feel like a man. I'm not one of
these new-wave brothers who feel comfortable having
their woman work while they sit around and scratch their
ass. It's not even in my DNA, and I'd never consider it.
And I'd be lying if I told you that I didn't worry about
how to take care of things, if things didn't go right—I've
been taking care of my family all my life. It's a hard pattern to break."

The tears that streamed down her face made him reach
out to her, but when she flung herself away from him,
he leaned against the sink.

"All my life I've wanted a family—something you and
yours take for granted. I grew up without close cousins,
sisters, and brothers, and couldn't wait for the day when
I could have my own family and do it differently. My
mother and father had only one child, me, for financial
reasons, for social reasons, because they're selfish people, Anthony. And when I met you, and you had this
big, wonderful family, and I saw how much you loved

kids . . . and how generous you were with all of your brothers and sisters and parents, I told myself, 'Here's a responsible, loving, kind man. I'm going to marry him.' "

The way her voice had fractured and split drove a stake through his heart. How could he get her to see what he was trying to tell her? He crossed the room and gathered her in his arms, and pushed her head against his shoulder despite the initial tension in her body. When her form yielded and earnest sobs crested against him, all of the fight drained from him.

Five

The drive to Jersey was just long enough to clear his head from the immediate heat of their argument, but only to make room to add the other worries. He was glad that Nina had gone out to run her normal errands, and that he could make this trip alone.

As his four-by-four pulled up into his parents' driveway, he thought of how he could begin the long overdue conversation with his father. He wondered how the old man did it, as he stepped over the driveway strewn with bicycles and Big Wheels and listened to the commotion of young voices and rap music within the house. More than thirty-five years with the same woman . . . through financial troubles, with a house full of their own kids, and his father working like a machine, while his mom took in laundry and watched other people's children. How did they keep it all together—even after their grown children returned with their children? Yet his mother always seemed to be in a good mood, and his father still looked at her as though he could eat her alive. What about this didn't he understand?

"Yo! Uncle Tony's here," the eldest one of his pre-adolescent nephews yelled, running to give him a high five on the porch.

"Hey, man! Look at you," Tony yelled back, roughhousing with the young man as a tumble of children poured past the opened screen door to greet him. "You gettin' taller every time I see you, Duane. Whatchure Momma feeding you? Where's Nana and Pop, and my sisters?"

"Nana and Mom and them went to the supermarket. Pop Pop is down in the basement watching TV," one of his tall, skinny nieces exclaimed, giving him a bear hug as she fought for dominant position against his side. "Where's Aunt Nina?"

"You boys behavin' for Nana and Pop?" He laughed, punching skinny male shoulders and slapping the tops of cap-wearing heads, then giving his niece a kiss but ignoring her question. "Y'all looking out for your sisters?"

"Aw, them uga-mugs?" a middle boy laughed. "Don't nobody want them!"

The comment started a commotion of tit-for-tat play fighting, arms flying around Anthony, who laughed and picked up the littlest girl to kiss. "Now, don't you be talking bad about my angels." He chuckled, pulling out some single bills to give to the brood. "Y'all give everybody a break, and go to the store. And watch out for these pretty girls—you're men, you hear. Make sure everybody gets something they like, Duane, and that everybody comes back here safe in a half-hour—no more than that. Cool?"

"You got it, Uncle T."

The eldest seemed to stand up a little straighter at the compliment that referenced his manhood, and began rattling off orders like a drill sergeant. Anthony watched the youngster preparing the troops to march toward the pile of kid transportation vehicles in the driveway, issuing commands about keeping up as they moved out to the store down the road. Anthony shook his head and remembered. It was just like when he was the oldest kid.

"Well, stranger." His father laughed, slowly getting up from his recliner to meet Anthony as he came down the basement steps. "Long time no see."

"Don't get up, Pop," Anthony said, chuckling, as the

old man embraced him, fully knowing that he was wasting his breath. "How's Mom and the gang?"

"Get yourself a cold one," the old man said with a grunt, returning to his chair and picking up his glass. "They the same as they always is. Gettin' on my last nerve and leavin' me with a house full of noise. I done tol' 'em a hundred times, if once, I didn't retire to open up no day-care center. Put in my time for Uncle Sam in WWII, then the factory. Anthony, I'm about ready to move out and leave them all here."

Anthony chuckled deep in his soul as his lips found the cool edge of a beer bottle. "Aw, Pop, now how would you make it without Mom? You wouldn't last a day on the outside."

His father laughed with him and shook his head. "There's just no reasonin' wit dat woman. Every time we git rid of one, she goes and opens the door to another chile we done coaxed out the nest. Suppose you and Cecil will be moving back here next, after Pebbles?" he added with a wink.

"Naw, Pop," Anthony said, laughing, then took a deep swig. "Not me, brother. I'm out for good. And, Cecil wouldn't last here two days. Might interrupt his nookie schedule."

His father let out his breath. "Like it don't inconvenience mine? Boy, I might be ol', but I ain't dead. And wit all dese kids in here, your momma done got holy, don't want the kids to know that Grandma and Grandpa ever lived no life. I keep tellin' her that we didn't git y'all six by immaculate conception. But her argument is that it would be a bad influence on 'em to hear anything like that. And, since we all livin' on topa each other—not that we didn't truly appreciate the addition you built for us last year . . . anyway, that's my problem. How you doin', son? How's the club?"

It was the conversation entry he'd waited for, but now that it was here, he didn't know how to begin.

"The club's fine, Pop," Anthony said in a more serious tone than he'd wanted. "You know. Can't complain. You taking your blood pressure medicine like you're supposed to?"

The old man gave him a sly look and clicked off the television, then took a swig of beer, making a face and issuing a sigh as he set it down on the card table next to him.

"That good, huh?"

"Yeah, it's cool."

"OK," the old man murmured through another sip. "How's married life?"

"Cool. No complaints."

His father rubbed the gray stubble on his chin and leaned back in his chair. "Then where are my grand-babies?"

"C'mon, Pop. Can't we just have a beer together, and watch the game before I have to go to work?" Feeling cornered, Anthony stood and walked over behind the bar to find a second beer.

"Don't never see you have a few before you go to the club. So it's either the club or your wife. I'm too ol' to indulge ballroom dancin' in a conversation, son. You know me, right?"

"Yeah, Pop, I know you." Anthony chuckled, downing the first beer, and then opening the second. "Straight, without a chaser."

"That's right," the old man said evenly, his line of vision trapping Anthony behind the bar. "And the way you just put away that brew, instead of nursing it, I'd say it was your wife. When's the last time she gave you any?"

"Oh, come on, Pop." Anthony sat down heavily on a stool and studied the beer in his hands. "It ain't like that."

"I see," his father said quietly, pulling himself up from his chair and sauntering over to take a stool directly across from Anthony. "You drive over here on a Saturday afternoon—which is when you norm'lly have your heaviest shipments comin' in at the club. Den, my house of rug rats clear out, after you no doubt paid 'em to go to the store like you used to when you had a date comin' by the house, and your wife ain't wit cha. I guess I must be senile, or somethin'. What do dis ol' man know?"

"How'd y'all do it, Dad?"

"Do what?" His father chuckled, feigned astonishment in his tone. "Now I know you not askin' me about the birds and the—"

"No." Anthony exclaimed, then stood to pace to the refrigerator behind the rec room bar.

"I'm sorry, I'm sorry," his father said in an easy manner. "I'll stop pullin' your chain. It's just so rare to see you all worked up like this, and I don't get much entertainment. C'mon," he implored, still smiling. "Man to man. Let's talk."

Anthony found his seat and kept his gaze fastened to his beer. "Seriously," he said in a barely audible tone, "how'd you and Mom handle it all, together, all those years, and still . . . I don't know, Dad."

His father's voice became mellow and serious. "When you switch up from callin' your ol' man Pop and go to Dad, I know you got a lot on your plate. For real, for real, what's happening in the recreational department?"

Anthony let his breath out slowly, but could not look his father in the eyes. "Before last night . . . it was four months ago." The admission brought the beer up to his lips as he glimpsed his father's stricken expression then allowed his gaze to slide toward the basement steps.

"Jeazie Christmas, boy! You got a woman on the side, or somethin'? You done loss yo' fool mind?"

"Naw, Pop. It ain't me."

This time Anthony looked his father in the eyes. "I love her."

The elderly man rubbed his chin, then looked down at his own beer. "She got somebody? I never figured her for the type that—"

"No," Anthony immediately corrected. "She ain't that way. We been fightin' like cats and dogs about having a baby, but how can a man just jump up and start a family with the cost of living the way it is, and the club is all I got. But my wife wants the child raising to be this perfect fifty-fifty of roles and responsibilities inside the house, plus me to work at the club, but that ain't real, not when the expenses are the way they are and somebody's gotta bring home the bacon. And when the bar is losing money like a man bleeding to death in the streets from a shotgun wound, and Cecil's ass can't give me a day of rest 'cause he's still chasin' tail and I can't depend on him to open and close so I can have a night at home with my wife—to even find the time to make a baby—'cept last night, which puts us on a schedule of once a quarter. But you worked three jobs when we were kids, and Mom worked too, but y'all made it—but Nina, she ain't flexible, and her art and career take priority, you know what I'm saying, and all my sisters need money to help you and Mom over here deal with a full house that's burstin' at the seams . . . you know? I'm tired, Dad. Really, really tired. How'd you do it?"

His father sat back, took a sip of beer, and set it down very carefully. "When I said you had a lot on your plate, guess I shoulda said platter, 'cause boy, I ain't never undertook such a mess of endeavors in my natchel black life. Whatchu gonna do next . . . leap tall buildings with a single bound?" His father shook his head and stretched, then held Anthony's gaze with his own.

A moment of silence passed between them, and suddenly both men burst out laughing.

"Damn, it does sound crazy, don't it?" Anthony admitted, playing back the diatribe in his mind. He wiped his hands over his face and took a deep swig of his beer.

"Crazy?" his father said, laughing. "Sounds downright incompr'hensible to me! Boy, if I had alla that on my shoulders, I couldn'ta got nothin' to stand up. You hear?"

"Yeah." Anthony chuckled sadly. "But what am I going to do? I can't kick Cecil's butt to the curb. You and Mom need—"

"Wait," his father countered. "Says who? Ev'rybody you tellin' me 'bout is grown, last I looked—and they issues fall under the category of Other Peoples' Problems, like that rap song, OPP. If Cecil is triflin', then put his ass out and get a manager you trust to open and close that establishment a couple of nights a week. That's one," the old man said, ticking off instructions with his fingers. "Two, stop sending gifts and cash over here. Me and your mom is fine. Your sisters are all grown and can work, but they know as long as their big brother is around, they really don't have to. But, like it says in the Good Book, let nuthin' stand between you and yo' spouse. And, for three, if the job is killing your nature and your marriage along with it, then git a new job. It's easier to do that than git a new wife. Trust me, son."

"Easier said than done, Pop." Anthony sighed as he stood to leave. "The club isn't like a job I can go find in the papers."

"Says who?" his father countered with a huff. "People gots businesses to sell in there all the time. Listen, I'ma tell you what's wrong with your generation. Somebody lied to y'all and told you you can have everything, all at the same time. I ain't been formally educated none, but I ain't no fool. I'ma tell ya, if you listen for a minute."

His father's stare held him, even though he tried to dismiss the concept with a healthy sip of brew. But he also couldn't leave. Not yet, anyway.

"Now, follow me for a moment, son, 'cause like you said, I'm a vet'ran."

His father paused for his customary dramatic effect while holding court. Anthony had watched the man for years keep their tribe enthralled at the dinner table while he gave his famous "The World According to Pop Williams" speeches.

After eyeing Anthony to make sure that he wouldn't jump in, his father leaned on the bar, took a swig of beer, belched, and began. It was the ritual Anthony had come there for in the first place. The age-old bond held them, one that his brother had never learned to appreciate.

"See," the sage before him stated, "in my day, we was clear about not being able to have it all at the same time. Like your grandmother, my mother, used to say, 'It's a buffet, so pace yourself and don't crowd it all up. You can git more later.' "

"Yeah, but in your day, Pop, women didn't flat out give you the blues about careers and whatnot."

His father looked at him hard, pushed his stool back, and laughed. "What? Are you crazy? Women ain't changed since Eve." When Anthony didn't respond, he continued. "Son, listen, your mother was the one who made me take the job at the plant, instead of at the hospital at night. There's a lot she made me do, and lookin' back, I'm glad she did."

"Mom?" Anthony was nearly speechless.

"Yes, your mother . . . fine as she wanted to be, my chocolate-brown, big-legged girl, told me it was this home and the kids, or a job that kept me away at night. After like a coupla months of arguin' and her not speakin'—or nothin' else, and me about to go blind from being horny—I went and found me a factory job up at Campbell's Soup in Camden. At first, I thought about other women . . . but, I'd seen the long-term effect of that.

Didn't like the prospects, so I stopped lettin' the little head think for the big one."

"You thought about cuttin' out on Mom? Damn . . ."

"I was yo' age once, and younger!" his father scoffed.

"But, Mom never had a career—"

"I beg your pardon," the old man countered, seeming to become peevish at the suggestion. "She had dreams, too. Plus your mother was, and still is, the real business head in the family. The girl's got organizing skills that, without, we woulda never made it through . . . too bad only the church got to see her in full bloom. But she wanted to work in an office, be a secretary, get a nice house with a yard, not a row house. I didn't know how I could do it, 'cause in them days, a black man just couldn't get any kinda job. So, we put our heads together. She decided that we'd save for the house here, instead of her going back to secretarial school at night. She made that sacrifice, and I always regretted that she had to." His voice became gravelly, and his gaze traveled off in the distance.

"If somebody give you somethin' special of themselves, boy, you gotta show them how much you cherish the sacrifice—and don't you never take a woman's nine months of carrying life in her body, and many, many years of givin' to your children, for granted. *Ever.* Rule number one—that y'all young men t'day done forgot, which has got a lot to do, in my opinion, as to why they ain't makin' mothers like they used to, neither."

Both men fell silent for a moment, consumed with their own thoughts.

"I decided to take the factory job and try to move up," his father admitted quietly, "even though it initially paid a little less than movin' bodies for the hospital. Then, on the weekends, I washed dishes for the diner, and delivered Sunday papers. She, on the other hand, sewed her own clothes and took in laundry for people so she could cut out extra expenses. We was a team. And, even though we was tired, we was in it together—which made her hard to resist when my head hit the pillow. You know what I mean? Even tired can't beat love like that."

"Yeah, Dad, I hear you, but times are different now. My club—"

"See, you need to change your vocabulary, first off. Start a sentence with 'we,' not 'me,' 'my,' or 'I,' when talking about your married life. Takes age to teach you that. The fact is, mostly all a woman wants from you is to not only listen to her, but to hear her. Youth'll make a man deaf, dumb, and blind."

Anthony had to laugh. "She said that to me last night, and again this morning."

"See. That's what I mean. You the businessman in the family. Restructure."

"Restructure?"

"What did I just say?" his father huffed with impatience. "Restructure."

"I can't just jump up and walk away from the club." Anthony was incredulous.

"Not exac'ly, but you can sell it."

"Then what?" he said, walking in circles. "And make money how?"

"First of all," his father chuckled, beginning a new list. "If you've built it up, then it'll bring a pretty price. If you have a knot, you can roll it over into an establishment that lets you work more days than nights, which'll mean it's easier to find help. And if Cecil cleans up his act, then he can still work shotgun right alongside you. Meanwhile, start trimming the fat. Ask yo'self, when did me and your mom buy a new car?"

Anthony hesitated before he answered. "Not until you retired, Pop."

"Exac'ly! So, trade 'em back in and get two clunkers that you can get around the city in. It'll lower your in-

surance, too. Why you need the stress of two brand-new
cars to take y'all to jobs you hate? Git rida excess. Ask
yo'self, you need a maid, or if you not passin' like ships
in the night, can ya both keep a house clean—y'all ain't
even got no real mess yet. Wait till you have kids. When
they git outta diapers and can reach the sink, make 'em
do the housecleanin' that's they job for being fed. And
pay off them damned credit cards and stuff. Cash only.
That makes the decision to say no a lot easier to things
you might want. Insulate the house, and cut the heat
back—it'll save you on utility bills. Clip coupons and go
to the supermarket together—you carry the bags. That'll
take the sting outta her cookin' all the time, 'cause if you
eat at home, it's cheaper. So she needs to shop, and then
you carry the load. It's the least you can do for your
wife."

"I don't mind carrying the bags, but I'm always at the
club—"

"I tol' you, sell it, if it's a bone of contention. What's
more important? If it's just a matter of money, there's
more than one way to skin a cat. But if your ego is tied
to that club, then that's a horse of a different color."

Anthony paused, and his father took the opportunity
to jump in.

"It ain't hard, and you been in the military. You know
how to bump off an inspection task, boy. Put out the
trash faithfully, and mop the floors, do the yard work,
and learn to hit the center of the toilet when you piss—
that's half the battle. The other half is pickin' up after
yourself. It's amazin' what a turn-on that is to a woman,
to come home to a clean house. Cheaper than buying
dinner, and a five-dollar bunch of flowers don' hurt from
time to time. Ev'ry now and then, git up early, and bring
her breakfast—when it ain't even her birthday. It'll be
the best morning shot you ever got, son, trust me. That's
why they teach you how to cook and clean for yourself

in the army, so when you git home, you kin readjust to civilian life."

By now, both men were laughing hard, and his father seemed unable to keep a peevish tone.

"And, about her workin', well she can," the old man continued on a roll. "But when the baby comes, that's not even a fight you gotta git into. As long as there's enough money around to keep the lights on, and to keep milk in the fridge, she'll decide for herself what's more important—jumping through hoops for some white man or being home with her babies to raise 'em to school age. There. Problem solved," the old man said with a grunt as he hopped off his stool. "I just cut 'chure household expenses by fifty percent, found time in your day, and made it easier for you to get some regular nookie. That comes from a vet'ran of thirty-five years of wedded bliss. It's all in the fundamentals."

Anthony embraced his father and headed toward the steps. "Yeah, just needed to go back to the buffet line a few times, instead of crowding my plate. Thanks."

"You gonna listen to her now?" His father made the comment with a sly wink as he went back to his recliner.

"Yeah," Anthony conceded with a shrug.

"You gonna adhere to the fundamentals, right?"

"I told you, Pop. Yeah."

"You gonna stop on the way home and git some flowers, and drop 'em home first before you go to work?"

"Pop . . . c'mon, now."

"Well?"

"Yeah, yeah, yeah."

"All right. You grown, and I'm outta your bizness. But I kinda like that girl. Don't want you havin' to move back home. We ain't got no room, no how." The elder man chuckled as he clicked on the television. "Done made me miss half my game. Damn kids, comin' home with drama over the basics. I tol' y'all, I'm retired."

"I love you, too, Pop. Give Mom and them my love. Tell her she's still my favorite girl."

"Naw, can't do that." The old man chuckled, flipping channels with his gaze fastened to the set. "Your mom's *my* baby girl. You go home and tell that to your own."

"Later, Pop," he murmured, becoming filled with emotion as he went up the steps to the now quiet house. "Give Mom my love," he whispered as he looked around once, then headed for the door.

He wondered if he could ever find that level of companionable friendship between himself and Nina, and if their home would ever be jam-packed with as much love and laughter and passion and dreams? For the first time in his life, he truly understood just how much his parents had sacrificed and all that it took to raise a family within an unbroken union.

Nina was right. It was definitely about more than money.

Six

Somehow, her car had maneuvered itself past the farmer's market, up The Drive, and down her parents' street. Nina sat in the vehicle for a moment with the engine idling, until she saw her mother's form appear in the side yard. It was indeed spring, and her mother kept a gardening routine that had not changed in all the years she had known her. When her mother turned and waved, Nina pulled her car into the driveway. To keep going was no longer an option.

"Well, look what the wind blew in," her mother said, laughing and rushing over to give Nina a hug. "We have to stop meeting like this."

The two women exchanged an embrace and a light kiss, and Nina's mother held her out from her.

"You look tired, dear. Is that good news?"

The excited expression on her mother's face made Nina's gaze slide away.

"I wish it was, Mom," she whispered. "How are you and Dad?"

"Oh . . . he's fine. Went to get some mulch for the bushes. Come on in," her mother said in a tender tone. "Let's visit. The garden can wait."

For the first time in a long while, her mother's offer was a balm to her emotions. Nina took her mother's hand, and the mere gesture made the older woman look at her, peck her cheek again, and lead her into the house like a child that needed a bandage.

They headed straight for the kitchen—The Mommy Clinic. Neither spoke initially, but Nina observed the routine of Mrs. Carpenter, who always made tea for talks. Nina looked at her mother's still-athletic form, immaculate silver hair that was stylishly coifed, and the way she kept her hair and nails so perfect—wondering if she could present herself so well at almost seventy.

Her mother wore a lemon yellow sweat suit and white sneakers, and had left a basket of garden tools and gloves in the yard, none of which appeared to have a speck of dirt on them. It must be a fifties thing, she concluded, realizing that she'd never really seen her mother undone.

When the tea was ready, Mrs. Carpenter took a seat across from Nina at the table, then stared at her. "What happened, honey?"

"Nothing, and everything," Nina admitted. "I don't know what's wrong with us."

"Was there a fight?"

"Fights. Arguments," Nina corrected when her mother visibly blanched.

"Oh," the older woman breathed, then took a delicate sip of tea. "That's just a part of marriage. The honeymoon is bound to be over sooner or later, honey. You know that."

"Yeah," Nina murmured, taking a sip of her own tea. "But . . . I mean, you and Dad . . ."

"Fought the whole way through," her mother countered, appearing blasé. "You only get six good months, if you're lucky."

Nina just stared at her mother, not knowing which direction to take the conversation.

"But . . ." Nina began, then trailed off.

"But what?"

"But you two are still married . . . I mean, doesn't it pick back up after the lull?"

"No," her mother said casually, stirring her tea unnecessarily. "It gets worse, and you just learn to adjust."

She'd known that there were icy moments between her parents, but she was not prepared to hear this at all. What she'd hoped for was that her mother would give her a magic solution and something solid to rebuild upon.

"But what if the passion dies so soon, and all you have is a test of wills between you? How do you accept that? How do you pull your marriage up out of that tailspin, before it's too late?"

She watched her mother's cheeks turn crimson and a hardness overtake her normally elegant expression. "You learn to sublimate those urges," she remarked flatly, "or run the risk of doing something that will hit the gossip columns, darling. I don't care what they say, it's still a man's world."

Incredulous, Nina sat back in her chair and studied her mother's frostbitten beauty. "Can we talk honestly, Mom?"

"Of course we can," her mother retorted. "Haven't we always?"

Nina let her breath out slowly, wishing Vonetta had been home when she'd called her. "Before last night . . . some time had passed since . . . well . . . Anthony and I have been passing like ships in the night."

"For how long?" her mother asked, employing her famous discretion and grace, and knowing exactly what Nina meant without it being said.

"Four months."

Her mother took a sip of tea, and her facial expression never changed. Then she sighed. "Is he having an affair yet?"

Nina blinked twice and simply stared at her mother, needing a moment to recover. "Why would he be having an affair? And why did you put it in the context of the word 'yet'?"

Her mother reached her hand across the table and covered Nina's. "Oh, baby . . ." she sighed. "The first time is the hardest, but you'll get over it. Trust me. Young women today are so rash, and leap right to divorce as an option. Your urges will subside, and there's plenty of work to do in the community—"

"Wait," Nina whispered. "Dad had affairs on you?"

Her mother waved her hand as if to dismiss the subject and stood, going to bring the kettle of herbal tea back. She took her time pouring each cup.

"There are private things that happen in a marriage that neither partner is proud of, but have, nevertheless, occurred." Her mother's statement was simple, elegant, and evasive, and had been delivered like well-edited sound bites from a presidential campaign. "And these issues leave both individuals with a choice: to ruin the life of another human being and their own reputations, or to do the only honorable thing—which is to stay and make the best of it. I chose to do the honorable thing. So did your father."

Her mother returned the kettle to the stove and took her seat again, this time staring directly into Nina's eyes. "But you don't have children yet, and this is a different era where women have choices."

Still shaken from her mother's casual admission, Nina's mind tumbled with a thousand questions from her youth that collided with the grown-up that she was now supposed to be. But tears came to her eyes despite all her attempts to take this new information like a woman. These were about her parents . . . her Dad . . . the one parent she most admired, believed in, and the one who always seemed to be the gentler soul of the two . . . who issued big kisses, called her Pumpkin, and indulged her like a goddess. Her Daddy . . . not *an* affair, but plural, affairs. The schism in her brain begged for closure, to know why, even though her mother had made it patently clear that details would not be forthcoming on the subject.

"There's no need to cry," her mother said quietly, wiping at the singular tear that had spilled over Nina's lashes. "That was years ago."

"But," Nina murmured, "didn't it hurt?"

"Of course it did," her mother whispered, her gaze going far off in the distance through the sunlit window. "I thought I would die. But," she said, her gaze coming back to the table with the strength of her voice following it, "I didn't."

"OK," Nina whispered, "but there was a price to pay for letting it go."

Her mother issued a hollow chuckle and narrowed her gaze in a way that sent a chill through Nina. In that flash of expression, her mother's age receded, and Nina could almost see an embittered young wife sitting before her. It was the side of a parent that no child ever wanted to really see. The human side, the not-so-omnipotent side.

"Yes, my dear," her mother said too calmly, "there's a terrible price to pay for acceptance."

When Nina only stared at her mother, she smiled sadly, her mother face returning. "You pay in ways that you can't even understand yourself. You lose your womanhood, and you transform into something else."

The two female gazes locked and held each other, one afraid to let go and hear more of the truth, the other afraid not to hold on, to teach and protect.

"I cried myself silly for months," her mother finally admitted, forcing Nina, by the low timber of her voice, to look at her. "Then came the ache—the indescribable ache of missing physical touch from the man you love, but no longer trust. And the devastation of feeling that all eyes know your life's story when you walk into a place, or at an event. It is the most brutal unveiling of privacy I have ever experienced. The first one was a young graduate student intern at the university—then at least he had the common decency after that debacle to remove his dalliances from public view within our social network. The local nightclubs provided a source of entertainment that I learned to live with, after that. But to this day, I can't stand the thought of what those establishments represent."

Suddenly, all of her preconceptions about why her parents were so opposed to Anthony's club evaporated. It was pure parental foresight . . . the past hashing itself out and making them face their own worst nightmares. Panic sent the words to her lips before she could censor them. "Why did you stay? Because you were pregnant with me?"

Her mother let her breath out in a slow, controlled stream. "No, honey. It had nothing to do with you. This was about male ego and societal options for a woman. Your father adores you, and always has. Don't confuse the three issues."

The response didn't make sense, didn't register. Nina's expression must have transmitted confusion to her mother, because she smiled and patted Nina's hand.

"But you two slept in the same bed for almost thirty years . . . and went to functions, and . . ."

"The first year, after you were born, I stopped sleeping with your father. I'm not proud to admit it, but my doctor actually had to write a prescription to dull the urge. Eventually, I had enough mental fodder to make myself lose interest in that part of my life. The species didn't interest me any longer. Besides, I had a beautiful little girl, the best thing that had come from our union, to keep me busy, and my work."

Stupefied, Nina sat back in her chair, trying to imagine her mother being a nun for almost thirty years, while keeping up appearances. "I still don't know how you did this, Mom . . ."

Guilt coursed through her as she thought of her doting and overprotective parents. She was their only source of joy within a loveless union. She was the woman in their house who loved her father back unconditionally, and kissed him, and laughed at his academic-brand humor, and kept him company in the study, sketching while he worked. She brought him tea and saw that he didn't work too late. She was the companion princess to her mother, the one who her mother could teach all the finer points of grace and society, while living through her female experiences of freedom within a changing era. The burden of being the center of attention because of a dysfunctional relationship revealed itself in full bloom right in the middle of her mother's kitchen.

"Not many women were going to college in our day," her mother reminded her, obviously responding to Nina's stricken expression. "Not many women were becoming professors at colleges, especially if they weren't all-girl academies. And my family had money. Don't you see, that's why I've always told you to get your education and career established first, before it got sidetracked, waylaid, or sabotaged by any man . . . and do you see why I said that water seeks its own level? Even today, in a new millennium, there aren't many men who can deal with the woman being in the lead in any significant financial or social way."

"But what if you love each other," Nina countered, trying to sort out the pieces to make them fit into the tiny spaces of sanity left within her brain. "What if each has different, but complementary abilities, each of equal value . . . I mean, didn't Daddy love you?"

She'd asked the question about her parents out of an attempt to understand their relationship, almost as much as she'd asked it to gain clarity on her own marriage. Her eyes searched her mother's face for an answer, and yet, all the years of her mother's seemingly selfish behavior became clear.

The woman before her was not only a mother, but also a wounded soul, whose effervescence had been curtailed long ago by the actions of another wounded soul, her father. With so many years and so much water under the bridge, who could ever sort out which party started it, or who was to blame . . . and did that matter? She loved them both.

The hesitation of her mother's response as she appeared to collect her thoughts was enough time to allow a thousand answers to slam into Nina's mind. Her mother had spent a lifetime making her father repay a debt, a heavy, Mafia-type debt with insatiable interest. The longer her mother pushed him away and cloistered herself in career activities to numb the pain, the more successful the woman became, and the more insecure her father became, and the more he sought reaffirmation elsewhere, which then led him to return the payment with interest— material acquisitions designed to pacify her mother, who could never be pacified by anything, as there was no replacement value for trust, friendship, and sacred touch.

And, in that moment, she mourned for her mother, and stretched her palms out to comfort the still graceful but aging hands in front of her, wishing with all her might that she could heal this hurt while removing the burden her father had carried for years. No wonder there were no children after her . . . it wasn't physical infertility, it was emotional infertility . . . something the doctors, in any era, could not fix. Both of them had participated in a cover-up by giving her excuses about not being able to have children. Tears blurred her vision, and she held her mother's hands tightly. "Oh, Mom," she whispered, "you gave up so much, too much for me."

"No I didn't. I love you . . . and of course your father

loved me, once," her mother murmured in a vacant tone filled with memories. "When we were courting, and then first married, things were so different. We were young and passionate and had our whole lives in front of us. And we made you . . ." she whispered, emotion catching her voice, then clearing from her throat. "And we dreamed about more beautiful babies, and I went back to work against your grandmother's advice. And the rest is literally history. Your father and I were adults, and we each made our choices. That's not your cross to bear."

"That wasn't fair, Mom," Nina whispered, squeezing her mother's hands within her own. "You had a right to do what you did without expecting to have to deal with that."

"Yes, I did," her mother murmured back. "And I paid the price for being on that first wave of women's lib," she added with a forced chuckle.

"If you had to do it all over again, would you?" Nina asked, her eyes searching the now-aged-looking eyes for the truth.

"Honestly, I don't know," her mother whispered, her gaze slipping away toward the window. "Was it worth it, is what you're really asking me. All I can say to you is this: to live your life in someone's shadow, because they're insecure, is not life. I always wanted more than that for my own daughter. After you were born, I'd look into your face and whisper, 'Be strong, little one. The best will be yours when you're my age.' Do you have the best, Nina? For you? If you tell me yes, then I'd say it was all worth it."

She considered her mother's words as the women's gazes again locked in a silent understanding. Suddenly her problems felt so small, and her own sacrifices so meager, and she wondered if she could ever love another human being enough to give away her own life like her mother had. Nina looked at the handsome beauty and proud carriage that still resided in the woman she called Mom.

The quiet between them created a telepathic space, where a new level of respect entered her soul, and all the years of mother-daughter struggles seemed so meaningless now. She cringed at the thought of her own childlike, selfish behavior. Her mother had fed, clothed, nurtured, and loved her, listened to her, encouraged her, and pushed her, hard, all the while enduring such inner conflict and pain. Nina could see it. During the teenage years, when she was flamboyantly exploring her own sexuality, her mother was her own age now, and a prisoner to celibacy, probably mourning the loss of her own desire—and remembering what it felt like to be young, and touched, and in love. And Nina now better understood that while she was in college, her mother was going through menopause, losing still more of her womanhood, as her own came into full blossom. Yet, that same woman who'd lost so much also stood at her daughter's wedding and wept tears of joy and remorse, never once taking that moment of joy from her. Nina thought, that is love, sublime. One that deserved respect, no matter what choices had been made.

"Mom, I don't know what I would do if Anthony had an affair. But I do know that if our marriage is going to work, it has to be fair, it has to be a team, and both people have to give—or I won't stay. With or without children. You taught me that, and I love you for doing so. Thank you," she whispered. "For everything. It took a lot of courage. You were ahead of your time."

Her mother nodded. "Then I have nothing to fear. This is indeed a different era, and my girl-child will be fine. Everything has its season. 'I'm in winter; you are my spring eternal,' my mother used to say."

Nina stood and walked over to her mother, and bent to stroke her silky hair before placing a kiss on her forehead. "But you, Mom, are still the most beautiful flower in any garden. I love you for being honest with me," she whispered against her mother's cool skin, feeling the older woman's fingers curl tightly against her hand as she reaffirmed her mother's femininity.

It was a squeeze of acknowledgement that no further conversation was required. In that subtle moment, and after almost forty years, the baton had been passed. They had just become friends.

Seven

What had he expected? Anthony carefully put the flowers in Nina's favorite vase and positioned the card within them. Of course she would have gone out. It was a beautiful spring afternoon with not a cloud in the sky. He'd abandoned the idea of trying to find her in the streets as she ran her errands. Nina was, after all, somewhat unpredictable. She could have gone to the farmer's market, or to her aerobics class, or to Vonetta's, or into the studios at the university, or simply stopped to admire a sidewalk art sale. The fact that he didn't even know her routine anymore truly weighed on him.

What troubled him even more was that, almost like clockwork, he could normally be counted on to be at the club. She knew that about him. His routine rarely varied these days. Hers did. It was one of the things he liked most about her—and the least about him. She was wired to the pulse of The Universe, as she called it. He was tethered to an assortment of electronic leashes—a cell phone, a pager, voice mail, the club telephone, electronic mail—all of which she shunned and refused to deal with, all but the phone.

He had varied his path slightly today, he noted, giving himself some margin of credit. He had, after all, stopped by his parents' house unannounced. Maybe he'd go visit his brother to have that long-overdue conversation.

Anthony pulled his vehicle into a tight parking space and looked down American Street. Cecil had been right. It would have been easier to live down in Northern Liberties, close to the club on Spring Garden, than to have to drive over from Queens Village, even though that was only a hop, skip, and a jump from where they both worked. But, at the time, he had building a family on his mind, and wanted a larger piece of property for that hypothetical family. Now even their house seemed to be in the wrong location, one that was perfect for two double-income-no-kids individuals. But it wasn't what he'd really envisioned: a house with a massive front and backyard, and tree-lined streets, and slow residential traffic that allowed children to spill out into the middle of the road to ride bikes, play stickball, and jump double-dutch.

Theirs had been a professional compromise, to get a place close to where they both worked, with enough interior space for her art and his music. When had they really added children into the equation? Maybe his wife's superstitions or new-age logic had been correct: The feng shui of their existence was out of alignment with their goals.

He almost chuckled as he walked down the narrow street and considered the heated debates they'd had on metaphysical topics. Then he glanced at the barred windows and designer grates that sealed doors off from the world. No matter how elaborate the wrought iron work was, it still reminded him of some sort of prison lifestyle. He wondered how his brother, a self-confessed free spirit, dealt with that reality, especially after growing up in an open, single-family home, with a screen door that was never locked and grass on every side of the house.

"Yo, can you spare a brother some change?"

Anthony looked at the bundled, dirty individual who

had slithered out from a side street alcove. He wondered
how a person could just allow himself to totally give up
on life, as much as he wondered why the homeless always
seemed to be dressed in opposition to the weather? Here
it was nearly seventy-five degrees outside, and the twisted-
looking goblin of a man before him had on gloves with
the fingers cut out, a tattered knit skullcap, torn corduroy
pants, boots, and a heavy army fatigue jacket, with layer
upon layer of filthy sweaters and assorted clothing beneath it. Anthony shook his head. How did his brother
deal with this on a daily basis, so close to home?

"C'mon, brother," the man lamented as Anthony appeared to ignore the request. "You give me a little somethin' somethin' so I can eat this morning, and I'll give
you a piece of advice. Don't the Good Book say we all
our brother's keeper?"

Anthony sighed and reached for his money clip in his
pocket, separating out a bill with his fingers without looking before pulling his hand out of it. What could it hurt?
He knew the drill. In the city, there was a troll at every
bridge begging for a toll . . . wanting to wash your car
windows, pump your gas, watch your car in a street parking space, all for a nominal fee, of course. Everybody had
a racket.

"Thanks, man!" the ghostlike figure exclaimed, crum-
pling up the bill in a dirty fist. "Hey," he called after
Anthony. "Ain't you gonna get your advice? A twenty spot
is worth at least a riddle."

Anthony groaned inwardly. Twenty dollars . . .
damn . . . that's right. He remembered. The kids. He'd
peeled all his ones and fives off to send them to the store.

"You got lucky, today, brother," he muttered, beginning to walk. "No service required."

"Naw, that ain't cool," the man chuckled through a
slur, following behind him. "I got my reputation to consider."

"What?" Anthony said as he stopped, turned and stared, the expression on his face obviously making the man's smile grow wider.

"I may be homeless, but I'm free," the urchin quipped. "And I have to give people somethin' when they give me somethin'. I call it the cosmic law of reciprocity."

"I don't do no drugs," Anthony sighed. "C'mon, bro, I've got things to do today. Go get something to eat. You don't owe me nothin', okay? Peace."

"I don't do no drugs neither, myself, just licka," the man said, laughing. "But here's a riddle."

Anthony folded his arms over his chest and kept his gaze roving the terrain. But he'd stopped. *This is how people get mugged and shot,* he told himself. *One distracts, while ten sons of bitches come out of an alley.* So why wasn't he moving, especially when he knew better?

"You've got all of thirty seconds," Anthony muttered.

"I'm about peace, too, brother," the man said with a smile. "You're probably packin', I know that, and I've been out here long enough not to get in some six-foot-four brother's way. But I have a riddle for you. Take it for what it's worth. Then I can go on. Deal?"

Anthony nodded but didn't respond, suddenly realizing why Nina could never get anywhere on time. She probably would have stood there and gotten the man's life story, then sketched him, bought him a cup of coffee, and ate with him at the diner. The thought made him smile, and unfortunately, the man before him took that as an endorsement.

"Here's my message," he chuckled. "Think about it, and apply it. 'Cause, out of the mouths of babes come words of wisdom. They angels, you know . . . and, somethin' gave this to me this morning, while they was out playin' in the streets, and since I can't do nuthin' with it, I knew I was supposed to pass it on to the first decent person I met. You him. Your generous donation to my freedom cause tells me so."

"All right, already. Like I said, I've got things to do, brother."

The man crossed his arms over his chest with effort, the bulk of his clothes making the task difficult. To Anthony's surprise, the bum seemed to sober himself for a moment before speaking. It was in his eyes . . .

"Step on a crack and you break your mother's back, 'cause all in time, three, six, nine, the goose drank wine, the monkey pulled the back off the street car line. The line broke, and the monkey got choked, and they all went to heaven in a little rowboat."

Anthony just stared at the man for a moment, then laughed. "OK. You have a nice day, brother. And spend that money on some food." He shook off the eerie feeling and began walking. Had to be his imagination, because the bum's original demeanor had returned. There was no response to a crazy person that would make one sound anything other than crazy himself.

"For real, for real," the man called behind him. "You good people, and it's a message for you, man. I can't do nuthin' with that stuff!"

As annoyed as he was at the delay, the little ditty kept replaying itself over and over in Anthony's brain, making him chuckle at intervals as he walked. It was an old jump rope rhyme, one that his sisters used to sing in the driveway. Well, at least kids still played in the streets around here. That was reassuring. But of all the stupid, insane, lame bunch of crap he'd heard from a grown-ass man! How did his brother deal with this every single waking day of his life?

Anthony stood on the front cement steps and rang his brother's bell, then began to pound on the grate until he heard movement. It must be nice, he thought, to sleep till three in the afternoon on a Saturday, with all that had to be done to prep the club for its heaviest night of the week. New irritation accosted him as his brother peered sleepily through the window, managed the locks, and cracked only the inside door, neglecting to unlock the outer iron gate.

"Yo, Tony, man, whatchu doin' over here at this time in the afternoon? Everything OK with Moms and Pops? Everything's cool at the club?"

"Yeah, man. Open the door so I can come in. We need to talk." Sudden aggravation made Anthony's temples throb.

Cecil hesitated, and leaned his face closer to the grate, but didn't open it. "Can we do that later? It's sort of a bad time."

"What!" Anthony found himself hollering. "No, we can't do this later, man. It's business."

"And like I said," Cecil repeated, "it's a bad time. I've got company. Later."

"Yeah. All right," Anthony muttered through his teeth. "Later. Just tell Maxine to have her ass at work on time to open up—and you're closing. Tonight, I'm going home to my wife."

"All right, man. All right. You don't need to go ballistic. But tonight ain't a good night for me to close."

"What?" Anthony replied in sheer disbelief, stopping his retreat down the steps to turn and look at his brother.

"Hey, man, I covered for you last night—tonight I've got things to do," Cecil retorted.

"Like I don't? When was the last time I took a whole weekend off? Huh? Tell me that!"

"Look, man, I said this was a bad time. You're blowin' the groove, and we can discuss this tonight," Cecil argued. "Later."

"Yeah. Later," Anthony raged, turning on his heels and bounding down the steps. Fury consumed him, and as he paced toward his parked four-by-four, he hoped that the friendly street person had moved on. The last thing he was in the mood for now was another cosmic riddle.

Nina set the phone down carefully and looked at the rows of produce bags on the counter. An attempt to get in touch with Vonetta had failed, and she was not about to call Tony—who was always busy when she did. She needed a warm body to talk to, instead of just voice mail or the kind of conversation interruptus that Tony offered when she called him midday during his pre-open phase at work. She knew better than that; it would just restart the argument they'd already had earlier.

Besides, she wasn't even sure what she'd tell her girl-friend if she did reach her. On one hand, she didn't want to betray her mother's most intimate trust. On the other hand, she'd been wounded to the bone to find out all that she did. Then of course, there was the issue with Tony that had gone unresolved.

Somehow, the lure of being out in the streets had lost its effect on her. She'd just wanted to get home and curl up in a little ball. Normally, she would have hit all of her favorite haunts, and maybe even taken a sketchpad to East River Drive. But there was nothing she wanted to capture on paper at the moment. And, although fatigue claimed her, her mind was too stimulated by a thousand cross-firing thoughts to really allow her body to rest.

The studio, she thought. Maybe she'd look around and pick up on a project in her sanctuary. At least she'd be home, in the solitude of her art and thoughts.

She made quick work of putting away the fresh vege-tables and fish, and stowing away the few all-natural pack-aged goods that she'd purchased. As soon as the last produce bag was put away, she headed upstairs.

"Flowers," she whispered, pacing across the room to lower her nose to the delicately arranged bouquet. "Jasmine . . . The Isley Brothers . . ." Nina carefully opened the card and took another whiff of the fragrant white blossoms. She read the note through once quickly, then again more slowly.

His note was simple, and contained their music.

> *No matter what we argued about, you're blowing through the jasmine in my mind . . . I love you. See you tonight so we can talk.*
>
> *Love, T*

Nina sat down slowly on the window seat, took up her sketchpad, and briefly closed her eyes. A man standing behind a woman, embracing her as she bent to smell jasmine came into her mind's eye. This one would be in color, and she would entitle it "Hope."

Eight

"Hey, Tony," Vonetta yelled over the din as she waded toward the bar. "Normally see you in back office and security mode. Where's Nina? I came here looking for her."

"Not sure, lady," Anthony said in a rumble a bit louder than the crowd. "Missed her this afternoon myself when I stopped home, then came here after a few runs, and it got crazy busy, so I haven't had a chance to call her. Your usual, or are you gonna surprise me?"

"Why don't *you* surprise *me*," she said, laughing. "Where's Cecil?"

"Don't get me started," Tony hollered back from the far end of the bar. "It's seven o'clock, the bar is loaded, Maxine is AWOL too . . . and Vicki called in 'cause one of the kids has the sniffles, and my other waitress just didn't bother to come in, which leaves two of them hoppin', plus, I'm down one chef 'cause of Duane being missing in action. My head chef, Eddie, and me did the setup, which left him all backed up on his food prep. I'm waiting on Cecil now, and my other bartender, Ron—who's also late—to relief pitch. So, girl, you gonna have to tell me what you want, 'cause I'm not exactly in a creative frame of mind at the moment."

From the corner of his eye he saw Vonetta's long, shapely legs, which ended with stiletto patent-leather heels, edge through an opening, using her burnt-yellow miniskirt as a blade to cut her way over to the bar and squeeze between two male patrons. Once her deep-plunge cleavage, which was wrapped in a tight, black tank top divided the men, Anthony knew it was only a matter of time. When one of the men got up for her, Anthony instinctively moved toward the threesome and took the men's orders. Tonight it was going to be top-shelf champagne for the lady—the whole bottle, since they were buying.

The constant hubbub and up tempo music from the jazz combo kept him moving and not thinking. He didn't even have to interact with Vonetta too much, or get into a conversation with her about Nina, because there was only a three-minute delay between bar requests, and her newfound male friends had plenty to say to her. The people at the tables were sending orders as fast as the people with their feet on the rail. He'd gone to get some clean glasses for the bar when he spotted his brother, and immediate relief mixed with indignation coursed through his body at the same time. Where was his second bartender though?

"Where the hell you been?" Anthony stormed under his breath to keep the patrons from hearing him.

"I got tied up," Cecil retorted, moving behind the bar at a nonchalant pace that further enraged Anthony.

This was not the place, Anthony told himself, and converted his interrogation to strictly business. "Where's Maxine, and Ron for that matter?"

"Probably on her way, and I'm not Ron's keeper," Cecil grumbled under his breath, then walked away from Anthony and took a drink order.

It was all Anthony could do not to throw the rack of glasses at his brother. Anthony set it down hard, and a few heads momentarily turned, then went back to their previous conversations. He watched his brother go over to Vonetta, and lean across the bar, kiss her on the cheek,

and begin a casual chat session—while the two males that
were buying drinks seemed to deflate. He'd wring his
brother's chubby neck, just like he used to when they
were kids!

"Yeah, baby," Cecil was saying as Anthony strode up
behind him, "tonight you look good enough to sop up
with a biscuit."

Anthony's eyes narrowed, and he could feel his pulse
in his temples. "Man, we don't have the time tonight.
Vicki called in, and Eddie's backed up in the kitchen—"

"Hey, man, I just walked in the door. Chill," Cecil replied, his voice dropping an octave. "I'll be with you in
a minute. The bar's not going anywhere."

Anthony moved away and walked across the floor to
hail a waitress. When she neared him, tray in hand, he
leaned into to her. "I'll put something extra in your hand
tonight, but I need ten minutes in the back room with
Cecil. Can you cover the bar for me for a minute, ask
Jean to cover for you, and I'll hook her up too."

"Yeah, boss," the waitress sighed. "I know you gotta
handle some thangs."

Anthony nodded, came up behind Vonetta on the patron's side, and motioned to Cecil. "I need to see you in
the back, *now*. Lisa's got this for ten."

"Screw all this rhetoric, man," Cecil argued. "I don't
have to explain my whereabouts to you. I'm grown, and
the last time I checked, you weren't my boss! We're supposed to be partners, so this partner didn't feel like coming in until I did."

"That's irresponsible, Cecil. And since we're on the
subject, you're damned straight, we *supposed* to be partners. That means half the weight, *partner!*"

"Oh, so because I'm livin' my life, unlike your ass, that
means I'm not takin' the weight? Or, are you goin' back

to the start of this thing, talkin' about the money? Which is it?" Cecil demanded.

"It has nothing to do with who put in what at the beginning. It has to do with the basics. What if I didn't show up to open this joint tonight, huh? Then what? Or if I didn't come in early enough to hear all the bull on the voice mail about who else planned to take this beautiful Saturday night off . . . and be here to come up with a Plan B? Or to set up, and make sure we had enough liquor stocking the shelves for this run on the bar tonight? Tell me that, Cecil!"

"I'd say, if you didn't show up, you didn't show up. Period. End of story."

He wanted to punch his brother out so badly that he had to put his right hand in his pocket and move away from him.

"There'd be goddamned people lined up around the corner to get in then, Cecil, and they'd leave and go to another establishment! Have you any idea how long it took to build up this level of clientele?"

"Oh, like I wasn't here from the jump?" Cecil folded his meaty arms over his soft chest and stood wide-legged in the middle of the floor.

"And you'd throw away a business that turns this much cash on the barrelhead for a piece of ass?"

"Didn't you—the night before? You left me so—"

"That was *my wife.* Don't you ever compare Nina to—"

"Just 'cause she's your wife don't mean a thing! You still rolled out of here early and left me to lock up and deal with the club, payroll, everything that had to get—"

"And, when's the last time I did that? A year ago . . . two years ago? Longer? I always close up!"

An eerie silence came over them, as Cecil's logic got cornered. Both brothers stood facing each other, gulping in deep breaths of sudden fury, and releasing it through rage-widened nostrils.

"I knew it would come to this one day," Cecil finally muttered. "Just because your money paid for everything to start up doesn't mean I didn't put anything into this. I've paid my dues, but you're still counting green. That's why my name don't mean nuthin' and you treat me like I'm an employee, not your partner. It's always been your way or the highway."

"The reason your name isn't on anything is because when we bought the building, your credit was so jacked up everybody you owed would have owned it by now. Then, even though you get a partner's cut and make no less than me, we had to keep the business in my name so your ass couldn't be hauled down to child support court. You asked me not to put you on any assets, because, as you claimed, bitches was always lying on you, and you didn't have no babies. That, too, is irresponsible, but I can't get in the middle of your personal business, like you've told me a hundred times. But if Moms ever found out she might have grandchildren in the street she never saw, she'd have a damned stroke. But I didn't tell your business—that was for you to tell. So don't blame me for not having you legally tied to this club—that was your choice, not mine. Am I correct, or am I the one who's crazy?"

Anthony watched his brother's gaze narrow on him with such imploded resentment that it momentarily chilled him. He'd always known and accepted that they had a brotherly rivalry between them. That was just a part of having siblings, especially a younger one with only a few years separating them, but it had been years since he'd seen the look his brother cast in his direction now.

When a light, female-sounding tap came to the door, Anthony glanced at his watch. "Need a few minutes more, Lisa. How you holding up?"

There was no answer, but the door opened slowly and a female form filled the frame. It took Anthony a moment to mentally calibrate the image of his wife. "This is a really bad time, baby," he muttered, fastening his gaze on Cecil.

"But I was just—"

"I said, it's a really bad time, Nina."

His line of vision had not moved from Cecil's face as he'd spoken, and he waited till he heard the door close before speaking to his brother again. "The club has been losing money to the tune of five thousand a month, despite the crowd. Wanna talk to me about it? *That part is my business.*"

"Hey, girl." Vonetta laughed as she tried to catch up with Nina, who was headed for the door. "Wait up!"

Nina slowed her pace, but her intention was still the same. To leave and get some space. She told herself that she'd stop long enough to give Vonetta a two-minute rundown, then she was out of there. She hated this club, what it did to her man's demeanor, and she hated the way it always seemed to create a divide between them. As soon as Vonetta was in earshot, she'd tell her.

"Chile, I have the scoop for you," Vonetta blurted out on a healthy chuckle. "Where you going so fast?" she asked in rapid-fire succession, not giving Nina a chance to get a word in edgewise while pulling her against the grain of the crowd to the bar. "You cannot jet now. I saw you come in as I was coming back from the ladies' room, and I tried to wave you down, but you didn't see me. I was trying to stop you from going in the back room and getting in between Tony and Cecil, 'cause I think I got Cecil in a world of trouble with his brother. But he's cool. He won't give up the tapes to Tony."

Vonetta's words were slamming against her ears too fast, and mixing with the loud saxophones and voices, twisting around her own hurt and disappointment, and falling on the hardwood floor. Only bits and pieces of what her girlfriend was saying entered her brain. "OK," Nina sighed. "One drink, then I'm going home after I go see my dad. I need a one-on-one with him . . . was going to ask Tony for his opinion, but I guess that'll have to wait." She didn't elaborate, and Vonetta had missed the nonverbal cue to inquire, so she let the subject matter drop.

"The night is young," Vonetta laughed, pulling Nina by the elbow and glancing around the room, oblivious to what Nina was trying to tell her. "I found two brothers who bought me a bottle of Dom, you know, you know . . . C'mon, while we can still get a seat—Lisa saved it for me. You sit down; I'll stand and fill you in. But girl, this is too rich to miss!"

Nina followed Vonetta's sassy hip swivel through the crowd and found herself plopped down on a stool. When Lisa greeted her and brought her a glass of champagne, all Nina could do was shake her head.

"Here's the deal, and I've gotta tell you quick," Vonetta whispered into Nina's ear. "Last night, guess who I went home with?"

Nina let her breath out hard. "Girl, I thought you were going to tell me something new, and I've got to—"

"You've got to listen," Vonetta said, laughing.

"OK," Nina sighed again and took a sip of champagne. "Who?"

"Your brother-in-law."

Nina did a double-take and both women's eyes met. When Nina covered her mouth, Vonetta winked and laughed out loud.

"Told you it was gonna be some mess in here tonight," Vonetta whispered mischievously. "All the way live."

"That's why you weren't there when I tried to call you this morning . . . I just thought you were out seeing clients, and—"

"Shut up, and listen." Vonetta chuckled, pulling out a cigarette, lighting it, then taking a sip of champagne. "I got all your morose, cryptic messages when I got home. I was at Cecil's. You know we had a thing a while ago when you and Tony first hooked up, but then, Miss Maxine—I call her Mommy—came into the picture, promising him the world and buying his lazy butt anything he wanted, and you know me, I don't support no man, they gotta come to me like that."

"Then why'd you go home with him?" Nina could not comprehend what the sexy, seemingly got-it-all-together Vonetta could want with yang-talking, pudgy, immature Cecil. That was her brother-in-law, and sure, she loved him . . . but, Vonetta and Cecil? She hadn't understood the attraction the first time around, but now? Especially since Vonetta had a man. Manuel Johnson was *fine*.

"Well, girl," Vonetta said in a sly tone, "the truth is, he's kinda cute, and we go way back, and it had been a few weeks since I had any, and you and Tony really kicked it off, truth be told. Manuel's been getting on my nerves, but he's my bread and butter at the job, can't mess that up."

"Me and Tony?" Again, her friend wasn't making any sense.

"I don't know what Cecil walked into back there last night, but he came back all quiet and depressed, and just wanted to talk. Maxine was sweatin' him about some of her usual silly nonsense, so while she was in the back office, and since you and Tony had left already, he said, 'Can we get out of here? You drive.' I did. We sat outside, in a space around the corner from his spot on the street, running our mouths, until this homeless dude got on our nerves. So we went inside, kept talking, which led to touching . . . and the poor man started telling me about that bitch Maxine and how he can't even get it up with her anymore, because she rides him for money all day, every day, so hard. Well," Vonetta said, laughing and cocking an eyebrow as she took a luxurious sip of her champagne, followed by a long cigarette drag, "he presented a challenge that I had to address. The doctor was in da houze."

"Oh, my God . . ."

"Then, after I wore his butt out, and we slept till three, who comes by looking for Cecil?"

"Maxine?" Nina's hand was still at her mouth, and her glass of champagne was getting warm where it sat.

"No. Your husband."

"Tony?"

"Are you married to anybody else?" Vonetta asked sarcastically, then giggled. "Yup. He wanted to talk, and Cecil told him it was a bad time. He thought Maxine was in there with him. I just lit a cigarette and listened to the feathers fly."

"Is that what I just walked into?"

"Yeah, girl, but it's more about the fact that Cecil rolled in here around seven-thirty, and all hell was breaking loose in the club, leaving everything on Tony, I suppose."

"Seven-thirty . . . Oh, Vonetta, I know Tony was fit to be tied."

"My name's Bennet, and I ain't in it," Vonetta said, laughing. "That fool knew he had to go to work."

"You came back here separately, I take it?" Again, murky dealings and new twists had accosted her senses for the second time today. First her mother's confession, now her best friend's liaison with her brother-in-law was unfurling in a way that was rocking the foundation of her husband's business partnership! It was almost too much to take in one day. Nina raised her glass to the barmaid to refill it as Vonetta rattled on.

"I came to the club after I got your last, and more upbeat, message, which had shifted like mercury from the tone of the first two. I assumed your mood had improved, and the doctor didn't need to make a house call to check on you," Vonetta said, chuckling in a conspiratorial tone. "Figured you and Tony might be back in love, and you'd be here, so I beat it over to the club to catch you. Only to find out that you never came in. But that ain't even the good part."

"There *cannot* be more?" Nina accepted her fresh champagne and nearly downed it. This was nothing short of pure conflama—confusion and live drama.

"I didn't make Cecil late for work. I left as soon as Tony cleared out."

"What happened? You put the poor man in a coma or something? Did he fall back to sleep?"

Vonetta's eyes flashed with a new level of mischief. "Nope, he'd recovered from that."

"Then what?" Nina laughed, growing impatient. "Why couldn't he get here on time to help his brother?"

Vonetta shrugged and accepted another drink from Lisa, who seemed to know to keep them coming. She stopped, looked at the bubbles in her glass, turning it around in the light for dramatic effect before taking a sip.

"I didn't make him late," Vonetta cooed. "So his job performance issues are not my fault. I solved all of his performance issues, trust me."

"C'mon, already, girl," Nina said, laughing deeply, feeling the effects of two quickly consumed glasses of champagne while working on a third.

"I guess his direct supervisor had issues when she couldn't get him to answer the door last night, and his phone was off the hook, and his beeper was turned off . . . and she saw me walk out the front door, kiss him, and wave at her as she almost hit a pole—while I sashayed my tired ass around the corner to my car, wearing the same thing she saw me in last night. Tacky, but effective. That mighta had something to do with why he couldn't get here on time. He had to handle his post-op business. I was just the doctor making a house call on the afflicted. She oughta thank me," Vonetta said, laughing. "I cleaned his pipes, and he's as good as new."

Nina let her forehead fall into her palms. No wonder Anthony was having a spasm if he even knew about this part. In one night, his rock-solid manager, Maxine, would probably be tendering her resignation, and his brother was screwing up so badly that the poor man couldn't get any respite.

"Vonetta," Nina said as she kissed her wild girlfriend's cheek, "remind me to lock you up and throw away the key when you get like this. Remind me, won't you, that you transform before every full moon. I know it isn't personal, but—"

"Well speaking of she-wolves," Vonetta cut in with a deep chuckle, pinching Nina's arm. "There's one in mid-change, fangs out, with fuzzy knuckles, raggedy gear on, and definitely having a bad hair day."

Nina's eyes scanned the room and when her gaze landed on her target, she held her breath and let it out slowly. The lean, brown form of a woman was drawn up tight, walking with purpose, and was admittedly not as stylish as she normally appeared. In fact, she looked ready for an old-fashioned beat down. What made it worse, there was no telling what Vonetta would say, or do, to escalate matters. Lisa also seemed to sense the precarious nature of things, and she swiftly went to the far end of the bar to head off the possible open-floor confrontation that could damage the club's reputation for being a chic haven.

"They're in the back, Maxine," Lisa said excitedly. "The boss wants to see you."

Nine

"Listen, just don't start a bunch of yang up here in the club. Promise me," Nina implored as she stood to leave. "I'm going to stop by my mom and dad's, then I'll be home in a couple of hours. They go to bed early, so call me when you get in. OK?"

"Yeah, yeah, yeah," Vonetta said as she polished off her champagne. "I'll behave myself, and I won't tell Tony about the Cecil thing."

"OK," Nina said, sighing. "But do me a favor. Tell Tony I'm not angry . . . that I just needed to stop in and check on my folks."

"Will do," Vonetta said in a bored tone. "Give them both my love."

"Glad that you could finally make it in here tonight, Maxine," Anthony said in a surly tone as she barged into the office. Before he could say another word, Cecil had stormed out of the room, slamming the door behind him. Although he was pissed beyond reason, her entry gave him pause. Something fishy was going on. Why would she be mad at him? Seemed like a lot of that was going around, and it was catching.

He studied her face, noticing that her light brown eyes were filled with tears. Her expression also carried hurt

within it, despite the fact that her arms were folded over
her chest and her chin was thrust upward in anger. He
knew the stance well. He'd seen it too many times from
Nina. In fact, Maxine and Nina were reverse copies of
the same form, he noted as he walked toward Maxine.
Nina was taller and a bit lighter in complexion, but they
had the same delicate bone structure, chiseled features,
and wide, light eyes. The only difference was that Nina's
were gray and Maxine's were light hazel. They even
seemed to wear their hair the same.

"So go ahead and fire me 'cause I was late on a busy
night," she fumed, her voice cracking as she spat out her
complaint. "Might as well. I can't work here anymore, no
how."

Tough on the outside, a kitten inside . . . He stared at
Maxine for a minute and watched her lower lip tremble
as she started to speak, then seemed to change her mind
upon a deep swallow.

"Why would I fire my best manager for a one-night
lapse?" he said quietly, easing his stance and putting his
hands in his pockets.

"Well, I quit anyway," she murmured, then looked
down at the floor. "I can't work where I'm disrespected."

"Who disrespected you, lady?" Anthony said in a calm
voice. "Tell me and they're gone."

This time, Maxine turned away from him and hugged
herself. From behind, he could see her narrow shoulders
shaking ever so slightly as her hands slid up and down
her upper arms.

"You ain't gettin' rid of him, so no need to go into
it."

Anthony walked around to stand before Maxine, so she
wouldn't be giving him her back to consider. He hated
to see women cry. What did his stupid brother do to the
poor girl this time?

"What'd he do?" Anthony asked quietly, placing his finger under her chin to lift her face.

Maxine just shook her head.

"Hurry up," Eddie hissed through his teeth, constantly looking back through the kitchen door. "I told you to never come for a load on a Saturday night, anyway! Y'all are supposed to come Fridays during the day, after the weekend shipment count—when Maxine goes home to change and I'm here alone prepping for dinners."

"We did," Duane fussed, walking quickly to shove a case out the back door to Ron. "But the son of a bitch is sleeping here, now. Cecil ain't our problem."

"You got maybe another three-minute window, then I'm locking the back door," Eddie whispered in a nervous voice. "If your asses get caught, I ain't got nothin' to do with it."

"Chill, man," Duane said as he hoisted up a heavy box of frozen shrimp. "It only took us five minutes to get ten cases of booze out. But like I said, the bar over there was running dry, and I need the rest of the meat. You got my chicken and steaks?"

Ron poked his head through the door. "Yo, you'd better get a move on. Saw Cecil come out the office, and Tony won't be far behind him. Maxine's in there with him now."

"Where's my knot?" Eddie whispered in a rush. "Y'all can get the rest later."

Nina rested her forehead on the steering wheel and looked at her parents' home. Nothing was what it seemed to be, and there was no more home for her, really. In one single confession, her sentimental memories of being a child there had been swept away. Now every tense look and seething statement her parents had exchanged took on a new meaning—despite the outer appearances of calm. Even the short answers, and many of the impatient responses her mother had been renowned for, all made perfect sense.

All Nina could think about now was how she'd blinded herself to the palpable undercurrent, all because she didn't want to see . . . if you couldn't trust the people under your own roof, then who could you trust? It would have been like acknowledging that she'd been sleeping with the enemy of mistrust for all these years. That was worse than ignoring it, then. Perhaps that's how her mother felt. But the reality of those affairs never completely went away.

She forced herself to climb the front steps and ring the bell. Her father pulled back the curtains and smiled warmly. Nina nearly convulsed.

"Pumpkin! What a surprise. Twice in one day," he crooned as he swept her into an embrace.

Nina hugged her father back, but without enthusiasm. He immediately noticed.

"Is everything all right?" her father asked in a soft tone, holding her back from him to look her in the eyes.

"Yes," she lied. "I just wanted to see you, since I'd missed you when I came by earlier in the day. Mom said she had an event to work on for the sorority tonight, so I thought I'd circle back and catch you."

Her father relaxed and smiled. "Yes, your mother's interminable social gatherings," he muttered good-naturedly, then led the way for her to follow him into the living room.

She watched his tall, proud carriage and the way he still had an Ivy League professor look about him, donning a neat pullover sweater and khaki slacks while at home. He made a sweeping gesture with his hand and motioned for her to sit down next to him on the sofa. When she did so, he followed suit, and she was amazed that she'd never really *seen* her father before.

Even at his age, he was still a very handsome man. His skin was a deep, golden bronze with tones of red that hinted at once-high cheekbones. His hallmark was his deep-set, steel gray eyes beneath dense black eyebrows, and his mane—a shock of glistening waves of silver hair, cut conservatively and neatly. She appraised her father from a woman's perspective now, instead of that of a little girl, and could see how his tall, athletic build, witty conversation, and still-brilliant smile could have swept the women of his era, including her mother, off their feet.

"So, we are visiting," he said with a dashing smile. "Glad to have a private moment with my favorite girl. Since she ran away and got married, I can't get her to myself anymore."

She allowed instinct to draw her to him to give him a real hug. Then she held on tight. She missed her daddy, the one that was now gone and changed into just a man. "I miss you too, Dad," she whispered through a swallow. "You don't know how much."

"Aw, pumpkin, I haven't gone anywhere. It's still the same old me, in the same old house, doing the same old things I've always done. So, how's married life?"

Nina's heart ached, and she sucked in a deep breath to stanch the pain. What could she say, or should she say, to get this heavy burden off her chest? If only Anthony had had a few moments, just a second to tell her what it might have been like from a man's point of view. Then she might have known better how to start this precarious conversation.

"Fine, I suppose," she said quietly, moving away from the embrace. "But can we talk, Dad?"

"Yeah, honey, sure," he replied with a tinge of concern in his voice. "Is everything OK with you and Anthony?"

She hesitated, and decided to speak from the heart.

"You know, I'm not being honest with you," she said quietly. "No, everything is not all right."

She watched the gleam of joy fade from her father's face, and he sat back, stared at her, and rubbed his chin with a sigh. But, to his credit, he was an excellent listener, because he added no commentary. She just saw empathy fill his eyes. In that instant, she knew what she'd been expecting from Anthony. That look, the eye-to-eye communication that said without words, *Baby, I'm sorry for what's happened, whatever it is, and I'm there for you . . . and I have all the time in the world for you to tell me.* That's what she needed when things were going wrong.

"At first, I thought he was having an affair with a woman who works for him at his club," she began slowly and cautiously. "But then, I found out that it was merely job stress that was affecting the way we communicate with each other. But the problem is, I don't know how to help alleviate his stress, and our communication is still in shambles, which still puts us at risk for finding a quick fix outside of our marriage. Do you understand?"

Her father's gaze never left hers and his eyes spoke volumes. "Yes, I understand," he whispered. "And I am so sorry."

His simple statement carried a lifetime of meaning for her, and guilt tore at her insides for having trapped her own father into discussing his worst pain. But she pressed on, not sure if she really wanted to know the answer to the question that haunted her.

"Dad," she asked quietly, "why do men have affairs . . . especially when they really love their wives?"

"I don't know," he whispered back, then, for the first time in her life, he looked away from her while speaking.

"You're a psychology professor," she whispered. "You have to know."

"But," he murmured, "I'm not God, although there were times when I've wished I were."

"Why?" The strange comment drew her in and placed her in a more observant, detached mode. Their conversation was almost becoming like an eerie out-of-body experience.

"What man doesn't want to feel all-powerful?" her father said in a quiet voice. "What man doesn't want to be proud of his accomplishments, and to sit back to survey all that he did, and say, 'It was good'—then rest on the seventh day? What man isn't seduced by the concept of wanting to build a financially secure future for his family, to provide his wife with all that she could ever want, to give his children the best education, and to feel some sense of dignity and respect within himself and his community? And what man doesn't want to feel like he's the alpha and the omega to solving all the problems that could ever befall his family?"

"But that's such an impossible goal," she whispered, seeing Anthony's face in her mind as she spoke to her dad.

"It is how this culture teaches us to believe in being a man, and it teaches women to look for men who can reach that Olympic bar without falter, as well. And, for many of us, we don't measure up. Black men of my era always seemed to fall short of this, simply because of the design of things . . . and not much has changed. But I'd have to say that, regardless of even race, color, or creed, this premise of what defines a man holds true."

It was the unvarnished truth, and it entered her marrow and congealed with her father's pain as he sat across from her with his hands folded and his eyes searching the horizon, just past the windowsill, for answers.

"Even at my age and yours," he continued in a faraway voice, "I want to be your savior, to remove your pain. I want to wave my hand and have my daughter happy, and laughing, and in love again. I want to snap my fingers and make her husband attentive and financially capable.

I want to blink my eyes and make her able to conceive, knowing that is her greatest wish. I want to dry her tears and make my little girl's face light up with sudden, inexplicable joy. . . . Oh yes, it's silly, but, that's what we all want."

She moved across the sofa and placed her hands over her father's, then kissed his cheek. He looked so tired from the sheer admission that she, too, for just a moment, wished that she could do all of those things for him as well.

"But what does an affair accomplish?" she murmured, forcing him to look at her briefly before his line of vision went back to the horizon.

"Nothing," her father said with a sad chuckle. "It's a foolish endeavor that makes you even less than a man."

"Then why?" she pressed, knowing that she was on the verge of a breakthrough within her own mind. Yet the question teetered so close to unveiling her father's privacy while exposing her own fears about Anthony that she immediately wished she could retract it. She understood just how close they both were to discovery when his gaze met hers.

"Because," he whispered, "as much as we may want to be God, we also want to curl up in a ball and cry about the responsibilities we've taken on—or were thrust upon us, by definition. We want Mommy to make it just go away, for a little while and to kiss away the boo-boo. We know we aren't supposed to cry—being men—or be afraid, or make a career mistake that can cost our family its financial future, and that the last people we can tell are those entrusted into our protective care. So . . ." he trailed off. "You run."

"But that only makes it worse, doesn't it?'

Her father nodded, and let out his breath heavily. "You run to a very temporary hiding place. It's a place where you are the all-powerful hunter, instead of the hunted.

You go there like a junkie—for your dignity fix, your fear fix, your pain fix—and the place where you run welcomes you with open arms, begs for you to stay awhile, feeds your wounded ego a king's meal, and greets you with the passion that those who really know you well enough to understand that you're an impostor to the throne, do not. It is a foolish but very seductive siren . . . one that has even called and captured presidents."

Nina cocked her head to the side, and allowed her line of vision to travel out of the window with her father's.

"Think about it," he said, now looking at her. "You have a white man, without race as a barrier, who has pulled himself up from his bootstraps to overcome poverty and an ordinary trailer-park existence, who then married well—as they say—to a beautiful, intelligent woman, who stands behind him, and as a result has a lovely family, lives in a modern-day castle with guarded care, has his every material need or wish granted internationally, and he is the ruler of the free world. But he still has an affair. Why is that?"

Nina blinked and shrugged her shoulders, now looking at her father intently. "Because he wanted it all, and then some?"

"Possibly," her father sighed, then let his gaze escape hers again. "Or, my guess would be, that he was afraid. Pick either President Clinton or Kennedy. It's the same."

"Afraid?" It didn't make sense to her. "Of what?"

"Of knowing that you, a single person, had the sheer power that could start or stop a war, or veto a bill that could either help or hinder millions. Of being the one that could go down in history for causing World War Three because of the wrong negotiating tactic at a United Nations Peace Summit. Afraid of getting assassinated, or having your family harmed. Afraid of getting older and feeling your virility waning, even if ever so slightly. Afraid of having the public suddenly stop adoring you. There are a million things for a successful man to be afraid of, but the issues are the same: A man is afraid of making bad decisions for his family, for those in his charge, for his career, for his sexuality, and the more that is expected of him, and the more he expects of himself, often the more vulnerable he can be because there is even more to lose. Success is a double-edged blade that cuts both ways. Just like poverty, where the less you have, the more inadequate you feel, and the more inclined you are to have that wound abated with a quick fix, because in your mind, you have nothing of consequence to lose. Ironic, isn't it—male logic?"

Again, she could only stare at her father, who without direct admission, had told her everything she needed to know. But he had done so in parable, oddly employing the same entry method she had used to begin their conversation. But then had she not learned this form and structure from him through a lifetime of watching and admiring him?

Her father had masterfully distanced and illustrated by example, but had also done so eloquently, with so much compassion and wisdom, another of his hallmarks. She could never take away his shield now to expose him, even though it was plain that he understood that she knew. He deserved that much of his dignity . . . it was in his eyes. A request for forgiveness without losing her respect as his daughter. But his eyes also held another request, for her to allow him to purge his soul.

"What did you really want to be, Dad?" she asked just above a whisper.

His gaze never met hers, and he let his breath out slowly. "I wanted to be a practicing psychiatrist with my own clients, while also on staff at a major medical facility with full tenure at the University of Pennsylvania, and to teach in their large medical classrooms, lecturing on the latest research topics. High hopes," he added with a wave of his hand and a grin on his face, but she noticed the tears in his eyes.

"And," he exclaimed dramatically, as though a child asking Santa for a long list of gifts, "I wanted to take my wife with me to international conferences, and to interact with my peers in the profession, and ultimately publish my findings and dissertation on the effects of racism in this country on the African-American family and individual psyche, because I felt it was important to be a member of DuBois' Talented Tenth—to make a true intellectual contribution to change in this country."

"But you can do that now . . . all of your research, and the history you've actually lived through, Dad."

He chuckled at the concept to dismiss it. "I'm retired, and I have blown my window of opportunity. Such is life. Penn has black professors these days, not a lot, but some. Plus, another younger black man, *and his wife,* have beaten me to the punch, and are already well-published on the subject now. My studies are old hat, passé."

Her father chuckled again in a self-deprecating manner, and kept his line of vision locked on some unseen point beyond the living room bay window. Nina's thoughts traveled with his gaze, wondering what he could have achieved by having the same drive simply placed in a different era, and how many other wounded heroes there were like him in a world of gatekeepers that only let a small few slip through?

"But that was before such dreams were realistic or achievable, beyond a very small margin." He laughed awkwardly when she remained silent. "Your mother, however, believed I could do it. Top social status was very important to her. There was a lot of pressure to hit one's head against a brick wall. And I tried anyway, knowing my margin of possibilities was about as good as the state lottery. And, after each failed attempt . . ."

His voice trailed off and he cast his gaze to the floor.

"She was always better than me at fighting battles, and we should have listened to my mother, who told us to go down to Morehouse College to achieve what I couldn't do here. Your mother was all for it and probably would have taken Atlanta society by storm. But the thought of crossing the Mason-Dixon Line with my family, at that time . . . no. I still wouldn't have done it."

"But Dad, you are a tenured professor at a historically black university up here. You're respected, well-liked, your students adore you—to hell with some Ivy League fortress that wouldn't let you or your ideas in. To hell with them!" Nina stood and paced, her heart breaking for her father's defeat. The look on his face drew her back to sit beside him, and she clutched his hands within her own. "Why did you let them do this to you guys?"

"You are so much like my Rose," he whispered, "That's why I adore you so much, pumpkin. She gave you the fight, and courage . . . and she said those same things to me almost half a century ago. Then, one day, she got tired of pushing me into battles I wasn't prepared for, and went for it herself, and landed a teaching post at Penn. She beat 'em, and me, in the process, which is not her fault, not Penn's fault. It's mine."

"If an affair occurs, for all these intangible reasons . . . then it could happen to any marriage. So what's to stop it?" she asked in a very quiet, but direct way.

"I don't know . . ." he whispered, but not with a disheartened tone. His professor voice of researching a problem in his mind had come forth, and she watched him work on the riddle with a strong, analytical mind. "Women always seem to think it has something to do with their sexuality, or the lack thereof, but it has very little to do with that—if men would be honest."

Nina allowed her body to slump back against the soft sofa cushions. Again, for the first time, she really heard what had been said. Her father's simple admission had been touted on talk shows and discussed ad nauseum in women's gathering and in books . . .it was indeed a worn forum topic. But this time, she listened with new ears. Hearing it here, now, and from this source, made it sink into her brain with the weight of an anvil.

"I believe it begins with real communication," he murmured, deep in thought, and oblivious to her awe. "But that's such a pat answer these days. What does that really mean?"

"I know what you're saying, Dad. Everybody's trying to communicate, and the divorce rate is going off the charts anyway."

"No. Don't confuse a high divorce rate with a seemingly higher lack-of-communication rate, or seemingly more affairs," he said promptly, returning his gaze to her. "No. That's two different subjects."

His response startled her. "How so?"

"People are getting divorced more today because the problems are out of the closet. There's no less communication between man and wife today than there was fifty years ago. In fact, there was less then. But divorce once had more dire social and financial consequences associated with it. We just see the outcomes in the open today, but there have always been frustrations, affairs, all manner of issues. People were simply more discreet with their problems. No. Let's get back to your original question."

Nina chuckled. "I love it when you're teaching," she said softly. "Did you know that? It's the way your voice takes on this tone of command and authority, and your eyes get all intense, and I always kind of expect you to stand and begin pacing as you lecture."

Her father smiled in earnest for the first time since they'd sat down, and a trace of white-knight twinkle seemed to shine from his eyes as he graciously accepted her compliment, as well as her forgiveness, which was embedded within it.

"That bad, am I?" he said, laughing. "Well, I do think better on my feet. Years of classroom habit."

"Stand and teach, professor." She chuckled, waving her hand for him to take the imaginary podium in the middle of the floor. "The problem and hypothesis solution."

"People are talking more," he began with authority as he stood and walked about the floor. His hands were clasped behind his back, and his gaze swept the room as though he and Nina were within a filled collegiate amphitheater. "But they are listening less. In the past, we didn't talk as much, so we relied on body language and small signs of consideration to fill the void of words."

"But there were still problems, professor, as you stated earlier."

"Correct, and duly noted," he added with confidence. "Because that mysterious language was equally misinterpreted for the same reasons that it is today."

"Then, if not with words, and not through gesture, how does one pre-empt what could be construed as the inevitable?"

"Women must—"

"But wait, professor, that is a sexist preliminary to your comment. Why is it up to the woman to heal all of these wounds? We have just as many fears and issues, and have fought hard for equality. What's the difference in who communicates first?"

"Maturity," he said back so quickly that it stunned her. "At any given age."

Again, she cocked her head to one side and asked for clarity without verbally stating the question. Her father's gaze softened as he stared at her and his sad smile was filled with pride in her as a student. He came to her and stooped before her, gathering her hands within his as their gazes met.

"Yes, maturity, my pumpkin," he whispered hoarsely. "And having a viable mate who is near your league, like

Anthony. What I'm about to tell you doesn't work if your partner is hopelessly beneath your grade, or if you two come from totally divergent customs, goals, and expectations."

"But you and Mom were so evenly matched in all of those things. How can I be sure we won't go down that same path, and—I love you both so much that it hurts to even ask this—I'm afraid now, myself. How do I know it won't happen to me?"

"Because you are not scared to admit out loud that you're afraid. Or to ask the questions that your mother never bothered to ask—but turned a blind eye to avoid. And because you know that your husband is in pain, you will go to him and not threaten his ability to provide with words that cut and burn in another's mind forever, until death do you part. Because you will tell him that it's all right for him to change his profession and that it is not his fault that the shoe he first brought into your marriage no longer fits. You'll say that you don't care what your parents think, or people think, and material things can always be replaced, but not him. And because you will have the patience and wisdom to understand everything that he is afraid of, you'll kiss his boo-boos instead of rubbing salt in the wounds of his failures. And you will have the grace and wisdom to know that you will always be faster, and smarter, and better at figuring out problems than he—not just because you are my daughter, but because you're a woman . . . and that's why God created your kind second—after the first flawed prototype He made, called man.

"And you will understand that a wise negotiator takes the high road, and that force only escalates matters, and with that wisdom you will be rewarded with a loyal follower who thinks he's in the lead. Maturity means freedom—being free to understand, without feeling that you are giving ground by occasionally giving in."

Her father stood and went back to his seat beside her on the sofa. In the quiet that wrapped around them, she wondered how many times she had not heard what had truly been said, had not seen what had been so clearly asked for, and how afraid her man truly was? Her father's hand found hers as they sat together a long while in companionable silence.

Ten

"I don't think your partner in crime is coming back here tonight," Anthony yelled across the bright room as he hoisted another chair on top of a table, then bent to grab the mop.

Vonetta Winston cringed inwardly, hoping that Cecil hadn't spilled the beans or that in Maxine's rage, she hadn't gone into excessively gory detail with Anthony; his opinion of her mattered.

"I'm cool, and I figured that, which is why I stayed." She couldn't be sure whether Anthony was talking about Nina or Cecil, and she decided to hedge her bets by playing the odds, then wheedling what he knew out of him.

"Yeah, well," Anthony said in a weary tone, "you'd better leave when the girls do. Eddie will walk you all to your cars."

"I was planning on staying until you locked up, then walking you out," she said, taking a slow sip of cognac. "We need to talk."

"Why is that all I've been hearing from women lately?" Anthony said in a disgusted tone as he slung the mop. "Anyway, I don't let nobody but the fellas lock up. It's too dangerous, especially on the weekends. A bullet doesn't care where it lands."

"Oh, puh-leeze," Vonetta scoffed, waving her hand at him.

Anthony looked up from the floor and let the mop handle fall against the nearby table, creating a clatter of wood against wood as he folded his arms over his chest. "I ain't making myself clear, am I, Vonetta? I said it was too dangerous, and I don't even let female employees do that, much less patrons."

"But I'm not an employee or a patron. I'm more like family," she argued.

"That's especially why I don't want you here when I lock up and make the deposit drop. If they pull a gun on you in the back alley or something, I'd never forgive myself." He let his breath out in a rush and grabbed the mop handle. "Case closed."

Vonetta stood and walked over to him and opened her purse, allowing a glint of metal to flash for a second in the overhead lights before closing it. "I'm an insurance detective, and licensed to carry it, and I know how to use it. I do bad guys in back alleys from time to time, remember?"

She smiled as he stopped, seemed stunned for a moment, then quickly collected himself and began mopping again. "I won't bother you," she said coolly, "and I can entertain myself until everybody leaves, you do your count, and are ready to roll. But we are going to talk. I'm not high-maintenance like our girl, Nina."

"Perish the thought," Anthony mumbled. "You ain't maintenance, but you are a piece of work."

Vonetta's smile widened and she sauntered over to the seat that she'd abandoned, hoisted herself up on a stool, and crossed her legs, leaning backward with both elbows on the bar to watch the man work. *God, he looked good.*

His shoulders defined precision as the muscles beneath his navy rib-knit sweater followed their way down the thick valley of his spine on each rhythm that expanded and contracted with a swipe of the water-laden mop across the floor. She watched the way his shirt clung to his torso, wishing at that moment that she were rib-knit fabric. The man was definitely poetry in motion. The view from behind him was particularly spectacular. Each time he bent and lunged at the offending floor, it caused his pants to cup against buns of steel, and the muscles in his thighs to strain the inner seams of them.

For years she'd tried to shake such images out of her head. A momentary pang of guilt made her open her purse and reach for a cigarette. After all, Nina was her girl . . . they went all the way back to high school. Vonetta closed her eyes and took a deep drag and let the smoke out through her nose. Regret swirled in the smoke she exhaled.

She should have never slept with Cecil, not the first time, and not now. There was just no substitute. Cecil knew it, and she knew it, even though she had looked into Cecil's eyes last night and had seen Tony. Yes, they had the same eyes. For two people so different in personality, they shared so much genetically: the same complexion and almost the same height. Their voices were also similar. But that was where the resemblance ended.

There was an inner strength about Tony that drew her. He didn't play around, didn't drink much, didn't give in to vices, kept in shape, and he was one helluva businessman. Nina was out of her mind to waste this for four months over a silly mess . . .

Vonetta took another drag and let it again out slowly, continuing to admire the body of the only man she'd fallen in love with. He was such a good friend, too . . . and put up with so much bull from everybody, but always seemed to forgive. That was a rare quality she'd never seen in her own home growing up. It had been cold and sterile, and a place where a large male like Anthony Williams answered a woman with his fists. It was also a place to have your womanhood stolen, as well as your money—if you weren't careful.

Vonetta stretched and, with a deep swig of cognac, shook off the unpleasant thoughts of growing up fast and hard. Nina didn't know anything about that side of life, so how could she possibly relate to this man who bore the weight of the world on his shoulders, and held it up like a fine, black Atlas? Spoiled, pampered bitch . . . the man even had the kind of parents that would take you in and make you one of their own, no matter who you were or where you came from. She had it all. Always did. And was whining about not having a baby?

Unconsciously, Vonetta's hand left her glass and rubbed her lower belly. If Cecil weren't such a loser, maybe she would have kept hers five years ago. She'd always wondered what it would have looked like . . . her or a genetic carbon copy from the DNA pool of Anthony? Then she would have had a real mother and a decent father, by way of the Williams clan, and a bunch of sisters. But even then she'd known that having Tony as just a brother wouldn't have worked. It would have messed her up for life, just like having Nina as just a sister-in-law was messing with Cecil's head now.

Vonetta downed her drink and watched Anthony approach her, not caring that he might notice the way she undressed him with her eyes. Hell, it had taken everything in her power not to call out the wrong name, the way Cecil slipped and called her Nina. But that was cool. They both knew why they were there: chasing dreams. Cecil was her buddy, and they shared that same secret pain of wanting what was not theirs to have. So it was all good, she told herself as she took another lazy drag off her cigarette.

She wasn't a bad person for feeling attracted to such a man, and she loved Nina like a sister, and genuinely liked Cecil—just not the way he needed her to. She actually felt sorry for him. Musta been hard growing up with such a tough act to follow. She knew that deep-to-the-bone hurt—Nina, as much as she loved her, had given her a dose of the same bitter potion since they were kids.

"OK," Anthony said in a solemn tone, pulling out a stool and sitting next to Vonetta.

He closed his eyes and lolled his neck from side to side, then hunched his shoulders forward and backward. It was positively mesmerizing. She studied the fatigue in his carriage, and the way his face still held a quality of patience and kindness, despite how tired she imagined him to be.

"Why don't I pour you a drink? Huh? You've been serving people all night, and who takes care of you, Tony?"

"I don't know, Vonetta. Yeah, that sounds good."

So did the sound of his voice. It was deep and mellow and relaxed. What was so hard about taking care of this man? she wondered as she went behind the bar and reached for the Johnny Walker Red. "I'm pouring you what you need, not what I know you're gonna ask for. No wine for the Rev tonight."

Anthony chuckled and accepted the glass, then raised it to her. Vonetta smiled.

"Lady, I'm beat. So if you're going to get on my case, I have no defenses left."

"I'm not here to get on your case," she crooned, leaning close to him as he sipped his drink. "I came here to offer an ear."

"It's that noticeable that I need one?"

"Yeah, it's that noticeable."

"I'm trying so hard, but I keep messing things up."

"You're not the one messing things up, Tony," she soothed, reaching across the bar and rubbing the length of his arm.

"Go ahead. Shoot. What did she say?"

Vonetta removed her hand and folded her arms as she continued to lean close to him. "Can we go in the back and sit down?"

"It's that bad, huh?" Anthony let out his breath and stood up. "Lemme turn out the lights and set the alarm. We can go in my office."

"And I'll bring my bottle and yours," Vonetta said, chuckling.

When he didn't object, she grabbed the bottle of cognac she'd been nursing, a clean glass, and the Scotch. Anticipation coursed through her as she followed him. She'd never have an opportunity like this again, and it had to be played very, very cautiously.

She slipped behind him and moved over to the sofa, leaving him just enough room to sit close beside her.

"She's pissed again, isn't she?"

His direct stare was so intense that she had to momentarily look away to keep from kissing him.

"Nina is complicated," Vonetta murmured. "She's like an orchid that requires a lot of care and attention."

Anthony nodded and took a sip from his glass. "And I've been treating her like a weed—letting her go unattended."

"You've had a lot on your mind," Vonetta whispered. "It's understandable."

"You have no idea." He looked at her briefly, then down at his feet.

"Try me," she said softly. "That's why I'm here."

"Vonetta, my business is going belly up, because my brother is the one that's probably stealing from me."

"Are you sure?" she asked softly, touching his shoulder.

He only nodded and then downed his drink. She read the cue and refilled his glass.

"That hurts to the bone, you know, Vonnie. I love that stupid bastard, and he messes up everything he touches."

Vonetta swallowed a sip of cognac to steady herself. He'd called her Vonnie, and looked her in the eyes when he'd said it, searching hers with his in a way that she'd always dreamed of. "Cecil has a lot of issues," she murmured quietly. "He's had a big brother who was fine, successful, and honorable looming over him all of his life. And he wants something of his own that he doesn't have to share with you—or credit to your help. It's not your fault. It's his head trip, but it affects you."

"But I'm his brother. I've always watched out for him, and had his back. How can he resent me for being what I'm supposed to be?"

The pain in his voice echoed through her soul and connected with a part of her that understood where all men's Achilles heels lie—down in the frightened little boy part that is covered by layers and layers of bulk muscle and attitude.

"One day, when he does something on his own, he'll look back and be thankful that he's been blessed with a brother like you, and he'll stop wanting everything you have, even Nina."

As soon as she'd said it, instinct made her want to take back the last part of her sentence, because his expression immediately hardened, and she knew that she was again dealing with his tougher side.

"You know," Anthony challenged, "I hear you, but I'm sick of taking the weight for Cecil's nonsense. I built this place with my own hands, Vonetta! Tore out walls, and put down insulation, and did the electrical work, and put years of hard-earned money into this joint. Broke my back to make it work, and all he ever did was BS around, give me a half day's labor for a full day's pay, and talk about my woman being too bourgeois, too flat-chested, too light-skinned, too this or that! Now he's stealing five thousand dollars a month from me—"

"You don't know that," she countered, trying to calm him and restore the previous opening.

"I don't know what?" he huffed, slouching back on the sofa and taking a deep swig from his glass.

"That it was all Cecil."

Again, she had his attention, and his eyes searched her face for a shred of hope.

"Listen," she said in an even tone without losing eye contact with him. "I do this for a living. Why don't you let me investigate where your hemorrhage might be coming from?"

"I can't ask you to do that," he said quietly, "and right now, I can't afford it."

"Did I say I was asking you to pay me?" Vonetta smiled and sat back.

"No, but . . . damn, girl."

"I'll tell you what, how about if I look at it as investment protection for that nice policy you'll give my firm for switching over to us for fire coverage. With that heavy life insurance instrument I know you have, plus auto and home owner's, you know, you know. . . . I can hook a brother up, if he hooks a sister up. Strictly business."

He laughed, and she eased closer to him.

"You have potential in here for multiple leaks," she said with confidence. Again she had his attention, and she shifted in her seat to give him the best view of her cleavage. "You've been missing cases of shipments, right?"

"Yeah. How'd you know?"

"Because I do this for a living, and that is usually the first sign of an inside job."

Anthony looked at her for a moment, then smiled and raised his glass. "I gotta give credit where credit is due. My bad."

"OK," she said, topping off his drink and taking a sip from her own glass. "That's one source. The person who has access to your kitchen freezers and liquor storage. Two, have you been missing register money?"

"Hell yeah," he sighed, flopping back again, this time closing his eyes as his head rested against the back of the sofa. "And Maxine just quit today because of some squabble with her and Cecil."

Vonetta eased back and propped her head up on her hand. So he didn't know . . . "Well, missing cash from the bar registers means it could be any of your bartenders, or your brother . . . or that the girls who are taking table receipts are pocketing some as they tally. And if there's money missing from the safe . . . well, that's Cecil—if only you and him have the combination."

"I've been through the same list in my head for months, and you're right. It's coming from everywhere," he said quietly. "The kitchen, the safe, the registers, and that makes everybody I trust, and called either a friend or considered family, a suspect. That's what's messin' with me, Vonnie. It's not just the money. I want to know who I can really trust in this world. Damn . . . Cecil and I are brothers. Maxine is like my sister. In fact, my own sister works the table circuit, and Eddie and I were thick in the military together, and kept each other from getting killed. Duane and I go back to high school, with Ron. It's like they're all my boys. We all make good money in here, split the profits, and it's like a second family. Now I'm not even sure if I want to be in the club scene."

"I know, baby," she whispered, again touching his arm as he lounged against the cushions with his legs outstretched before him. "You might have to let it go, or change everybody in here."

"I know . . . been thinking about selling it, but don't know what else I'd do for a living. I'm scared that I'd sell it too low and not have enough of a knot to transition into something viable, or go into the wrong venture. Hell, I never went to school, and the bar business was a safe bet. But to go and research something I never did before, and bet my household and whatnot on some potentially fly-by-night scheme. Oh man, Vonnie, there are so many variables."

"You are a capable, solid businessman, with plenty of options," she whispered, leaning near his face. "I've seen a lot of so-called educated fools out there, and deal with them every day, and I haven't run across your match for courage yet."

"I've been trying to get your girl to understand that I just need a little time to figure things out before . . . I need some head space to make a business transition and handle my next move, so that when we land, it ain't some stupid high-wire act with no net, especially if a baby would be involved. You can't roll like that, putting your family at risk, but the more I try to explain, the more I piss her off. Then we get to arguing, and the cold treatment starts, and I get cut off for four months."

"Like I said," she whispered, "it's not all you."

They looked at each other for a moment, then he closed his eyes again.

"Four months is a long time, Tony. Even iron wears out." The dull ache between her thighs reverberated through her skeleton each time the bass notes of his voice caressed her ear.

"Last night was the first time she let me near her, and by morning, we were back to arguing, then when she came in here tonight, I was in the middle of dealing with Cecil, and trying to keep my head on straight."

"You were handling your business, Tony. She can't fault you for that. I certainly don't."

The sound of Vonetta's voice, and her simple statement, was like receiving absolution. Why couldn't his wife understand him the way her best friend did?

"I'm so tired, Vonnie. I can't wage war at home and in here. I'm not trying to make excuses. I'm just being real. Do you understand what I'm saying?"

She allowed her finger to trace his forehead while his eyes remained closed. "I understand more than I think you do. Do you understand what I'm telling you? It's all right, and what goes on here stays between us."

Damn, he was exhausted, and the hand on his forehead felt so relaxing as it swept across his brow, taking away the headache that had nagged at his temples all day. Just to be able to say what was on his mind and get a viable solution, instead of a feminist manifesto of rhetoric. . . . The heavy scent of perfume collided with cigarette smoke until the warmth of lush female breasts against his chest made him open his eyes and break his reverie.

"Vonetta," he said gently, touching her face. "We can't go there, baby. Not like this, and not for these reasons. We'll both hate ourselves later."

"So you're sending me home to my vibrator again tonight?" She chuckled and touched his lips with her finger to keep him from speaking. "I won't tell if you don't. We're both hurting," she whispered, running her finger along his cheek, finding the opposite grain of his beard.

"Vonnie, I can't. We can't." He sat up straight and took a deep breath.

She swept his mouth with a kiss that stirred in his groin like a momentary ember that soon burned itself out.

"You really love her, don't you?" Vonetta whispered, pulling her mouth away from his.

"I really love her, and you love her too, honey. This is just my Johnny Walker talking to V.S.O.P. In the morning, you'd be crying on my cell phone voice mail explaining how you were about to slit your wrists," he said, pulling himself up further and away from her. "But you wouldn't get me, because I'd be on the Ben Franklin Bridge, about to jump for ruining my marriage with my wife's best friend, and sleeping with my brother's ex-girlfriend. We're too old for the talk-show circuit."

"I guess we are," she said with a smile. "But you still need your questions answered, and my offer to investigate for you still stands. We're still friends, right?"

"Yeah, we're still friends, and this never happened. It was my fault. Dropping all this yang on you, and both of us crying in our liquor." Anthony shook his head and chuckled with self-conscious remorse. Damn, that was a near-miss. . . .

"I'll answer all your questions about the business for free if you just answer one little one of mine."

"Depends on what it is," he hedged, smiling as he collected the bottles and put them away on an office shelf. He needed distance and a good night's sleep before he did something foolish, like give in.

"Haven't you ever wondered about what might have happened if we'd hooked up instead?"

The question gave him pause, and he looked at the gorgeous, smart, outrageous, funny, tender woman sitting across from him with her blouse half opened and her long legs crossed. But even with all of her sassy bravado, there was something vulnerable about Vonetta. It was the faintest glimmer of a long-ago hurt that would probably never heal. Instinct told him he couldn't fix that darkness within her, even though he wished he could. She was not a bad person, just a destroyed one. Men were her self-esteem fix. He understood more and more as her eyes searched his.

Anthony closed the distance between them and touched her face. She kissed the inside of his palm as it cupped her cheek. This time it was a nonsexual gesture, and it transmitted the warmth of a thank-you, which he understood. The sweet depression her mouth made in his hand said thank you for not thinking badly of me, or exposing me, or taking advantage of me, and for still loving me like a sister, even though I crossed the line. You are safe.

"My brother is a very, very foolish man," he whispered. "And he has a penchant for blowing opportunities of a lifetime."

"You didn't answer my question," she whispered back while looking up at him, her wide irises shimmering, asking for something solid in this world to hold on to.

"Some questions are better left unanswered, baby."

What else could he say? She knew, even though his voice had been tender. And she stood, thanking him with a glance as she fixed her blouse—for not putting into words what would have cut her to the bone—that in comparison to his Nina, she never stood a chance. All men knew: the naked truth was not always the answer a woman wanted to hear.

Eleven

The light April drizzle pelted his windshield as he toured the city streets. Somehow, at that hour just before dawn, there was a calm that befell the environment, and hence his mind. It was the time when he loved the city best, for it was so still and the massive buildings looked down upon quiet sidewalks as if with awe. Soon it would be dawn, and everything would stir again. But at the magic hour of five A.M., there was a transition to momentary peace.

He wasn't ready to go home. The near-miss with Vonetta had rattled his nerves, along with his conscience, and he needed this fresh air space to put his life into perspective. He knew that a drive just before dawn would do that for him. There was much to consider, but one thing Vonetta had said had been right. Either he'd have to clean house or sell the business.

But, perhaps he'd been thinking about the problem from the wrong side of it. Rather than trying to focus on how to save what was dying, why not focus upon where he'd want to go next? His mother had a famous saying: "Let go and let God." He'd never mastered the art of just letting things go. He also remembered her warning about not letting things go, which was just as simplistic as her first piece of advice. She'd also say to him, "Son, if you don't turn loose what God is ready for you to leave alone, then He'll make you sorry you didn't listen to Him."

Anthony peered at the strip of commercial shops that framed the province of University City, then headed west, only to find himself on City Line Avenue going up The Drive. After a full loop of Germantown, he took the back roads to Huntington Park, segueing through north central Philly to hit the east side, then down The Drive again past Boathouse Row, down the Benjamin Franklin Parkway to loop back through Center City and head toward his Queens Village home.

What did he really want? A new place to live, that was for sure. As beautiful as their house was, and as nice a block as it was on, he wanted more of an old-fashioned neighborhood feel. He wondered what Nina would think of a move. But, as for a business that could support that, he wasn't sure. However, he did know that he'd passed the age for the club scene. Mentally, it just didn't do anything for him now. It was time for something that fit his lifestyle and what he wanted to contribute to, and receive from, a family. *Let go and let God,* he told himself as he pulled onto his street.

A bluish gray tinge of morning light streaked across her face and made her turn over to avoid it. Nina yawned and snuggled down deeper into the covers, and stretched her feet across it hoping they'd collide with a warm body. When the chill of still-fresh sheets ran up her leg, she withdrew it from Anthony's side of the bed and then balled herself up into a fetal position. How long would it take before the club killed what they had? she wondered, letting out a long sigh in the process.

But the sound of metal hitting metal brought her around to full consciousness . . . and Santana? She sat up in bed, listened for a moment, and laughed. He was home.

She grabbed her silk robe and adjusted the straps on the sexy nightie that she had purposefully chosen to wear to bed, and looked over at the vase filled with jasmine that she had brought into the room. Peering into the mirror quickly, she ruffled her hair and snapped off a small blossom to tuck behind her ear, then paced into the bathroom to splash water on her face and to take a swig of mouthwash.

The clang of metal got louder with the music as she neared Anthony's in-home sanctuary—his weight-room.

As she entered it, she stopped and watched her husband. He was lying prone on the weight bench, legs straddling the narrow cushioned surface, and he was keeping time to "Smooth" as he lifted.

His light gray shorts had a charcoal vector of sweat around the waistband, and rivulets ran down the sides of his torso. She watched the next lift, becoming hypnotized by the way the muscles in his thighs and calves expanded and contracted to carve out more definition in his already perfect mahogany structure. Beads of perspiration had formed on his forehead and the bridge of his nose, and there was a shallow pool of moisture in the deep cliffs of his chest, giving his entire body a wet sheen in the rising golden rays of the sun. God, he looked good . . .

She perched herself on the seat of the nearby exercise bike and simply indulged in watching him work. Soon she noticed that her body was swaying and keeping time to the Spanish guitar. Oh yeah, he was *smooth*, every rich, dark chocolate inch of him. Heavy percussion rocked her, and she began snapping her fingers and singing along. She noticed that he smiled and glanced at her between lifts before shifting his focus back to the hovering metal. Damn, that guitar was awesome.

Her body swayed itself up to stand, drop her robe, and

dance in the center of the room. Reflections of her rico-
cheted off the mirrored walls and the jasmine fell from
her hair. The metal had stopped keeping time and she
closed her eyes.

Was that *his* wife? He breathed hard from the weights,
as well as from the sight of her as he stopped and looked
at the woman who undulated her body in the sunlight,
her image shattering his concentration. The jasmine he'd
given her had fallen from her hair, and her thighs were
barely kissed by the sheer white silk that grazed past them.
Her fluid movements created a visual harmony with the
guitar that was crying in Latin. Oh, yeah, he'd prayed for
the first time in a long while, and an angel had appeared.
God had heard him.

He watched the way her long lithe arms seemed to
beckon him as she pulled her fingers through her tresses.
With eyes closed and mouth pouted, she dipped back,
before she spun and rotated her hips while her thighs
bore her weight down into a deep, rhythmic slow squat
that rose in time to the guitar's scream, and went into a
cha-cha move, then transformed into a hustle spin to return to pure liquid motion. *Oh, girl, step into my groove!*
She was feeling the music, and he was definitely feeling
her. And then she opened her eyes and smiled at him as
she turned again. *Yeah, Santana, I won't forget about it. To
hell with the club, 'cause this life ain't good enough I live . . .
not for her . . .*

"Good morning," she whispered as the CD went into
the next slower cut.

"Don't stop dancing," he murmured. "You're a work
of art in motion."

She appraised the new dimension of his damp shorts
and walked over to the CD player with a smile, and
backed up the music to "Put Your Lights On." She then
proceeded to show him the way she felt through slow,
aching dance movements just beyond his reach.

Her father had been right—people talked too much and didn't listen. But she was sure from the way her husband swallowed hard as she lost her negligee to the middle of the floor as she danced that he heard her loud and clear. "La la la la . . ." Her voice blended with the music, the words meaning nothing and everything, and his eyes said it all. As the next cut brought a fast flurry of Spanish words she didn't understand, she allowed her body to interpret them for him, giving him the naked truth of how she felt about him.

She closed her eyes and felt the sun, and allowed the brisk morning air to kiss her nipples and spin her in the middle of the floor in a salsa. There was so much she had to give him, so much passion stored up and released in her work and dance classes, and the drums in the music brought it to the surface of her soul, and she spoke to him in the way he could understand. She then moved to his side and pulled him up from the bench where he lay watching, to make him participate and move his body to the rhythm as she sang the words to "Smooth," which had come on again. And she danced against him belly to belly as his tongue forcefully found hers and his hands gripped her behind hard enough to almost keep her from dancing.

But she had to move, to feel the freedom of motion, and she twirled out of his grasp and came back to hold his hand so that he could spin her in the middle of the floor. The breeze against her bare skin felt good, and the music in her soul felt like a living entity within her, and she laughed as she panted and evaded his grasp, causing him to chase her and laugh himself, until cornering her against the mirror with his hands on either side of her head. They both stopped laughing when she flipped him and pressed his back to the mirrored wall and found his mouth, then pulled back from him enough to tug his shorts down to the floor.

"You watch," she murmured, directing his gaze away from her toward the opposite wall of mirrors.

A deep tremor coursed through him as she slid down his torso, found his pain, and continued to keep time with the screaming guitars. In response, his fingers found her hair and gripped it tight to the scalp, and when her name began with a shudder that ran the length of his body to audibly fuse with the bass lines, she knew there was nothing left for them to talk about, until later.

Tears ran from the corners of his eyes and there was not enough air in the room to fill his lungs. He took it in like a dying man, allowing his neck to arch and his head to hang back to rest on the wall mirror as his lungs fought for the limited resource. Not since they'd first dated had it been like this. "God, I love you," he panted as she slid her nude form up his thighs, then over his belly, nipping his nipples and licking the side of his neck before sending her hot breath into his ear and blanketing him.

"I love to watch you work out," she murmured. "It does something to me."

"Then I'd better do that more often," he said, still gulping air. "But I'll need a medical alert bracelet if you keep this up. I haven't been in here in like a month."

"I know, baby. You need more time for you."

His eyes rolled back in their sockets as he closed them. She was taking care of him. Deep, sensual kisses trailed his body . . . *Dear God in Heaven* . . . And he felt her lead him by the hand. He followed without a will of his own, and let her push him down gently on the bench. She smelled so good, like jasmine—natural—and her fragrant wavy hair brushed his face as she straddled him. The wetness between her thighs sent a signal to the exhausted muscle in his groin that had just been worked, and begged it to respond. And slowly but surely, as she repeated the stanzas close to his ear and moved with insistence to the music, hovering, slightly grazing, then lowering, the message was received and answered at the source.

"Wishing it was . . ." she murmured. "Don't you?"

She mixed the music with her body like an aphrodisiac. Oh, yeah, it was effective, and she forced him to keep the slow percussion pace on the downbeat as she controlled the upbeat and sang the song's refrain in his ear until she could not form words. Then she allowed him to set the pace: a chaotic tempo that he composed, which didn't allow him to pull enough of himself into her fast enough.

They lay there on the bench breathing in staccato pants that soon relaxed and collided into a pattern of deep melody, him sprawled on the bottom with her draped over him, limp.

After a moment, she pushed herself up and placed her palms down flat on his chest and stared at him.

"Damn . . ."

He laughed, nodded, and echoed her sentiment. "I know whatcha talking about, girl. Where did that come from?"

"I don't really care," she said. "Help me!" She laughed and waved a hand in the air. "Take me with you the next time you shop for CDs for the club, OK?"

"Definitely, baby. But, you are music . . . and you are art. You are . . . I don't know what to say," he whispered, leaning up for a kiss. "You just are."

"You know what you are to me?" she whispered back, becoming suddenly emotional.

He didn't speak, but touched her face.

"You are the most important thing in my life. You are my friend . . . my lover . . . my family . . . the one I trust, the one I fight with, the one I laugh with, the one I trust to enter my body, the one I can fall back against with my eyes closed. You are simply a part of me. That's what I mean, Anthony, when I say I love you."

Her admission blurred his vision as unshed tears of gratitude and emotion filled his being. She had told him what he had needed to hear so badly, to understand from her for so long. He'd heard her say that she loved him, but until this moment, he didn't know what that truly meant. But having her speak it so plainly while he was still inside of her made him want to weep for every time he'd left his orchid unattended. He pulled her head close to his chest. "I'm selling the club for both of us. It's over. Our marriage can't take that type of business, and there's nothing—not even money—worth losing what we have."

He felt her shoulders shake with repressed sobs, and he rubbed her back as she let out her pain on a wave of sudden relief.

He had finally heard her after all these years.

He watched his wife dance as she beat the eggs to the pulse of the music blaring in the kitchen. She hopped about, whipping them in a metal bowl like she was playing an electric guitar, and the sight of her almost made him cut himself as he laughed and simultaneously attempted to chop mushrooms and peppers for their omelet. He continued to laugh as she giggled and poured the eggs into the hot skillet from way too high, then jumped back to keep from getting popped with hot butter.

"Be careful," he warned with a chuckle, his soul feeling amazingly light. "Don't be damaging that soft skin I have plans for after breakfast."

She squealed as a stray pop sent her running, and he turned down the heat while he dramatically flung vegetables into the center of the eggs like a professional chef.

"We oughta do this for a living," he said, laughing.

"Work out to mind-blowing music every day, then fix gourmet meals and health shakes afterward." He chuckled as she added strawberries and bananas to the fresh-squeezed orange juice in the blender. "And we could put your art in there to make the place chi-chi for upscale clients who—"

"Anthony," she screamed. "You have found the feng shui!"

"What?" he said as he put his head in the refrigerator to find the turkey sausage.

"Think about it," she said with a wide-eyed expression, removing the eggs from the hot burner and turning off the flame. "Your idea is brilliant!"

A sense of pride washed over him as he looked at his wife's face. It was the way her eyes sparkled and hope praised him from deep within them. He sat down, and gave her his full attention. "OK, baby. Shoot."

"Listen," she said with a glee-filled twirl. "One must align one's life system to every energy pattern that you surround yourself with to be in balance, and the stars may have aligned on this one!"

He laughed and shook his head. "In plain English, baby. You might as well be speaking Spanish. Although I do like your use of that language."

"OK, OK, OK," she said. "From a purely business perspective. Here it goes."

He nodded with satisfaction as her tone remained excited, but the way she approached the problem now began with a logic he could comprehend: business.

"Our new mayor is on a mission to bring good health into the neighborhoods, especially after that article came out about a year ago listing Philadelphia as the most unfit city in the nation. Correct?"

Anthony rubbed his chin and nodded slowly, the light-bulb beginning to go on in his brain. She was on to something. "That's true, and good for public relations to go along with a pre-existing bandwagon—especially one coming from the top. Yeah . . . ?"

"And you like the day, but rarely get to enjoy it, and you love to work out, and have kept yourself in excellent shape, and want something we can do together, right?"

"Yeah," he murmured, deep in thought.

"Well, that's an alignment of energy between the way you live your life, find that same energy in your purpose, and run your household. A lot of people could use assistance with that."

Even though he'd been up for more than twenty-four hours, and that after a workout, his wife had worked him out again, he was now running on sheer adrenaline, instead of stress. His mind snapped together the fragments of the puzzle she'd begun to lay out. "Location is the key, so, if I found a large single Tudor, with a lot of ground around it, like the kind they have up in Mount Airy, there would be ample parking, close to public transportation, and a diverse clientele that would probably already be into holistic things. And it would have the tree-lined environment, like we'd talked about. I am so tired of cement."

Her smile spurred him on. He appreciated that she let him talk it out, think it out, as his brain raced. He was creating on the fly . . .

"Then we could blend our interests. There could be a fitness center, with graduate student instructors majoring in rehabilitative therapy and phys ed from the nearby universities. You always have to consider where your staff is going to come from, and ways that you can create a win-win for them, and you."

"I love the way your mind works," she murmured, sitting down across from him. "Keep going."

"Then," he said with a sweep of his hand across the table, "we could offer smoking cessation classes, meditation, martial arts, stress management, and definitely cultural dance," he added with a wink that made her giggle. "That all could go on the second floor, while on the first floor we could add on a sunroom, and make that a health food café sporting a juice bar, with the front rooms converted into a positive materials bookstore and herbal remedy shop, with, of course, gallery space. If we were lucky enough to find a three-level location, we could use that portion of the space for art classes, cooking classes, dance classes, and all sorts of mind, body, and spirit fitness-related activities. Then, are you ready for a really big dream?" he asked, laughing.

She laughed with him. "Like you always say, shoot."

"In the basement would be theater space."

"What?" she murmured, looking so excited that he thought she might jump out of her seat.

"For visiting professors, lectures, small conferences, and a once-a-month independent film series."

She stared at her husband.

"Well, what do you think?" he asked sheepishly.

His grin lit up the room, and it made her pop out of her chair and round the table to hug and kiss him profusely.

"I take it you like the idea?"

"I take it you're a genius!" she exclaimed. "I know so many artists, as do you, who don't have the venue, want to display their work, and want to teach in an unconfined environment. Oh, Anthony!"

"OK," he said slowly, pulling her into his lap. "Now, let me put my business cap on again. Forgive me, baby, but I've gotta work the numbers, too."

"That's cool. What do you think it will take?"

"OK," he began cautiously, "we'd have multiple product lines to feed the place, revenue-wise. The theater and small conference space is one revenue stream to help get us a return on the investment. Then the bookstores and natural food herb shop—those are retail operations. The café is like running a small restaurant, but provides another stream of income. The art, in and of itself, is a retail operation—the gallery part. Then we'd have the fitness center, which can generate a lucrative sum all by itself, as well as provide steady income through annual or monthly memberships. Private trainers offer an addition, and if I allowed a chiropractor, reflexologist, and aromatherapist to sublet space, that's another source of funds that complement our other product lines, and gives us rent plus a cut of their clients' visits. Then the classes are a revenue structure too."

"Anthony, if I didn't know better, it sounds like you already have a place in mind?"

He laughed and hung his head. "Guilty. I cruised the streets after the club closed last night, and saw this mansion up on Johnson Street, just before you get to Wayne Avenue. Then I thought, nah, what would I do with a monstrosity like that? When I came home, I was so wired I couldn't sleep, so I decided to work out to pump away the stress. Had I known you were in the mood, I would have let you do that."

"See what happens when you don't come straight home?" she said. "You miss out."

"I know," he murmured, thinking about how different this whole morning would have been if he'd made the wrong choice. "The best part of this plan to me is that none of these services have to go beyond seven o'clock in the evening, and, if they do, it can be the membership, prepaid stuff, not the retail operation, which means I can come home at a reasonable hour, and nobody would be at too much risk for a holdup. Even the Saturday and Sunday operations can be turned over to a solid manager. I can find one of those easy enough from the Restaurant School."

"You sound like you're cleaning out your staff slate

from the club, like you don't intend to bring anybody from the old business to the new one."

"A new start and new energy is needed," is all he would say, and he looked down at his cup of coffee and took a slow sip. She was so happy, and the whole theft ordeal was not for the breakfast table. *Let go and let God,* his mind repeated. Everything that had happened at the club was history.

"What about if you also had a family therapist come into the new place, to help people keep their homes together, like say, once a week? I think positive mental health within families is as important as good physical health and everything else, don't you?"

He looked at her eyes and the way they searched his face. "I think that could be arranged, especially if the person were a wise, well-respected doctor."

"How did you know I was talking about my dad?" Her mouth brushed his lips and her head found his shoulder. "He might love to teach once a week, and give little seminars, and see couples privately, and I might even be able to coax him to finally write his book, which we could sell through our bookstore. You heard me when I hadn't even said it. How did you know?"

"Because I know how close you are to him, and that you have always wanted him to be near you. That's why I was sorta thinking we might move up to your parents' end of town—to be near enough to the new venture to baby-sit it."

Nina sat bolt upright and stared at him. "You would move up there, after all you put into this house?"

"Don't you want to be close to them, since my parents have my brother and sisters to look out for them, but your parents just have you to care for them?"

Two big tears formed in her eyes even though she smiled. "I love you," she whispered. "Thank you."

"Besides," he said, "if we're gonna make this baby, I

want your mom near you, and you near to a job that doesn't keep you on your feet all day, fighting crazies downtown, and it would be nice if you could walk to work, wouldn't it?"

She kissed the bridge of his nose, then his eyelids, and his forehead. "Anthony . . ."

"I love you, too, baby," he whispered, finding her mouth. They both laughed when his stomach growled.

She moved off his lap and went toward the stove very slowly, and slid the cold eggs onto a plate to microwave them. "It's all happening so fast," she whispered, fixing the food in robotic motion as though stunned. "I never dreamed that something like this could be a solution . . ."

"I'd have to put the club up through my broker," he said in a steady tone, working the math mentally as she added food to the table, praying all the while that he could deliver this risky dream.

"What about Cecil? And Maxine?" she whispered, and she stopped midstep to look at him.

"I'll give my brother a partner's cut, and take care of Maxine. That's why the sale has to be very profitable. But this business is me and you as partners, starting it together, picking the location, and choosing the décor and renovations, menus, and classes. I want you to be a part of this, Nina, to create it with me, and not to be on the outside with your nose pressed up to the glass looking in."

Her expression of quiet joy said it all and brought forth another rush of planning as his mind whittled away at the details. "We'd have to start looking for locations and houses, then put this on the market. But, the club sale and the house sale are going to have to cover extensive renovations at the new site, plus provide at least six months of working capital, and, of course, we'll need inventory, furnishings, new telephone lines, equipment for two kitchens, which will cost a king's ransom, and—"

"And it will happen, because it's right, and because you are an excellent businessman with a good reputation, and you've helped so many people," she said calmly, landing another kiss on his forehead as she set a plate before him. "Good deeds come back tenfold."

He looked up at the eyes that glowed with appreciation. As long as she looked at him like that, he could accomplish anything.

Twelve

Incessant banging and ringing created a fissure in his skull. Five hours of sleep was not enough time to recover from Nina, or really not sleeping right for months. He felt Nina stir and her weight leave the bed. "Thank you, baby," he mumbled. "Tell that stupid Cecil that I'm not coming in today." A kiss on his forehead had been her reply as she slipped out of the room, and he slipped back into unconsciousness. In the remote part of his mind, he heard her running, then her hands were pulling at him.

"Wake up, Anthony, baby, c'mon on, wake up."

She had not yelled the command, but the tone of her voice immediately wiped the haze from his mind as he turned over and sat up, then stood up, reading the look on her face as he grabbed his shorts and followed her to the front of the house. Two police officers stood on the landing, and he opened the door, motioning for them to come in.

Both officers appraised the couple, as though making a mental note, stepped through the door into the wide vestibule, hesitated, then proceeded and stopped once the foursome was in the wider front hall section of the house.

"You Anthony Williams?" The tall male officer had asked the question without removing his dark aviator glasses, even though he'd come inside.

"Yeah," Tony said confidently, his gaze bouncing off the officers, then Nina. "What's this all about?"

"Your brother was shot today around 3:30 P.M. at the establishment you own—The Jazz Note," the female officer said evenly. "Using a cell phone, he put out a 911 from where he dropped, and said to inform his brother of the incident. We took him to Hanneman Emergency less than twenty minutes ago, and couldn't get past your voice mail on the number he gave us, so we pursued your address."

Anthony felt Nina's arm wrap around his waist, and it was the only thing that stopped the ringing in his ears long enough for his mind to form a question. "How bad?"

"Three gunshots hit him. One in the back, two in the front. They're working on him now," the other officer replied. "We're here to escort you to the hospital, then down to the station for questioning."

He couldn't sit as Nina went outside to use his cell phone to call his parents. He watched her from the wall that he leaned against as she connected with his mother and father—speaking softly yet firmly to them in an apparent attempt to calm them, but there was no way to calmly deliver this type of news to anyone. He thanked her in his mind as guilt continued to torture him. He should have left his beeper and cell phone on, and never taken the house phone off the hook, and he should have been there to open up . . .

His mind reflexively grasped at every possibility as Nina called her parents, then Maxine, and ultimately Vonetta. Everything around him seemed to be happening in slow motion. All he wanted was for one of the white coats to come out and tell him some good news.

He could feel his heart slam against his ribs from the

inside as a doctor approached him. It felt like the bottom had dropped out of his stomach as he watched the face of the man coming toward him. The clinical expression on it was deadpan.

"Mr. Williams," the doctor began in a halting tone, "your brother is in a coma. He lost a lot of blood, and took a bullet in the back, which narrowly missed his spine. That's the good news. But it punctured his lung, which filled up with blood and almost drowned him. The other two bullets that lodged in his body came from a frontal shot, which hit him in the stomach, damaging a significant part of his small intestine, and the other shattered a portion of his hip, which we will have to replace. But, like I said, he's lost a lot of blood."

"Is he going to make it?" Anthony asked. His voice sounded detached even to his own ears.

"It's touch and go, so I would alert any relatives or meaningful individuals, because we can't make any promises."

Anthony looked directly into the blue eyes that were set in a too-young face for his comfort. "Saving my brother's life is not an option, and not a classroom project. Just do it!"

He felt his wife's hand at his shoulder, and the way it squeezed the bones beneath his skin. It told him to be cool. It would be all right. It told him not to take out his frustration on this young person in front of him and it assured him that an older, more experienced doctor was probably in the back working with a team on Cecil. Don't kill the messenger, her hand said, and Anthony could feel his breathing slowing down enough to allow another sentence to pass through his lips. "How long till we know anything, doctor?"

"He'll be in surgery for another few hours, at least. Someone will come out in intervals to inform you of any progress—or to ask the family to make any decisions they need to."

He watched the young man turn and swiftly walk away from him. Had it not been for the close proximity of the wall, and Nina's steady grasp on his shoulder, he might have fallen as his knees buckled. It was the last part of the doctor's statement that got to him.

All she could do was sit quietly, holding Anthony's hand, and wait. That was the part that she knew was killing her husband. The wait. The wait to know the fate of his brother. The wait to see his mother and father come into the hospital. The wait to know who'd done this to Cecil, and the wait for the detectives to arrive.

When two dark suits approached, Anthony stood up, and she pulled herself up next to him.

"I'm Detective Len Collins. This is my partner, Detective Roberto DeShields," the tall, clean-cut brother said evenly. "Let's talk."

"So, let me get this straight," the one called DeShields said casually. "You left at approximately four A.M., then drove around the city for almost an hour, made the call to your insurance company to leave a voice-mail message to convert your business coverage to another firm—but left your homeowner's with your present firm? Is that correct?"

"Yes," Anthony replied, glancing at both men, but not at his wife. "What's your point?"

"Then you came home and worked out, and went to sleep with your wife, until a squad car woke you up?" The other officer had ignored his question by issuing one of his own.

"That's right," Anthony said with impatience. "I overslept. Now what leads do you have on who shot my brother?"

"That's what we're trying to ascertain now," DeShields noted monotonously. "Does your brother have any ene-mies?"

Anthony thought about it for a moment, and let his breath out hard. "Cecil got himself into a lot of things . . . I really can't say I know everything that he was up to."

"Can anybody vouch for where you were last night, or who you were with?"

Anthony looked at the black man who'd posed the question to him. "Why is that so important? I was at the club, closing down for the night before I came home. My brother got shot at three-thirty this afternoon, like the officers who came to my door said. So what has the night before got to do with anything?"

Both officers glanced at each other. The one named Collins spoke as DeShields watched Anthony's eyes.

"Because, when the officers arrived at the scene, your brother was lying on the floor, and the safe was open. We did an initial sweep of your establishment for intrud-ers and found cocaine, marijuana, and other drugs."

"Not in my club, you didn't." Anthony stood and be-gan pacing. "That stupid son of a bitch . . ."

"We then temporarily sealed the premises with crime scene tape," Collins remarked without emotion. "But somebody with a key got in and out undetected, and started a fire that gutted the building—they knew we'd be coming back in to sweep for prints and gather more evidence. They had to know how to best torch your es-tablishment."

"My club is in ashes?" Anthony whispered. Nina's gasp went through his skeleton.

"So," DeShields said casually, "we're working backward here, Mr. Williams. Whoever confronted your brother was probably someone he knew. I take it only a few people had the combination to the club safe."

"Right. Me and him," Anthony stated with caution. He

sat down hard next to Nina and rubbed his face with his hands. "Make your point."

"When he was hit, the first shot in the back spun him around. In the 911 call, he said that as he was going down, he could only see a hand that he couldn't make out through the partially open door. The other two shots got him as he fell—facing the door to your office. The only person he wanted to speak to was you. I'll replay the dispatch tape for you if you want, Mr. Williams. It goes like this . . . 'I'm shot, my back, my stomach, I can't breathe.' Then, dispatch asks for a location, he gives the club's name. Then dispatch asks if his attackers are still there, and if he saw who did it. Your brother says, 'No, I was going down, just saw a hand, too dark . . . get to my brother,' then rattles off your cell phone number. By the time we got there, he was in a coma. Who normally comes in at three-thirty to open?"

"Why are you asking him all of this?" Nina blurted out as she cut in. "My husband was with me at three-thirty, and your officers came to our house and could see that—"

"Mr. Williams, who opens, normally?"

"Me, or my manager," Anthony whispered, then squeezed Nina's hand to beg her not to jump in again.

"Ma'am," DeShields said in an even tone. "Since we found drugs, we cannot rule out a premeditated hit. It doesn't matter where your husband was, if there was probable cause for him to have somebody shoot—"

"Wait. Now I'm a suspect?" Anthony said.

"Any reason you have to shoot your brother?" The officer named Collins had begun scribbling on his pad as he'd asked the question.

"That's the operative word, man," Anthony said through his teeth. *"Brother."*

"Yeah," DeShields shot back nonchalantly. "In this line

of business, money comes before blood. We see it every day. Who's your manager?"

"She doesn't work there anymore."

"Oh?" Collins replied with a sideways glance and stopped writing. "When did that happen?"

"Last night, around seven-thirty, eight o'clock. She and Cecil had an argument, and she quit."

"Isn't that convenient . . ." DeShields muttered. "We need a name, and a list of everyone who ever worked at your establishment. And we want the name of anybody you know at the insurance company you were attempting to switch your policy over to, as well as a rundown on your relationship to that individual. We can do this the easy way, or we can do it the hard way, but we will do it. This isn't just a case of a simple robbery, Mr. Williams. You see, it's gotten complicated. We're talking attempted premeditated murder, drug charges, arson, and possible insurance fraud. The list of potential felonies is very long here."

Collins stood. "Whoever returned to set the fire had to have a key, and know that something had gone down in there—and they definitely didn't want the police to investigate further. And, you changed over your fire insurance and business insurance policies at four A.M. on a Sunday morning, when most people usually wait until Monday to conduct standard business. Wanna tell us why you needed an increased policy and decided to make a change the night before your brother was shot?"

"Wanna tell us how much was stolen out of the cleaned-out safe we encountered, in real dollars?" The other detective asked in rapid succession. "We'll have a better opinion of you as potentially not being our primary suspect, trust me, if you cooperate, and don't do that plead-the-fifth bull—and help us find out who shot your brother, *if* you didn't do it, as you claimed."

Silence crept over the group, and both detectives were

standing over Tony and Nina now. A thousand answers to their questions battered Tony's brain. He couldn't look Nina directly in the eyes, nor could he have a full-disclosure conversation in front of her.

He glanced at her stricken expression and knew she had doubts. He couldn't blame her. All she had to go on was his shaky behavior of late, and she knew a little bit about the financial problems that the club was having. She'd even witnessed the argument between him and Cecil. Her eyes had said it all when the detectives started talking about the four A.M. telephone call he'd made. *Stupid move!* How could he explain that he'd made the call in front of Vonetta as a show of good faith, and to assuage her damaged self-esteem? The intent had been a peace treaty, a way to say to Vonetta that they were still cool, and that he still trusted her to investigate the money leak.

That discussion in front of Nina would open a whole can of worms, and by now, she probably thought he'd intended to finance the big dreams he'd come home with by using drug money and a fire-insurance settlement. He glanced at his wife's face and only saw a thousand more questions within it. The original confidence and praise that had shone from her eyes only hours ago had been replaced with fear and marginal distrust in who he really was to her now. He was only glad that his parents weren't here yet to witness the police questioning him. This whole scene was way out of control, and he needed hard answers for everyone, especially himself.

Anthony stood slowly and allowed his gaze to lock with the detectives'. "I need to call my attorney."

Thirteen

"I don't understand, Anthony," she whispered. "What has been going on down there?"

"Later, baby," he whispered back as he saw his parents approach. "I was lucky that they just gave me a warning to stick around, instead of picking me up. Let me get up with Earl, and take care of Mom and Dad, and see that Cecil is out of the woods."

"You are going to talk to your lawyer before you talk to me . . ." she said quietly. "Now I'm really afraid."

His mother filled his opened arms, and her face was streaked with the white salt lines of tears. His father added to the huddle, hugging them both, as sisters and nieces and nephews all gathered to wait, hold on to each other, and pray.

"They're saying my boys were into drugs," his mother whispered into his ear through a thick, mucus-filled swallow. "Tell me they lied, and what they say on the news is all a terrible mistake," she pleaded as she turned her face up to his.

Without looking at the rest of his family, he knew every member present was holding their breaths, their eyes on him to wipe away the possible sins of the world. He felt his mother's petite frame and ample bosom heave against his chest as she wept, and his father's eyes held an urgent plea for him to restore his wife's heart and peace of mind. Anthony kissed the top of his mother's head and caressed her back with the width of his palm, and told her the only part of the truth he knew. He could only vouch for himself, not Cecil, but he didn't need to complicate his answer with such detail. What he was about to say to her would be an evasive half answer that he was sure she'd accept. That's all he could give her now with his love.

"Mom," he whispered. "Your boys weren't into drugs. I love you and Dad too much to go there, and you deserve better than that for all your years of hard work. Drug money never bought that addition, or anything else I've ever given you and Pop, and it's not the way I ran my club. I swear that to you on the Bible."

Again, her face turned up to his, and her palm reached out and traced the line of his jaw. Her eyes overflowed with such hurt and confusion that it ripped at the soft tissues within his chest. In that moment, he saw his mother as a dual entity for the first time in his life—one part mother, the other part woman, asking a man for the truth, the simple truth, as her bottom lip quavered and her gazed locked upon his and held it.

"Then why's God taking both of my sons away from me? My good children . . . my babies that I held in my body and promised him I'd care for? I prayed every day that nothing like this would ever come near any of my babies, now the law wants one and death is chasin' the other."

Her voice had broken off into a muffled wail of pain that went through his bones and caused his tears to over-flow. All he could do was rock her and kiss her, and look to his father for help.

"C'mon, Natalie, baby," his father whispered, gently guiding her away from Anthony to coax her to sit down. "Cecil is gonna be all right. They have good doctors here.

We just have to hold on in the darkest hour, and have the faith of a mustard seed, honey. And you know our Anthony is an honest man. You know that," he added with emphasis, glancing at his son with a warning that said, *If you've lied to my wife, and if you've hurt her in any way, I'll kill you.*

Anthony understood the warning all too well. He had a wife of his own. Nina's stunned expression and her tears of doubt haunted him as his mother moved away from his side and took a seat next to her husband and their daughters. The focus turned to his mother, but not before his family glanced at him with unspoken questions. He also noticed that Nina had not moved from where she stood. After hugging his parents and his siblings and all the children, she had taken a remote post, standing away from him and watching too.

The wait was interminable, and none of the Williams children could get his mother to eat or move from where she sat with her eyes closed and hands clasped. All he could think of was that God must be able to hear his mother's 911 call—the call of the faithful, the call of a woman who got down on her knees every day to thank Him for the sun rising—hers was a call for help in the wilderness from a woman who'd dedicated her life to hard work and clean living. How did those bastards live with themselves? he wondered as he stared at his aged parents across the room. Making mothers weep and sending fathers to early graves, all for the glitter of silver.

"She won't even take a sip of water," his sister Vicki said, coming up to him and handing him a bottle of spring water, which he also refused.

"Mom's taking this so hard," he whispered, his gaze traveling to caress his mother.

"How else is she supposed to take this, Tony?" Vicki's expression had hardened and it drew him to study the barely concealed rage on her face. "It's breaking her back. Cocaine, reefer, and her son is shot? Then an arson cover-up?"

"Try to get Nina to go down to the cafeteria with you, hon, please. This is wearing them both out," he murmured, nodding in his mother's direction, then Nina's.

"I've tried already," Vicki said in a low voice. "She's waiting for her parents to come. They were at a luncheon today, and all she could do was leave them a message. That's why she keeps stepping outside to use the cell phone. She's pretty shaken up too . . . it's like a double tragedy," Vicki added with a swallow. "Everybody's messed up, especially the kids. You and Cecil are their heroes. The oldest boys are taking it the worst."

His sister's last comment sliced through his dignity and his soul, even though he knew what she'd said was true. His nephews and nieces now saw their successful uncles as low-life drug peddlers, who were no better than the constant images that besieged his community on the nightly news. The children's eyes had never met his, and their shoulders slumped like all the joy had been stripped from their young lives. And those stereotypes had been played enough times until they seeped into the subconscious of his loved ones and permeated their marrow.

He wanted to break down and cry. He'd tried so hard. But he knew that their guards were up until a plausible answer could be found. His family didn't want to be played, like so many other hopeful ones had been, believing in the lies of men-children who looked into the face of the aged and claimed, *'Momma, I'm innocent.'* And those old women had faith and love, and thus mortgaged their homes, which had been bought by scrubbing floors on their knees, only to be heartbroken by their sons who'd skillfully deceived them, or turned a blind eye to a pain they couldn't acknowledge.

Those lies of men had now become viewed as his lies, and had shaken his own mother's faith, his father's

trust, and his wife's love. He was judged guilty by asso-
ciation, without a trial or jury—associated with the nega-
tive image carried in the media and attached to the
tribe of African-American urban males.

Emotion caught in Anthony's throat. His mind tore at
the option to call his attorney, Earl Jones, but he was
afraid to—for fear that the family would see him making
a business call and assume that it was a drug-related tip
to warn his crime family of a police raid.

"I'm innocent," he murmured thickly. "I swear to you,
sis. This all looks so bad, but I never financed the club
like that. Tell me you believe me?" His eyes searched her
face for affirmation that never came.

"Dee and Pebbles and Rhonda took the kids downstairs, just to give them a break. Why don't you try to see
if you can get Nina to go down, then I'll work on Daddy,
and I'll take him down when you guys come back to sit
with Mom. Tell Nina I'll let her parents know where you
are if they come while she's gone."

"I did not do this," he stated with conviction, holding
his sister by the arm. "Look at me," he pleaded when
her gaze swept the floor.

"Go take Nina downstairs," Vicki whispered, then
moved away from his side.

Anthony stood by the wall for a few moments and
watched his family, especially his wife. A hollow filled him
and disconnected him from them, and it allowed him to
move past them like a ghost, out to the fresh air beyond
the emergency waiting room, to call Earl Jones.

How many women had been lied to, but wanted so
badly to believe, that they opted for ignorance? Nina wondered. Told this same sad tale that always ended in an
indictment, then a conviction? New tears filled her eyes
as she watched her husband on his cell phone outside

the glass, and she thought of his soaring club success and his dreams.

By any means necessary, she mentally whispered, but that's not what the phrase originally referenced. They were so wrong. There was a more noble cause, of uplifting one's people, than the used-out-of-context quote had been stolen from, and which was now maladapted to address underhanded deals and self-serving crimes. How many black men were in prison today because they rationalized away the truth with that five-second sound bite from a civil rights speech while not even understanding its author's intent? How many women and children were victims of this mentality? Her insides wailed to the universe for an answer.

And what would Tony tell her after the truth came out? What rationalization would he use to try to make this OK with her? She leaned forward in her chair, wrapped her arms around her knees and pressed her face to her thighs and rocked.

Morose thoughts turned into a hundred pinpoints of light behind her tightly closed lids in the darkness. Maybe that's why she couldn't have a baby, either because God was saving her from being a mother who had to ride with her toddler on a prison bus to see his father once a week, or because her husband also used what he sold. How many women were in that position, some of them not seeing the truth until it was too late?

She rocked harder as she thought of all of Anthony's flimsy excuses about not wanting to take a fertility test. They'd see traces of substance abuse in his specimen, for sure, which would lead to questions and issues that he didn't want to deal with. He didn't have to be the one who shot Cecil. That was never a question in her mind— she was with him this morning, and knew he didn't hire anybody. But if he was running that type of business through his club, then he'd killed them all—members of his family, anyway. Their hopes, their dreams, their belief system, everything. No wonder God didn't give her a baby, his baby, because she'd never be able to sever herself from this toxic situation.

A slim woman, showing slight signs of early pregnancy, passed him as he re-entered the waiting room. She had a small boy in tow, and for some reason, his focus riveted upon her as she stopped before his mother and father. Anthony approached but stood back, observing as his mother opened her eyes, and the rest of his present family members gave the young woman curious glances.

"I'm Jackie," she said in a soft voice.

His mother looked perplexed, and his father's arm covered his mother's shoulders while the little boy hid his face in the folds of his mother's pants leg.

"They told me Cecil had been shot. My sister heard it on the news," she offered quietly. "I wanted his son to see him. They said it was bad, and he might not make it."

All Tony could do was watch as his mother's face crumbled with a new level of despair as she reached for the child and brought him to stand before her, inspecting the child with love.

"What's your name, sweetie?" his mother whispered, tears streaming down her face without censure or shame.

"Daekwon," the little boy answered, stepping out to the older woman before him slowly, while glancing back at his mother.

Anthony watched in agony as his own mother covered her mouth. From the corner of his eye, he could see Nina staring at him, before she looked away into the distance. Then his mother fastened her gaze on the young woman.

"How come we never saw this beautiful child?" his mother whispered.

"It was the way Cecil wanted it, and the way we left it," the girl murmured back. "As long as he took care of things, I went on with my life, and have a new man now, but when I heard he was shot, I figured that his son had a right to at least see him once . . . you know, if things didn't work out and—"

"You had a right," his mother said firmly, now standing to look the young girl in her eyes at the same level. Signs of fatigue wracked her elderly face as she held her head high and drew a breath, ignoring her husband's attempts to comfort her. "And I had a right. This child had a right. And this family had a right. And Cecil had no right to keep this from any of us."

Mrs. Williams cast her gaze around to the members of the family who had gathered, telepathically asking which of them knew, before her gaze went to her husband, who looked away. "Sit with us," she said, "or we—me and you—can take this child down to eat with the other children in the family. It may be hours. Cecil's in surgery, and no sense in making the children suffer through this," she commanded, regaining her inner strength.

"Do you want me to go with you?" Vicki asked quietly.

"No. I'm done here. There are no more words that I can say, or prayers that I can pray. I done turned it over to the real Father," her mother pronounced. Then she guided the young woman away with her to the cafeteria without looking back at Anthony or her husband.

"Did you know about this?" Anthony asked his father and sister quietly.

"For about six months," his father admitted in a faraway tone. "I didn't know how to break it to Natalie. I knew it would just kill her to know that Cecil had been so irresponsible, and had kept the boy from her."

Anthony put his arm around his father's shoulders. "What about you, Vicki? Did you know?"

His sister hung her head. "Me and Maxine did; it almost broke them up four months ago."

"Why didn't you tell me?" He glanced from his sister to his father, then to Nina, then back to his sister again. He'd noticed that Nina had been attentive throughout the entire conversation, but still sat back, observing.

"Because Cecil was tapping the registers to give the girl money. As the boy got older, she started making more demands, and then she started seeing Ron, and—"

"Wait," Anthony shouted, then lowered his voice as heads turned. "You're telling me two things I cannot comprehend at once, Vicki." He stood up and leaned down into his sister's face. "Number one, you knew our brother was hitting the registers—"

"It was only a couple of hundred a week, and you can afford it," she shot back in self-defense. "I didn't know you guys also had another operation running in there."

"We didn't!" Anthony shouted.

"OK, fine, if you say so. But after Maxine found out about the girl, she started demanding that Cecil pay her the same amount to make up for his affair. That's what strapped Cecil, and he had to dole out to both of them on the sly for a while till things calmed down. He was gonna put it back after they got over it. But he knew you'd flip if you found out that he was strapped because he'd gotten himself into a jam like this. Then it got crazy out of control. Sometimes Maxine helped herself when Cecil couldn't bring himself to do it, then other times he just handed her a knot."

Anthony stared at his sister, too angry to sit or form another question.

"That's probably why she quit. Because by Ronell hooking up with Jackie, it put things too close to home for Max, Ron being a bartender there too, and the money just wouldn't be enough for her, after a while. I told her that going in," Vicki said. "But you know about a scorned woman. That's probably why Jackie hooked up with Ron in the first place, to rub Maxine's nose in it."

"Maxine quit last night," Nina murmured, bringing both Vicki and Anthony's attention to her, even though Mr. Williams only hung his head where he sat.

"Yeah," Vicki said, sighing. "She and Cecil got into a big fight, Lisa said, and that's why Maxine came in late and threw her keys on your desk."

"Oh . . . God . . . damn . . ." Anthony said on a slow rush of breath as he flopped into a waiting room chair beside them.

"The fight between Cecil and Maxine wasn't about the girl," Nina offered quietly. "It was about Vonetta."

Anthony, Mr. Williams, and Vicki just stared at her.

"Vonetta?" Anthony asked in disbelief.

"When you went by to discuss the club's shortages with Cecil Saturday morning, and he wouldn't come out," Nina said in a tiny voice, "Vonetta was the one in there who'd spent the night with him. Maxine saw her leaving and went off. Vonetta told me last night. That's why I waited up for you, Tony, because I wasn't angry, and I knew you were dealing with some heavy issues over there. Didn't Vonetta give you my message?"

Mr. Williams just shook his head, as Vicki covered her mouth with both hands.

"You have got to be kidding me." Anthony let his head fall forward. "My club is in ashes, my brother's shot, and my ass is on the line because of Cecil's booty calls?"

"I think you ought to tell Earl Jones that there are a lot of possible suspects other than you who might have shot your brother, baby," Nina whispered as her hand found Anthony's.

"But where did the drugs come from, Nina? My brother? This is like a nightmare that can't get any worse."

His sister sighed as she put her arm around her father's

rounded shoulders. "C'mon, Dad. Let's get you something to eat so your sugar doesn't go wacky. OK? Besides, you got enough on your heart right now," she said quietly, motioning with her head toward the door.

Anthony and Nina looked up, then glanced at each other.

"You talk to Maxine," he murmured. "Let me handle Vonetta. Where the hell is Earl Jones?"

Fourteen

She relented without an argument to her husband's peculiar request. Vonetta was *her* best friend, and only his friend. It stood to reason that if anyone were going to talk to Vonetta, it would be her, not him. What's more, Maxine was his brother's woman, and his former employee, not hers. An eerie feeling of dread connected to her synapses for the second time today. Things just weren't adding up. Her undelivered message, his irrational phone call at four A.M., and the way her friend greeted her with the subtlest hint of distance.

She shunned the dark question from her mind, and refused to give it lodging, then reached for Maxine's hand to go sit and speak with her more privately.

"I know that's your girl, and all," Maxine said angrily through her sniffles. "But that bitch has no right to be here. *I'm* his woman!"

"I know," Nina soothed, rubbing Maxine's clenched hands. "We're going to get to the bottom of this, but there's something you should know before we go down to the cafeteria to see Mom Williams."

Maxine stared at Nina for a moment, her eyes pleading for a respite to pain.

"Jackie's down there with her, and she brought her son."

"Why didn't you tell me that Nina wasn't angry?" he demanded in a quiet but firm tone as soon as his father and sister left with Nina and Maxine.

"You know why," Vonetta said softly. "But like you said, it never happened. So get over it. I did."

Frustration bore into his temples, and he let his breath out in a rush. "You're right. We have bigger problems. I called my attorney, Earl, off the green, and he should be here soon."

"I don't need a lawyer," Vonetta said. "Unless Earl is fine. What I need is—"

"To listen," he snapped with impatience, cutting her off. "When I placed that phone call to your firm in a show of good faith at four A.M. so that we could get this investigation rolling, my insurance company told the police—and gave your firm's name, which I left in that voice-mail message. Their own investigators are probably already on it, after they heard about one of their big policies going up in smoke on the news, and being potentially linked to illegal activities. They'll tie a settlement up for months with the investigation, just so they don't have to pay out. Meanwhile, my business interruption coverage, my brother's disability coverage, everything, will be held up. Cash deposits could even get seized by the police, at the same time, because of drug allegations—"

"What's that got to do with me, directly?" Vonetta asked nervously. "I understand that you'll have some financial problems as a result of—"

"How long do you think it's going to take before they figure out that you're employed by that firm, and that we sat up in each other's company last night?" He dropped his voice an octave and stared in her eyes as he spoke.

"Between the fact that you're going to be living off your wife after your well in the bank runs dry, and an insurance settlement is out of the question, and I'm going to lose my job, if not my license, for being anywhere near this, not to mention the fact that we could both wind up in jail, I'd say maybe a talk with Earl Jones wouldn't hurt. And it also wouldn't hurt for me to go snooping around, either. Our asses are in a proverbial sling." Vonetta threw her head back and quietly chuckled. "All because I wanted something I wasn't supposed to have. Poetic, isn't it?"

"You pick up on things fast, lady, and I'm sorry about all of this."

"Does Nina know who kept you up talking last night, or which insurance company you were gonna switch to?"

Anthony cast his gaze toward the glass windows. "Haven't had a chance to get that far in a conversation with her about that yet."

"Step outside with me," she said in a weary voice. "I need a cigarette."

"You think the guy is lying?" Detective Collins asked his partner as they sat across the street from the hospital in an unmarked car.

"It's always hard to say," DeShields remarked over a slurp of coffee. "He doesn't fit the MO, but I think we can nail his ass on insurance fraud. He looks like the white-collar crime type to me."

"Let's call for another stakeout unit to watch the hospital traffic and visitors' list. Whatever's going on with these two guys is convoluted at best. And somewhere in the mix is a potential murder suspect, if the brother bites it." Collins shook his head, and started the engine.

"The guy's Mom and Pop look like nice people," DeShields murmured, reaching for the dispatch radio.

"Ain't it always that way," Collins muttered. "Nice family, and messed up kids breakin' some old lady's heart."

"Yeah," DeShields agreed. "Let's nail the bastards."

Earl Jones watched Vonetta leave, and he sat with his hands folded between his legs as he leaned forward on his arms, which balanced his weight on his knees. He addressed Anthony in his usual quiet professional tone, but his eyes had questions neither of the friends could answer.

"How long have we known each other, Anthony?" Earl asked in a confidential manner.

"We go way back, man," Anthony murmured, leaning forward with Earl.

"Then tell me why," Earl urged.

"It's not important, and I really don't know why I even went there for a moment. It was just stupid."

"Do you know what you're about to lose?" Earl whispered.

"Yeah, that's why you're here, man."

"No," Earl said in a low warning, then sat back. "That's not why I'm here. I'm here because you don't know why, and don't have the answers that will come up and indict your ass. And I'm going to ask you questions that you don't even want to tell your Jesus."

Anthony stared at his attorney and his friend.

"Because," Earl continued, "what I don't know will get you locked up. Any surprises on the stand, should you have to take it, could cost you your freedom."

"I hear you, man." Anthony sighed, rubbing his face with both palms. "I am so freakin' tired, man. You just don't know."

"Got a good wife, had a thriving business, money, good

family. Coming from you, Anthony, I'm frankly disappointed," Earl murmured.

"Don't you think I'm all messed up with that same head drill? But I didn't run any drugs through my operation, nor did I shoot my brother or try to burn down my establishment."

"That's not what I'm talking about," Earl said on an exhale that was filled with disgust. "I'm talking about Nina, brother. The weakest part of your alibi has to do with her best friend. And you haven't even told her. Now that's bull. Of all the goddamned choices. . . ." Earl stood and paced in the waiting room, then returned to his chair after his moment of rage had been tethered.

Anthony looked at his friend's dark, solemn face, and how the loss of respect for him had left it looking a tad older and more haggard than he'd ever seen it in his life. Shame washed over him, and he found a crack in the floor to observe. Anything was better than staring at Earl at the moment.

"OK," Earl said. "Lecture's over. Now I can say that the drugs that were confiscated only circumstantially link you and your brother to them, since there are many employees in the establishment. Since neither of you have any priors, it's very plausible."

"At least that part of my reputation precedes me, and it may help," Anthony said with defeat. "Maybe all those years of trying to do the right thing will pay off somehow."

Earl put his hand on his shoulder, then removed it. "This is not the time to go into a pity party. All right? So pull yourself together and pray that Cecil lives—for more than one reason."

Anthony nodded as Earl continued to badger him with his strategy.

"We can show from your bank drafts how the money that started the club, and was going into the business afterward, came from legitimate business revenue from the club. We can also show that you didn't even skim from the profits, as your household expenses and taxes line up to match your owner's draw."

Again, all Anthony could do was nod as Earl spoke.

"Now, as far as your whereabouts during the actual shooting and subsequent fire, you have a rock-solid alibi: You were home making good love to your wife. And all of the employees there can be brought in to testify that you were missing money and didn't know where or why, and now we know that was Cecil's doing—for domestic drama reasons. Two women, possibly three, are involved. But that doesn't clear him from being a suspect in a drug operation. The only thing this suggests is that you weren't stealing from your own club to fund any illegal activities."

"Then since everything links up to the truth, and there are witnesses, eventually things should be cool, right?"

Earl let out his breath in exasperation. "Not."

"Talk to me, man," Anthony whispered.

"You made a phone call, which has been entered into police evidence. This call you made, in some stupid, horny show of bravado at four in the morning, is your albatross. Listen to how this sounds, and think. You made a call to give something to a woman—who is your wife's best friend."

"That's not a crime," Anthony countered.

"Hear me out," Earl said evenly, and held him with a glare. "A woman who recently slept with your brother, was an ex-paramour of your brother, at a time when your club was losing money like rainwater, and during a period when you hadn't slept with your wife for more than four months. You make a call to give this woman's firm a large commercial account, which she will benefit from by way of a finder's fee, the same morning your club burns down, and your wife doesn't know about this."

Earl ran his fingers through his close-cropped hair and let his breath out hard. "Now if I were the prosecutors, I'd lean on you and twist this evidence around your balls until you cried for mercy, and I'd charge you with either being an accessory to arson—to get a three-million-dollar settlement, to take your brother's tactic of paying for two women at once to the multimillion dollar level, or I'd assume that you were an accessory to your brother's sideline hustle, and planned on keeping up this liaison with said woman by buying into the illegal business at a higher level—using her commission and insurance settlement as a down payment. Either way, there's a plausible motive, all because you didn't go home when you were supposed to."

Anthony stood and walked in a circle.

"Now, you're getting it. They are going to try to nail your ass to the cross with this part of it, Tony. And I can possibly counter with the fact that being a good businessman, the fire happened too quickly for the transaction to be done, therefore, ergo, you would not have benefited from the insurance company changeover, thus knocking that out as a plausible reason for all of this ugly business."

"Right . . . right! That's what I've been saying, man," Anthony exclaimed as he paced back to sit beside Earl. "That's how you know. I'd have to sign papers, documents would have to be transferred. It takes time, and the fire happened the same day."

"That's how I know, and the only reason why I'm sticking by you on this one, my friend," Earl said quietly, "is because if I thought you were messing up that badly, then our friendship, and my retainer, would be history. Do you understand?"

"Yeah, I do," "Anthony admitted, his voice trailing off with his thoughts. "But they can still try to make the case that I'd intended all of these things, but maybe my druggie arsonist jumped the gun when he came in and my brother was there instead of me, and got nervous, shot Cecil, and did the white-lightning job anyway. So it was a botched plan, instead of me really being innocent. That's how they're going to see it."

"Now you're thinking like an attorney," Earl murmured as he stood up to leave. He looked at Anthony, then gave him a quick embrace. "The doctor is coming down the hall, and I have my work cut out for me. Cecil won't be in any condition for me to question him. If it's other than good news, let me know. That will change things by an order of magnitude I can't even ponder now. Keep me posted on his progress. Give your family my regards, and give Nina my love—and tell her the truth, man. Promise me."

As the young doctor approached, Anthony stood and braced himself.

"Mr. Williams, your brother was under for almost nine hours. We've moved him to recovery in the intensive care unit. It may be days before he's well enough to respond to questioning from the police, your family, or attorneys. Inform your relatives and you can go in two at a time for five minutes each. Then, I suggest you all go home and get some much-needed rest."

Fifteen

By twos they assembled and waited their turns to go in to see Cecil's lifeless form. First his parents, then Maxine and Vicki, his other sisters, followed by Vonetta—who had left the hospital, then returned to go in alone. After her followed Jackie and Cecil's son. Anthony watched the strange processional pecking order. It would probably be the same at the viewing, he thought, then shook the terror of that shadowy whisper out of his head. To chase away the demons, he hugged each procession member as they exited the room.

Nina stood away from the group by her parents, and they all spoke to one another using inaudible, hushed tones until it was their turn to go in. He wondered what she'd told them, and if perhaps she'd even asked to move back home for a while. He'd waited to be the last in line, thinking that his wife would go in with him. However, at this juncture, that was presumptive.

He wasn't sure why else he'd waited. Perhaps it was because he wasn't ready to see his brother attached to machines that helped him breathe, or to have to sublimate the rage that was still mixed with hurt, or worse, acknowledge with his own eyes that all of this was actually happening. So he waited.

Nina withdrew from her parents, and came toward him. He wasn't sure if she was about to tell him she was moving out, or what. It was the unreadable look on her face that left him teetering on the edge of a plastic chair he'd finally agreed to sit in, looking off in the distance, and glimpsing her from the corner of his eye.

He stood with great effort. Everyone was beat. It wasn't just the length of time, or the waiting, it was the emotional drain of not knowing. Adrenaline collected in muscles, and arms, and backs, and legs, and created upset stomachs, and had flushed tears from swollen eyes, making tongues lick cry-cracked lips, and round down shoulders, until his family looked like refugees camping out. The ticktock of a life balancing on a thin line, the never knowing if the doctors quickly rushing by will stop to deliver bad news, all contributed to the feeling of wanting to curl up in a little ball. So they did.

His mother had found his father's shoulder, and made herself small, despite how angry she had been at Tony earlier. His sisters fit their bodies into uncomfortable plastic chairs so that their laps could hold dead-weight, sleeping youngsters, and allowed older ones to use their slim bodies like concrete pillars to lean against, while holding up the lot by sheer will. Vonetta had had the presence of mind to make her visit brief, which in turn allowed Maxine to leave—only after Jackie and her child left the hospital first. He understood that part, as did all assembled. It was an unspoken code amongst black people. Only the family-deemed legitimate woman had the first right of refusal—she was always the one who got to see the body first, after the mother, and leave it last, regardless of marital status. That meant he, the eldest son, had the duty to perform the last viewing after all the unspoken codes of honor and processional courtesy had been properly addressed.

Nina stood before him and waited. They would be the last family members to go in, and she knew that it was up to him to move away from the chairs and join her.

Her acceptance to be his escort was simply communicated through her hand on his shoulder, which seemed to propel him forward, and she knew he was ready when he caught her hand as it fell to his side to lace his fingers through hers. Her support of him, and her empathy for his pain, were transmitted to him through a gentle squeeze of her hand.

Once inside the room, his hand slowly left hers, and she knew that he wanted her there, but also needed personal space to walk over to touch his brother's face. His deep inhale was her signal to rejoin his side, and she watched her husband's eyes rove over Cecil's prone form, then assess the machines.

She had never seen so much hurt collected in his expression. His complexion went ashen, and silent tears streamed down his face, and he kept shaking his head slowly, as if saying, "This cannot be. . . ."

Nina looked down at the sunken face in the bed that had once been so vibrant and so alive, and felt her lungs close off as she remembered the smile now obstructed from view by a mask and tubes. Her husband said nothing, but leaned down and kissed his brother's brow. Then he turned, wiped his face with both palms, paced to the door, dry-heaved as he momentarily lost his balance, caught himself on the inner frame of the door, then quickly took a deep breath and straightened his back, and walked out.

When she came out seconds behind Tony, all eyes were on him. It was as though nothing the doctors had said mattered. The family was waiting on a pronouncement from Anthony. That's when she saw it. The indefinable strength Anthony possessed. For as shaken as he was, he'd gathered his internal forces, his eyes burned clear, and his voice was strong.

"Mom and Dad, you both can either come to our house, or if you want to be close to the hospital, I can put you in a hotel—but you must get some rest. He is in the best care he can be in now. We have to turn it over to God."

Then he looked at his sisters, and dispatched the same order. "You all go home. Go put the kids in bed and get some rest. Me and Nina will come in the morning, and will call everybody over in Jersey. Mr. and Mrs. Carpenter, thanks for coming. It means a lot."

And, without words, everybody began to move. The rag-tag platoon of battle-weary refugees stood and stretched and dabbed eyes with balled-up damp tissues, and began the business of checking on ride partners, and kissing friends of the family and parents good-bye.

Mrs. Williams stood slowly with the aid of her husband and accepted condolences from the Carpenter clan. She held on to her husband's arm, looking bewildered but ready to lay her burden down for the night. But first, she approached her son. So, again, Nina waited.

He didn't know what he could ever say to his mother to take this away from her, so he decided to opt for the language of touch, which communicated more than words. And this time, when he pulled her into an embrace, her body yielded completely. All the fear and tension and disbelief that had made her carriage stiff when he'd hugged her before, had given way to something he'd never felt in her before: defeat.

"Mom," he murmured against her temple as he stooped to kiss her. "Cecil's gonna be all right. Everything will be all right."

He was glad that Nina had come over to rub his mother's back and send a message of love to her through the laying on of hands. When the two women's gazes met, he knew his mother had received the conferment of deep caring that Nina was trying to send. At that moment, his appreciation for his wife could not be defined. And oddly, during the passing hours in the hospital, it seemed as though she, too, had come to accept something he couldn't explain—but it was not defeat. Yet Nina's presence in their three-way embrace had a strange effect on his mother.

Instead of nodding and weeping as she had before, his mother did something that he was totally unprepared for. It was the expression of sad peace that had come over her face as she pulled back from him, with dry eyes, and looked at him directly as she touched his face.

"No, baby. It's never going to be like it was. Don't you understand that?"

He was going to interrupt her, but she shook her head and smiled as he took a breath, stopping his words and hypnotizing him with her gaze. Never in his wildest dreams would he expect her to verbally claim defeat. It just wasn't like her.

"My baby son—my chile, Cecil—lied to me. First he lied, and then his father—my husband—lied to protect his lie. Then his sister lied to protect her father, and on and on and on. A lie, honey, is like a crack in the foundation of a family. One small crack leads to another crack, and it spreads slowly and quietly, until one day you step on what you think is just a teensy weensy little group of small cracks, and what's beneath it is a giant sinkhole. If the foundation ain't right, the whole house soon gives way, and you find yourself at the bottom of a hole you can't climb out of—'cause you done broke your back in the fall. No, baby, this family now has a lot of cracks, and it all needs repaving. Don't start no cracks, Anthony. Nowhere," she whispered, then turned and looked at Nina, then her husband.

Too stunned to move, Tony could only stand there as the women kissed each other and walked away from him. Their bond was palpable, and he was their outsider now. He could only assume that his father must have picked up on his confusion and distress, for he sauntered over to him slowly and put an arm around his shoulder.

"Guess we both almost killed the goose that laid the golden egg," his father said, not caring whether or not the women heard. "All 'cause our Cecil done cut the natural monkey. Son, take your wife home, and I'ma do the same. No sense in even driving by to see what's left of the club, either. Do that in the cold light of day—after you let your mind rest before the next battle. Everybody gotta lot of thinkin' to do tonight, then tomorrow morning is another day. That's when you talk—in the light of day. And we jus' gotta pray that the Lord is merciful upon all our souls, most especially my wounded boy laying half dead in there. That's all we can do, son. I'm too old to fight battles bigger than me."

All Anthony could do was nod, and as the family moved out and his mother rejected his invitation to stay in town, stating that she just wanted to go home, he hoped that she meant to Jersey, not home to Jesus. He said a silent prayer, while walking next to Nina. He prayed with all his might that his mother's heart would hold up through the night, and his father's high blood pressure and sugar wouldn't send him into a stroke or coma. He worried that the sheer disappointment of it all might be enough to take those two battle-weary spirits away in their sleep. So he asked the Father to let his brother see another day . . . and that He'd give him some words of wisdom to make it all right with his wife.

"C'mon, baby," he whispered as he closed the door and turned the locks. "Let's go to bed."

Nina walked ahead of him, but toward the kitchen, not the stairs. He appraised her gait, which was not filled with attitude. Instead, it was fluid, and yet fatigued, but not tense.

"This goose," she said quietly, grabbing a tall, clear water glass, "is going to drink some wine first. It doesn't even want to think about anything till morning at this juncture, Tony."

Her voice was even, nonjudgmental, and calm—too calm, perhaps. And he watched this new dimension of his wife, which he'd never seen. Normally she poured her wine into long-stemmed crystal, sipped her Chardonnay chilled, while relaxing or reading, or in the tub. But he was watching her belt it down while straddling a kitchen stool, one hand on the bottle, the other on her glass.

"Baby, you might want to take it easy. Tomorrow may be a long day," he said with concern while leaning against the door frame.

Then she laughed and stood up, and poured another glass, and wobbled, caught her balance, and brushed past him.

"Nina," he called after her as she mounted the stairs, teeter-tottering on each rise. "Baby, you're scaring me."

" 'Cause we've had a rough day, and I'm drinking some wine?" she said, downing the third glass on the stairs and trying to pour another where she stood. "And I'm scaring you?" Her giggle was hollow, filled with hurt, and faraway sounding.

"Baby," he whispered, approaching her slowly to keep from making her fall. "Come to bed, and give me the wine. You'll be sick in the morning. You'll be in no condition to go to the hospital to see Cecil, and I know you'd want to. Baby, please, give me the glass."

Nina shrugged, and started to hand it to him, then snatched it back and strode quickly up to the second-floor landing. "Nope," she called over her shoulder. "I'm cool. I'm not on the steps, so you don't have to worry about me falling."

"I'm not just worried about you falling," he murmured, trying to get close enough to her as she hop-ran into the bedroom, spilling wine down the hall as she downed the fourth glass while trying to run.

"It's just wine, Anthony. This has been one helluva day." She flopped on the bed and shook her head.

He just stared at her. Then she laughed.

"You know what jumped into my head just now?" Her eyes had an unusual sparkle to them, a frightening, half-about-to-cry, half-ready-to-run-screaming-into-the-night look.

"Baby, I'm so sorry . . ."

"Step on a crack, you'll break your mother's back." She chuckled, swigging what was left in her glass and dropping it on the rug as she stood up to begin to turn imaginary double-dutch rope in the center of the bedroom floor. "But all in time, three, six, nine, the goose drank wine, and the monkey tore the back off the street car line." She looked at him and laughed.

His heart was beating so hard within his chest that it made his ears ring. The sight of his wife in this state. . . . He'd never seen her drunk, but the words . . . the words . . . they all came back in a terrifying slow-motion recall of the way the last twenty-four hours had begun.

"Three, Tony," she said, picking up the fallen glass. "I don't know who six and nine are, but I think the number three deserves a toast, since your dad called me the goose . . . the stupid goose!"

Her words had begun to slur, but her eyes had a level of clarity that he was determined to reach.

"You need to put down the glass and let me tuck you into bed, and we can talk about all of this in the morning."

"Fine," she said with a capricious nod. "I guess it would have been all right for me to get a psychiatric prescription while I was at the hospital, take a few Valium, and go to bed. That's more socially acceptable than self-medicating with wine," she scoffed, placing the glass down hard on the nightstand, and flopping into a chair. "But it's tacky that the goose drank wine, huh?"

"No, baby," he whispered. What could he say? He needed to have this fight in the morning. He needed rest—time to heal his own wounds, and to know if his brother would live, and if he'd be on his way to prison. Time to break it to her that he was virtually penniless. Time to explain that the drugs in the club were not his. Time. All he was asking God for now was time, and yet he didn't have the right to ask her for it. A damned homeless person had given him a warning that he was too arrogant to accept, and he'd discounted that freakin' gift—one that he was paying much more for now than the twenty dollars he'd begrudged a bum.

He looked up at his wife, who had begun to cry, and he sat down on the foot of the bed, slowly, testing that it might even be his right to still do so. When she shot up and sought a chair, he let his head fall into his hands.

"Tell you what," she said evenly. "I will not drink any more wine. And we will go to sleep so that we can meet your parents at the hospital tomorrow when we check on Cecil. But I have one question—actually, it's more like one of those Zen riddles—then I can go to bed."

He looked up at her and remained still.

"What do me, you, and Cecil have in common?" She waited.

"What?" he stammered slowly, feeling as though he'd been on the twenty-fifth floor of a high-rise when the elevator had suddenly dropped to ground zero.

"Three . . . the three of us?" she repeated in a deadly whisper.

"I don't—"

"Vonetta."

Sixteen

The aroma from the ginger tea that Anthony had placed before her steamed up to her lowered face and helped her open her eyes. Daylight was harsh, she thought, taking an unsteady sip of the strong brew and putting the cup back down on the kitchen table with care. Especially if you were stupid enough to chug down four glasses of wine on an empty stomach. What was she thinking last night? That was clearly not the answer, and she hadn't attempted anything so foolish since her college days.

She could feel the vibrations of him taking a seat across from her through her bones, which shot heavy percussion into her skull.

"Ohhh, be quiet," she groaned, covering her hair with one arm and easing her head down to the table. She lay there for a while, just breathing slowly and trying to keep from vomiting again. With much effort, she finally pushed herself up using both hands against the edge of the table. But she kept her eyes closed for a moment, feeling around for her cup like a blind person.

"We have to talk," he said in a mercifully low tone. "There's so much I have to tell you."

Now he wanted to talk? Oh, heaven help her. Not this morning.

She shook her head no, with care, and held up her

hand to stave off his voice, then took another sip of tea. Again his movements jarred her skeleton as he got up, went to the counter, and made noises that sounded like he was preparing toast. She was right . . . the smell of toasting bread wafted to her nose, and she panted as she bent over and dry heaved. There was nothing left in her belly, which was a good thing, because she certainly wouldn't have had it in her to sling a mop.

He watched his wife from the corner of his eye, and brought the dry toast over to her. Rubbing her back, he helped her sit up in her chair. What had he done?

"I figured coffee would have been too much for your system," he whispered, "since you're not a coffee drinker. But your books said ginger takes away nausea. So I made it strong. But try a little bread to get a base on, and once you can keep that down, I'll run you a bath."

Although she didn't answer him, she accepted the small piece of crust he'd broken off for her and carefully placed it in her mouth with her eyes still closed. He never ever wanted to see her like this again, especially not on his account. His mother had been right, and he wondered if his father was at home doing the same thing— tending to the emotional wounds of the person he'd inflicted them upon. But the only real medicine would be to perform emotional triage, using the truth as a scalpel, and his arms as sutures, if she'd allow him to close the incision.

Again he sat down across from her and waited. She needed to be prepped for this surgery, and he needed a clean environment to work in, lest outside-of-the-relationship bacteria infect his patient.

"Whether you believe me or not, I did not sleep with Vonetta. Not last night, or ever."

Again he waited before speaking, and she opened her eyes, which now had a dull glaze to them instead of their normal sparkle. Her body moved back in her chair, and

she took a sip of tea, looking over the rim of her cup at
him as she munched another piece of toast. She didn't
have to say a word. Her expression said it all. *Shoot.*

"You know," he murmured, "yesterday, I had a lot on
my mind, and I went to Jersey when I left the house. I
went to go see Pop, because I just needed someone to
talk to—another man," he added for clarity. "I was feeling trapped—by the business—and I wanted to understand how he and Mom made it all these years, while still
providing for us. Until I went down into the rec room
and talked to the old man, I didn't even realize how much
stress I'd been under, or how much stress I'd put on our
marriage."

He sat back and stared at her, looking for any nonverbal response to cling to. She offered a nod, and he held
his breath, waiting a moment before speaking again.

"I went to my parents, too, that day," she mumbled.
"Twice."

OK, he thought. Common ground. Hope. The beginnings of détente. The fact that her eyes did not contain
a hard glare gave him the courage to press on.

"Then," he said in a low voice, taking his time to
gather his thoughts, "I understood, from talking to my
father that I'd been carrying my brother and taking care
of other grown people's problems, for way too long, and
neglecting my primary responsibility, my marriage. The
club had outlived its usefulness, and it was time to move
on and make a change. I couldn't hold the line on the
club and carry Cecil, who was breaking my back, and
have a happy home. Something had to give."

"You've been carrying a lot of people on your back for
a long time, Anthony," she said. "I've known that since
I met you—ironically, it was what drew me to you. You
had compassion enough to do it, but . . ." she whispered,
shaking her head, "somehow, you couldn't make the
break, and you let them ride you like a Septa trolley, pull-

ing everybody along by a thin wire, and balancing on narrow rails between the club and here, and you never could understand that that self-sacrifice involved me, too. If you sacrificed yourself, and I'm a part of you, then you've let them ride both our backs."

He nodded and looked down at the small fissures in the wood of the butcher-block table. How did women master this level of wisdom and communication even with a hangover?

"You're right," he murmured after a pause. "That's why I went to Cecil's that morning after I left Pop. I wanted to set the record straight, to have a man-to-man, brother-to-brother conversation with him about either taking some of the weight, or us just dissolving the partnership and selling the club."

Anthony sat back and looked up at the ceiling, and allowed a pain-filled chuckle to escape. It was a way to send a thousand questions up to the sky, and let out the tension winding its way around in his gut.

"But instead of being able to talk to my brother," he said, this time looking at Nina directly, "I wound up accidentally giving this homeless guy a twenty because I didn't want to pull out a wad of bills on the street, and I forgot I had given my nieces and nephews all of my small bills. That's how much I had on my mind when I left Pop's. So I reach in, peel a bill off in my pocket, and hand this dude a twenty without looking. There's a lot I haven't been looking at, Nina."

His gaze met hers, and he wanted so badly to reach across the table to grasp her hand, but fear of her reaction held him back. She furrowed her brows, and cocked her head to the side, then looked at him squarely.

"When you gave this man the money, what happened next?"

He shrugged. Her expression and question were odd,

eerie even, as though she were working a puzzle in her mind.

"Just some crazy drug talk."

"What did he say?" she pressed.

"Baby, why are you focused on this little detail when—"

"Because," she stated in a firm tone, "you gave some-one a gift, then your whole world fell apart that same day. Doesn't make sense. It's not the way of the cosmos."

He let his breath out hard and sighed. This was why he never disclosed anything of import to her. He loved her optimism and the way she believed so hard in all this fairness mumbo-jumbo, and he was the last one who ever wanted to tell her that the world was ugly, dangerous, and had a slimy underbelly to it. It would be like telling a kid there was no Santa Claus. Why take away her inno-cence or faith in unseen forces? She and his mother were the only women he'd ever known that seemed to have any.

"Baby," he began with patience, "that doesn't matter, what I'm trying to say is—"

"What, *specifically*, did the man say to you?" Her ques-tion was more like a command and her gaze was direct. Now she was leaning forward, forcing him with the pas-sion of conviction in her stare to not look away, but to answer the question.

"He gave me a kid's jump-rope song for twenty dol-lars," Anthony said.

"Repeat it for me," she said quietly.

Her stare and tone captivated him. She'd never been this intense, even in their other arguments. But there was a nonjudgmental quality to her voice that he clung to. It was as though Earl Jones were sitting across the table from him, getting just the facts, and nothing but the facts.

"He said, 'step on a crack, and you break your mother's back . . . but all in time, three, six, nine, the goose drank wine, and the monkey pulled the back off the street car line, and the line broke, and the monkey got choked, and they all went to heaven in a little row boat.' An old kids' jump-rope rhyme, like I said." He pushed himself back in his chair and watched her and waited for a response so he could get to the rest of what he really wanted to tell her. But she rubbed her chin and stood up. She walked over to the sink and leaned against it—looking at him like a cop.

"It was a warning, Anthony," she whispered, staring at him intently. "A cosmic gift of prophecy."

"Baby," he murmured, now really becoming concerned about his wife's state of mind, "I know you're looking for answers, and we're all grabbing for straws, but we have to stay in the here and now, and we have to come up with real—"

"This is real," she snapped, walking back to her seat, leaning forward and grabbing both of his hands across the table. "You, Cecil, and your father, stepped on a crack—lied—and it broke your mother's back. She said so last night, how lies represent a crack in the foundation of a family."

Now he was listening.

"And," she pressed on, "your father said I was the goose that laid the golden egg. Sure, he meant by that metaphor that your mother and I had enriched your lives immeasurably, but he called me *the goose* nonetheless." She hesitated and seemed to be waiting to be sure that he wouldn't interrupt her again.

He didn't, because her wacky train of thought was opening new possibilities within his mind. Being awestruck at her perception, and the way she drew analogies, gave him a new respect for her gut instincts. Unorthodox as it was, many a decision had been made in his own life simply based on a hunch. He nodded to give her the encouragement to go on.

"And, did I not drink wine, too much in fact, last night?"

Again, he could only stare at her and nod.

"And what was the last thing I said to you before I threw up, and you had to tuck me into bed?" she asked on a whisper.

"You kept yelling about three, the number three," he recalled in a very quiet voice.

"Three, six, nine . . . Tony, the three are me, you, and Cecil. The goose is me, you are the streetcar line, and Cecil is the monkey that got choked." Her gaze went out of the window, as though she was looking at some invisible mural unfolding before her eyes.

"What?"

"Think about it," she said more confidently as her gaze traveled back to his. "Strangely, I just equated you to a trolley, carrying everybody on a thin wire, the club—the line—which Cecil pulled the back off. By not being there to support running the club with you, stealing from you, and generally causing chaos in there with his women, he pulled the back off the streetcar line. He didn't have your back, Tony. And by not having your back, and cuttin' the monkey, as your father put it last night, he got choked."

He watched his wife fold her arms over her chest, stand, and begin to pace in slow motion around the kitchen. He'd seen his mother break down biblical parables in this same mysterious way, equating a random Bible passage with some current family problem, and coming up with a very wise, yet unfathomable, solution. But never in his forty-one years on the planet had he ever seen a person dissect a nursery rhyme given by a street bum. The concept was ludicrous! However, it made so much sense that it scared him.

"OK, OK," he said quickly, feeling too much adrenaline in his system to continue sitting. He stood and paced with her in the center of the kitchen floor. "Then who makes up six and nine? That's possibly nine people—when it's all said and done, Nina. Do you know what you're saying?"

"I know Vonetta is a possible person in this, which we have yet to fully discuss," she said in a calm, dissecting tone that worried him. "I know that Maxine is, too. She has a definite motive. And we have this new girl, Jackie, to consider—because Cecil did some foul mess to her. That's all I know. But if you add up the first three, plus these three more women, you have six to investigate. You need to tell Earl Jones this."

He walked away from her, then spun to look at her. "I can't tell Earl to base a freakin' legal case on a nursery rhyme from a homeless man, Nina! Do you hear yourself?"

"Leave out the rhyme as a source when you tell him where to start digging. But tell him who to start looking for clues from."

Exasperation coursed through his veins, lifting his fist and propelling it into the wall. The crunch of bones and flesh against the plaster released his frustration into it, and he pulled his hand away, taking deep inhales of air in through his nose. "My life is crumbling around me, Nina. The bar is burned out, the insurance companies won't settle till they have answers, and my bank accounts could be seized. Everything I've worked for, and the way I support this household, is gone. I could get indicted, my brother is lying in the hospital, holding on to life by a thread, and all I have to go on is three women linked together by the long stretch of a nursery rhyme? Then when this is over, we'll all go to heaven in a little row boat?"

He threw his head back and laughed, and as he did so, a deep sob quaked loose from down in his soul, forcing him to laugh harder and louder until he was crying against the wall he had just mangled.

"I didn't sleep with her, Nina," he gurgled. "I swear to God. She was there last night, trying to get me to forget I was married, and I thought she was going to tell me why you were so angry at me all the time—because she was the only one who I knew you confided in. The next thing I knew, though, she was in my face and pouring me Johnny Walker Red, so I tried to get her out of there, and to get my head together. By calling my insurance agent to switch policies, I thought it would be a peace offering, to let her know we were still cool, but that it couldn't go like that—ever. And in return, she was going to investigate for me, and find out who was stealing five thousand a month from the club. The club has been hemorrhaging for the last four months, but it wasn't all Cecil."

His confession had left him spent and panting and his wife silent. He couldn't even look at her now.

"Why didn't you tell me when you came home?" Nina whispered.

"Because how do you tell the person you love more than life itself that you almost did something that stupid? Or explain to her that the one girlfriend she has in the world isn't necessarily her friend?" He first addressed his questions to the wall, then the floor.

"And how do you explain to your wife that you don't have all the answers, and that you might not know what you're doing, and that you're afraid you're going to fail? How do you admit that you're most afraid that, one day, she'll walk—and replace you with an educated, professor-type guy, who shares her same interests, schedule, and the way she was used to living, especially when all of your friends, your business associates, even your own damned brother, are all just waiting for you to mess up so they can have a shot at taking her from you? How do you look the woman you love in her eyes and tell her that?"

Nina absorbed his statement and matched it to the con-

versation she'd had with her father, and remembered
what he'd said to her . . . and knew. She felt herself cross
the room, and her hands found the shoulders of the man
whose back had just been broken, causing another round
of sobs to vent themselves on her shoulder as she rocked
him and hushed him with her murmurs, and stroked his
head and neck.

Seventeen

"I'll be back in a few hours," she promised, kissing Anthony's cheek, then kissing her in-laws. "Let me take your cell phone."

He looked at Nina for a moment and complied. She never carried the cellular. But right now, with his brother still unconscious, and his parents sitting bedside just praying, it made sense for her to have a way to call the hospital if she needed to be later than expected.

"Come back when you can," he murmured, pecking her on the cheek. "Don't stay at the university too long. You know how they pull you in and keep you from leaving once you get there."

"I won't," she whispered, leaning over Cecil's body to kiss his forehead. "I'll be back in a flash. I just have to deliver some papers to my boss so that the students can get their grades on time. I may be gone from work for a while, given all of this, and I also need to show them where the files and stuff are."

He nodded and watched her leave, wondering how long it would be until she just gave up on him, his family, and all the problems they'd brought to her life.

Nina turned on the car engine, idled it in the hospital parking lot, and let her forehead rest on the steering wheel. She'd lied to him. But it was the only way. After seeing his face as they kicked through the charred rubble of the club, she'd made her decision. Anthony hadn't burned his life work—not even for insurance money, nor had he put a bullet in his own brother's back. And she knew her husband damned sure didn't run drugs.

The problem was that the police didn't know it, and Earl Jones might not have the time to prove it—at least not before Anthony's reputation was ruined, he was financially bankrupt, or temporarily imprisoned. And if they put her husband away for even a short stint, like a few weeks or months until a trial, anything could happen to him. He could be violated, gang raped, or murdered in some jailhouse brawl, and what would such indignities inflict as a permanent scar on his soul? He'd never be the same.

The specter of those possibilities helped her decide to shift the car into reverse, pull out of the space, and head for her target. The university could wait.

"The wife is on the move," Collins said to his partner. "That means it's our move. Just hang back and let her lead us."

DeShields nodded and brought their sedan around slowly, keeping several car lengths out of sight.

Anthony squeezed his mother and father's shoulders as Cecil stirred. No one spoke, but as his brother's eyes fluttered, his mother's hand covered her mouth, and his father began rocking in his chair.

"C'mon, Cec," Anthony urged in a whisper, then came closer to his brother's face. "We're here, man. Mom and Pop and me are all here."

* * *

Nina stood on Maxine's steps and waited. After several moments, she rang the bell again, and began knocking. Her pulse beat in her ears as she heard movement, then saw the curtains stir. What was she going to say?

The door opened a crack, and she could see Maxine's form motioning for her to step in. When Nina moved forward, Maxine grabbed her arm, pulled her through the small opening, slammed the door and turned the locks quickly.

"Oh, my God, girl. It was just you," Maxine breathed with a sigh of relief. "I thought you were the cops."

Puzzled, Nina cocked her head to one side and looked at Maxine hard. "The cops? Why here?"

Maxine let out her breath and walked past Nina to the kitchen. "C'mon to the back and I'll make us some coffee."

Following behind her, Nina appraised the tiny row house that was neat and well-appointed, like Maxine. Maxine was good people, a hardworking sister. What had been on Cecil's mind? Maxine also ran that club like a drill sergeant, and if there were anything shaky going on, Maxine would have had to know.

Nina was too wired to sit, and she simply leaned against the wall. "Max, listen, Tony's in big trouble," she began without preamble, unable to wait for the slow process of coffee to be made and for chitchat. She didn't even drink coffee, which was not the point of Maxine making it. She recognized that the woman before her was wired, too, and needed something to do with her hands. So she waited and watched, and gathered that Maxine had a piece of the puzzle just from the way she maneuvered inefficiently around her own kitchen.

"Did you hear what I said?" Nina pressed on when Maxine hadn't answered her or turned around. "Anthony

Williams is going to go to prison for shooting his brother and burning down his own club!"

"He didn't shoot his brother," Maxine said quietly without turning around as she scooped coffee grounds into a filter.

Nina's stomach did flip-flops of anxiety as she looked at the woman who was carefully measuring out coffee and painstakingly putting the scoops into the filter-lined holder. "Stop already, Maxine! You're like my sister-in-law. Please. Talk to me. Your man is almost dead, and mine is getting ready to go up the river. What about this don't you understand?"

"I don't understand how you can root for Vonetta to be with Cecil, after I thought you and I were so tight . . . that I was family. And I don't understand why I'm supposed to help Tony, at my expense, when it looks like Cecil's gonna die anyway."

Within a split second, Nina's brain replayed the night before the incident. Maxine had seen her sitting and drinking and laughing with Vonetta, then Maxine had stormed out, leaving the club and all the guilty parties, according to Maxine, there to snicker at her humiliation. The seeming betrayal of trust was evident, and her voice found the truth that she didn't even want to hear herself.

"Vonetta lied to me, Max," she said simply, and came around to stand by Maxine at the counter. Nina waited for Maxine to look at her directly before she spoke again.

"I never knew she'd started up again with Cecil, or spent the night with him, until after you came in, then stormed back out again. Even Tony didn't know until the shooting."

"He didn't?" Maxine whispered, searching her face for evidence of deceit.

Nina shook her head. "You know I wouldn't have condoned it, because even though Vonetta *was* my girlfriend, respect is respect. You're good people, Maxine. You are my brother-in-law's woman. All his sisters, his parents, and the kids think of you as family—Aunt Maxine—and you've been in our lives for years. Vonetta had no right, and she has a man. Why she had to step into your yard is beyond me. And, trust me, she and I will have words on the subject."

"That bitch." Maxine said through her teeth. "Do you even know what she did when I caught her over there?"

Nina shook her head no.

"She waved at me, Nina. Laughed and waved, then trotted around the corner. Then she shows up at the club to rub my face in it. I was so hurt that Cecil would even go there with any woman, but her . . . or Jackie. But do you see what I'm saying?" Maxine's eyes had filled with tears of rage, and she allowed them to overflow and stream down her cheeks, obviously feeling safe in the company of another trusted woman.

"I know how Vonetta can be," Nina said.

"I noticed you said *was* when referring to her as your friend?"

"That's because I meant *was,*" Nina whispered, actually saying the words out loud for the first time. "She put a move on Tony that night after I left, shortly behind you, and never gave him the message that I wasn't angry about a fight we'd had. She stayed until closing, and convinced him to give her firm the fire-insurance policy so she could get a cut of the commission from whichever agent she's in cahoots with now."

"What . . ." Maxine opened her mouth, closed it, then walked around in a hot circle. "That stinkin' heifer! Tell me that your Tony, our Anthony, didn't do her?"

"I don't know," Nina whispered. "You know the effect that Vonetta has on men, and the only reason Tony told me was because he had to go through his entire whereabouts up to and after the shooting. I don't think my husband went there. In my mind, I pray that he didn't.

But all I have is his word to go on, and right now, there's a lot of stuff that just doesn't add up."

Maxine walked back over to Nina and placed a hand of support on her shoulder. "Listen, girl, don't go there yourself. It'll make you crazy. Tony isn't like that. I mean, he has a lot more self-control, and knows the difference between right and wrong—unlike Cecil. Same family, but cut from a different cloth."

"I have to find out the series of events, Maxine," she whispered. "I can't let Tony go to jail."

"But, he was with you that morning, then afternoon. Right?"

"Yeah." Nina shrugged. "But I'm his wife. My testimony will be viewed as a lie, no matter what. And even if he was with me, they're saying that Tony coulda had somebody clean out the safe, shoot Cecil, and burn—"

"No," Maxine whispered, walking away from Nina. "That's not what happened."

"If Cecil could have just stayed conscious to tell 911 who got him, but then he passed out—"

"Cecil never called 911. My brother Darrell did."

Nina stood very, very still and stared at Maxine.

"My brother didn't shoot Cecil. We don't even own a gun. But we both went over there that morning to give back my second set of keys, and Darrell wanted to cuss Cecil out. He said what he had to say to him was a man-to-man thing, and he told me to wait in the car. I did, and we were in the front, not even in the back. We came in through the front door this time. Then Darrell came running out and said Cecil had been shot and the safe was open. He wasn't in there long enough to have cracked a safe, and nobody but Tony and Cecil had the combination, plus I never heard gunshots fired. So I said call 911. We can't leave the man to die, no matter what he did to me."

It was hard for Nina to find her voice, but a sense of relief washed over her. There was an eyewitness.

"Why didn't you tell the police?" Nina finally managed. "Darrell didn't do it, so—"

"When's a black man received a fair trial, when he's on probation for other things, and all the evidence points his way? My brother has been working so hard to get his act together, and he was only over there for my sake. *I dragged him into this crap.* The police have already been here once, questioning my whereabouts and whatnot. I was scared, Nina. But we never killed Cecil. As odd as it sounds, I love that fool. Can you understand that?"

"Yeah," she whispered, fully understanding just where Maxine was coming from. "But they said Cecil called 911—"

"That was Darrell, pretending to be Cecil so they'd never trace it to us. But if they ever look up the number, it's my cell phone. I figured I could always tell 'em Cecil had access to mine, and had it on him, since he was my man, and that would clear my brother. Darrell had turned him over, saw a shot in his back, and two holes in his front, and told them that much so the paramedics could get to him quick and know what to do. Then we jetted."

"Thank you, Maxine," Nina said quietly, and drew toward the door. "You two actually saved Cecil's life. That's gotta count for something."

Maxine followed behind her, and touched her shoulder to make her turn around.

"Nina, I know you have to tell the authorities, but promise that you won't let them make Darrell take the weight for something he didn't do."

"We won't," Nina said with false confidence. How could she promise what wasn't hers to give? Strange things happened to black men in the system, and yet it was either Darrell or her man. There was no contest, and both women's gazes locked, understanding that.

"Tell me this," Nina asked, hoping that Maxine would

give her the right answer. "You didn't allow your brother to run his old business through the club, did you?"

"Hell, no!" Maxine exclaimed, stepping back from Nina, and looking at her hard. It was not a stare of indignation, but one of absolute truth.

"You need to have Tony have a conversation with Ronell about that. I have warned Ron, and told him that I'd tell Tony that, just because he started dealing with that bitch Jackie, which also benefited me, I was not going to allow him to have that mess in the club."

"Wait," Nina said in confusion. "While you were dating Cecil, I know he'd hooked up with Jackie, and yesterday, we *all* found out that they had a baby together. You knew about the baby? Since when?"

Maxine let her breath out hard. "When Cecil started skimming money off the top of the registers, I went to him about it because I knew Tony didn't know. At first, he said he was doing it because Tony wasn't giving him a fair cut. Then I found out that there was more to it than that because Tony has never shorted Cecil, and I can count. One thing led to another, and it all came out that it was hush money for this broad. Child support, I call it. But he had to send her some ends. That's why we were always at each other's throats. Finally, I guess when she saw that Cecil wasn't going to leave me for her, baby notwithstanding, she hooked up with Ron, to rub Cecil's face in it. Then she got pregnant with Ronell's baby."

Nina shook her head. "I be damned. So, Ron needed more money, right? And he couldn't go to Tony for a raise—not dealing with one of Tony's brother's women."

"You got it. This is man stuff, Nina. Ron always wanted to be a big-time player, like he thought stupid Cecil was, so he decides, in his infinite male wisdom and good access as a bartender, to run a side hustle through the club."

"But why didn't you tell Tony right away?"

Maxine hung her head and sighed. "I wasn't thinking, lady. I was more concerned about me and Cecil. I can't have babies. My tubes are scarred up so bad from my past life, and this girl had her hooks into my man's brain with a little boy. Ronell served three purposes. He kept Jackie out of Cecil's face, kept an eye on Cecil—'cause if those two fell out, I'd know Cecil was back to his old mess with Jackie. And he helped me to rub salt in Cecil's wound for even having the affair with Jackie in the first place. So I just told Ron to cool out, and take his business to the private club with Duane and Eddie. We had somewhat of an unholy alliance, sorta like honor among thieves. I'm not proud of it, but we didn't kill anybody or burn down anybody's club."

Nina ruffled her hand through her hair and let out her breath slowly, then leaned her head back and shut her eyes. This is what her husband had been mired in? Treachery, deceit, sexual escapades among crazy adults, drugs? No wonder he didn't want her anywhere near the place.

"Eddie and them have a private club? I take it Tony doesn't know?"

"Probably not," Maxine murmured. "Nina, love makes people do strange things, you know?"

She found herself curbside, sitting in the car, and making the call to Earl Jones's office. She'd needed fresh air so badly that she almost ran out of Maxine's house. How did people get so screwed up, in such short order, over such crazy things? Now, even children were involved. It seemed so painfully ironic that she and Tony couldn't have any, while those who took such a gift for granted used their children as bait and weapons. Her temples throbbed as she left an information-filled message on Earl's voice mail, and headed for Vonetta's.

Eighteen

"Are you Edward Hunter?" Detective DeShields asked as he flipped open his badge while standing at Eddie's front door.

"Let's go downtown," Collins said. "We're booking you on drug trafficking, arson, breaking into a safe to lift twenty-six cold ones, and attempted murder."

"Hold up, brother," Eddie pleaded as the two detectives drew weapons and turned him around. "I just boosted some liquor and some meats from the club, never took no cash, and don't run the drugs."

Collins turned Eddie around to face them. "You had a key, you had a motive."

"What motive?" Eddie argued.

"I hear there's a little after-hours spot you and your boys run at night up in West Oak Lane that doesn't have a permit, liquor license, or—"

"OK. OK. We was making good money at The Jazz Note. But if we burned it down, then we'd lose our access to free supplies. That don't even make business sense, man. Think about it."

"Maybe one of the owners came in and caught you red-handed, so you forced him to open the safe, cleaned it out, then shot him, then tried to cover your tracks by burning down the joint," DeShields said casually as he inspected his gun before putting it back in his holster.

"Or maybe your private club was getting too much competition from The Jazz Note," Collins offered in a blasé tone.

"Naw, man, you got it all wrong. The clients for The Jazz Note ain't even the same kinda people who come through our spot. I'll go down for moving some supplies from the boss, and even helping to run an illegal joint, but not for attempted murder. In fact, none of my boys shot Cecil, or stole cash money from him. We came in, all three of us, about two-thirty that day. Moved a bunch of liquor out—not enough to hurt 'em bad, money-wise— and I left the back door open so Ronell could come back and get the meat before Tony came in around three- thirty. The coast was clear, wasn't nobody there, plus Ronell had a package to pick up, which I don't even deal with, but he left it there from Saturday night, on account his old lady is expecting, and he don't transact his busi- ness at home no more. Me and my boys told him he couldn't do it at the club, so his clients had to make their pickup from The Jazz Note. That's his business. I don't mess with drugs. They'll get your ass killed. So, we didn't have no drugs in our spot."

"You're going downtown," Collins said with disgust as he looked at the gleam of sweat polishing Edward Hunter's face.

"Hey, man," Eddie protested. "Cecil was my boy's brother—and me and T go way back."

"How do you call yourself Anthony Williams' friend when you admittedly were stealing from his estab- lishment, even though you said he paid you well?" DeShields asked incredulously as they walked Eddie down his steps to the sedan.

"Yo, man," Eddie protested as they pushed him into the backseat. "Tony was phat-paid. He could handle the littl' somethin'-somethin' we broke off to get our own thing going. Woulda paid cuz back once the dough came in. Plus, it was only for like a few months or so—wasn't like we was lootin' him the whole time. Ronell made a run, got into some mess with his old lady, then went by the club, and couldn't even go in, or lock the door like we told him to because the joint was in flames when he rolled up on it."

"And we're supposed to believe your crew is so honorable, wouldn't shoot a man, clean out a safe, and burn down a building to save your sorry asses?" Collins muttered, feeling pure disgust rise in his throat and begin to coat his tongue.

"Did you find any drugs left in the joint after it burned?" Eddie hollered from the backseat.

"Why?" Collins muttered. "You want a receipt so you can show it as a business loss on your taxes?"

DeShields laughed, and both cops shook their heads.

"Naw, wise guy," Eddie said with a huff. " 'Cause if you found some then that means we didn't burn the joint. If we was all that, like you saying, it would have gone down where we shot Cecil, hit the safe, and Ronell got his stash, then torched the joint, and you'd be IDing Cecil's dental records. I'm telling you!"

"Yeah, right," Collins said, turning the corner. "That's some ghetto logic if I ever heard it."

"OK, then lemme ask your boy," Eddie pressed on. "Since we talking about dealers, what drug dealer have you ever known to burn his whole shipment for the week after killing somebody. Just leave it there to go up in smoke, when he could cut it ten times and make a mint? Do that make business sense?"

When both officers looked at each other, Eddie sat back in his seat. "I rest my case, gentlemen. Like I said, we ain't no arsonists, and we ain't no murderers. And we wouldn't steal cash money from our boy. He had the access to liquor and supplies that we couldn't get, and he could spare it. That's all we took advantage of. You have to draw the line somewhere, boss."

"How's he doing?" Earl Jones murmured as he approached Anthony.

"Going in and out, but not talking yet," Anthony said quietly and stood. He walked over toward the door with the attorney and leaned against the door frame to get out of earshot of the nurse. "I promised Mom and Pop I'd stay here until they came back up from the cafeteria. My sisters were finally able to convince Mom to eat. What's up?"

"Well," Earl began, obviously choosing his words with care, "as soon as everybody comes back, you and I need to make a run downtown to police headquarters."

Anthony could feel the knot in his stomach start to travel up his esophagus. "I have to wait till Nina gets back, man. I can't go in the joint without having a chance to hold my wife," he whispered.

"No, we need to go now, so that you'll never have to go again," Earl whispered back. "We need you to listen to a voice on the tape and tell us if it's Cecil."

Confusion tore at his insides and made it hard to breathe.

"Listen," Earl commanded, taking Anthony by the arm. "Nina called my office from your cell phone. She went to Maxine's this morning and turned over a strong series of leads, which I thought was in your best interest to turn over to the police. We want to show as much cooperation at this juncture to clear your name and aid your case. They have Ronell, Eddie, and Duane in custody, the last I heard, and they're looking for Maxine's brother Darrell."

"All me and my brother's boys . . ." A sense of deep

betrayal swept through him, and he glanced at Cecil lying prone in his bed, still lifeless. "Where's my wife?"

"That's what we're concerned about," Earl admitted. "She's out in the streets like some junior play-detective, trying to keep you out of jail, but could be running into some very unsavory characters."

"Nina?" Anthony pulled Earl out of his brother's room and into the hall. "My wife didn't go to the university?"

"No," Earl replied in a soothing voice. "She went on a witch hunt to save your ass."

"Then the hell with the police station. I need to go get her!"

"No. You need to let DeShields and Collins send a squad car to pick her up, Tony. There's strong reason to suggest that the shooter might have been aiming for you."

"And?" Anthony shouted. "I'm not worried about that. I'm worried about Nina being out there stalked by somebody mad enough at—"

"Listen," Earl said matter-of-factly, "DeShields and Collins tailed her to Maxine's, then broke off to question Maxine. After pumping Maxine, they headed for the nearest secondary suspect, Eddie. But they radioed for a backup unit to keep a tail on Nina, and they spotted her car going into the lot for Vonetta's building."

"Then at least let me call her." He would not be moved until he received Earl's nod of agreement.

"Do it on the way to the station. You can't call her on a cell phone here," Earl said without emotion. "You'll flat-line every patient in this ward, including your brother. Go tell one of your sisters to get up here so we can go. Now."

The wait for the elevator in Vonetta's building was interminable. It had taken the doorman long enough to grill her, then raise Vonetta on the telephone to get permission for her to go up. Now she had to wait until the unit came down from the twenty-fourth floor. As Anthony's cell phone rang in her purse, she realized that she didn't even have the code to his voice mail, and she dug quickly to get the noisy electronic gadget out and figure out how to press the right button—only she clicked it off accidentally. She hated these things, and just prayed that it was Tony's normal business volume trying to reach him.

Then it dawned on her that it might be Tony. She did a fast star-six-nine and waited.

"Hey, don't say a word, but Nina is on her way up here," the female voice on the other end of the phone stated. "As soon as you can, I need you to come over—to talk. Something's happened." Then the female voice hung up.

Sudden fury collided with hurt as the elevator doors opened. It was as plain as the nose on her face—three with a star, six-nine . . .

Nina held the phone in her hand, struggling with the decision to go up to the twenty-fourth floor and slap her friend's face, or to march back to her car, drive to the hospital, and kick her husband's ass. She'd believed in him, through the tears, through the self-recrimination, even stuck her neck out to try to get him out of the mess that he and his brother had gotten themselves into! *Liar.* No, he wasn't a murderer or an arsonist or a drug peddler, perhaps, but he was no husband.

When the phone immediately rang again, she punched the button and connected, hearing Anthony's voice. She cut off his questions about where she was with a severe warning. "You know where the hell I am, and why I'm here. Don't you have the nerve to ask me where I am! You liar!" Then she hung up and switched the unit off.

The elevator doors opened, and Nina bolted past them

with purpose welded to each long stride. Vonetta had been her friend, an ally, a confidant, a sister, a cut-buddy, and mentor, a businesswoman she'd admired, a trusted, dear significant part of her life. *How could she?*

When Vonetta opened the door to her incessant banging, Nina stopped, looked at Vonetta's face and gasped.

Anthony and Earl stood shoulder to shoulder and peered at Darrell as DeShields grilled him on the other side of the glass, and Collins leaned against it from their side.

"Try her again," Earl whispered. "She wasn't making sense, Tony."

"We'll keep a tail on her," Collins said in a low but oddly supportive tone. "Something else might have gone down to add to this ball of yarn. Damn, your brother had a lot of stuff going on."

Anthony kept his eyes fastened to the glass, watching what now felt like a nightmarish *Twilight Zone* episode where he was both a spectator and a character trapped within the framed insanity he was witnessing in the two-way mirror.

"This is a woman's handgun, brother," DeShields yelled, holding a small, silver ladies Derringer in a plastic bag before Darrell, who kept shaking his head no. "You can wait for your lawyer if you want, but you're gonna go down for some silly things that your sister led you into. Why not let her take the weight?" DeShields stood and paced around the room, talking as he was walking. "Oh, right, I get it. You're the man in the family, and have already been to jail, your sister has a clean record, so you drive her over there, let her snuff her man and take twenty-six out of the safe. You make the call to cover for her, and do the honorable thing by going back into the joint? Just a natural knight in shining armor."

"It was like I told you, man. And I can prove it," Darrell finally retorted.

"How, you lying son of a bitch?" DeShields cut back. "Tell me."

"Because," Darrell hollered, his voice cracking. "Dust it for prints, for one! Hers and mine won't be on it! And for two, I took the money. Maxine would have never allowed it."

"Oh, no," Collins whispered. "The dumb bastard told on himself."

"Well, now we're getting somewhere," DeShields said more calmly.

"Check my apartment. The money's under the mattress. Maxine is not a thief, but after all that Cecil did to her, all the women he ran on that poor girl. I took it for her. She was due and I would have bought my sister anything she needed with it. I'da held it for her. She raised me, and is like my mom and a sister . . . so, don'tchu be implicatin' her in this bull, man!"

"OK," DeShields said quietly, taking a seat across from Darrell. "I have a sister. I love her too. But you sure you wanna do attempted murder and arson for her? That's a long time to be away, man—even for blood."

Darrell's head found his hands, and DeShields stood and left the room, joining his partner, Anthony, and Earl Jones.

"Looks like your client is one lucky bastard," Collins said in a dejected tone in Earl Jones' direction. "Once we sweep his apartment, run the voice analysis on the 911 call, and check that cell-phone number, we'll have Darrell's butt in a sling. It's all over but the paperwork."

Earl cast his arm around Anthony's shoulder to guide him out, but was forced to stop when Anthony didn't budge.

"You have Eddie and Duane for stealing liquor and opening the back door of the club, Ronell for cocaine and other drugs because his boys sang. That's three, right?"

Both detectives and his attorney looked at him.

"I just identified that the voice on the tape wasn't my brother's. Right? Which leaves Darrell—who says he didn't shoot Cecil or burn down the place, but just took the money."

"Yeah," Collins said, shifting a glance to DeShields.

"As your attorney, Anthony, we need to have this conversation in my office—alone. Do you understand?"

Anthony nodded, but shrugged Earl's arm off. "Darrell makes four. I think there may be a five and six. Darrell didn't shoot my brother, nor did Maxine—she loved him. I don't care about the twenty-six thousand; Cecil owed it to her. He treated her like a dog."

"Anthony," Earl insisted, "the balance of this conversation is for you and me to have under the auspices of attorney-client confidentiality. Do you read me, Captain?"

"I read you. But like you said, it's about cooperation. I'm innocent. These brothers know it. And my wife, who seems to be a damned good detective herself, gave me a hunch this morning. Three plus six equals nine—"

"I won't allow it," Earl spat, his voice raising an octave as his gaze swept DeShields and Collins.

"Me, Nina, and Cecil are the three victims, and I think you've only found four of the six criminals. I'd place money on it that that's who Nina is searching for now—numbers five and six. I know my wife. No sense in any man going to jail for what he didn't do, just so the paperwork's neat, and the case gets closed fast. Right?"

"I abdicate any responsibility for the direction of your defense, then, Tony—as your attorney, I'm begging you to—"

"Let me see the gun," Anthony said quickly to DeShields, cutting off Earl's words, while both detectives shot another meaningful glance at each other.

"I saw this gun last night," Anthony whispered. "Go get my wife, *now.*"

"Can you ID it?" Collins asked as he cast a glance at his partner.

"Yeah. It belongs to Vonetta."

Nineteen

Nina covered her mouth and stood in Vonetta's doorway and stared at her friend's once-lovely face. The sight of her made Nina cringe and want to reach out and touch the distended, purple skin around her friend's eyes and jaw that was tinged with an eerie yellowing circumference of battered flesh.

Vonetta's lower lip was cracked in the center, and her nose was crusted with dried blood. Around her neck were bluish rings, and as Nina's gaze traveled down her friend's cleavage, she could see that more damage had been inflicted, hidden under the soft silk folds of her fire-engine red kimono.

"Dear, God, Vonetta. Who did this to you?"

Without asking Nina in, Vonetta turned abruptly, leaving the door open as she picked up a lit cigarette and headed toward the white bar that rimmed her living room. All Nina could do was watch as the electric-red fabric trailed behind her friend, who from behind looked like a graceful geisha. But when the woman before her turned around, the hideous condition of Vonetta's face drew a shocking parallel to the beauty that now seemingly merged with the ugliness that had always been inside of her friend. Yet no one deserved this, Nina thought, slowly entering the luxurious bachelorette pad and closing the door behind her.

All thoughts of kicking Vonetta's butt had been temporarily swept aside. Something more than she realized was going on, perhaps . . . then again, maybe not. All she did know was that right now, Vonetta needed to be seen at a hospital.

She watched Vonetta pour herself a stiff drink, belt it down, and pour another one.

"Painkiller," Vonetta said after a moment to the still stunned Nina. "Better than Advil."

"You need to go to the hospital," Nina whispered. "Like, now."

"You need to let it rest, honey. Got my ass kicked already for being at the hospital. Ya know?"

"Who did this to you, Vonnie?" Nina's voice was soft, but steady.

"You know who did this. Does it matter, anyway?" Vonetta took a long drag off her cigarette, and let the smoke out slowly as she lolled her neck and sat down very carefully on a white-on-white bar stool. "Been gettin' my ass kicked for years, in one way or another. My dad, men, jobs, you name it. But this old girl can hang." She laughed bitterly, then took another puff. "What brings you here this fine afternoon? A showdown?" Vonetta stood and brought the entire bottle of booze to her side and poured a drink, looking at the glass instead of Nina. "If you want a fight, you've gotta take a number."

"Why weren't you honest with me, Vonet—"

"Honest, Nina?" she scoffed, sipping her drink more carefully. "Be honest, you say? Are you sure you want to hear the truth? Because right now, Nina, for the first time in your life, you just might get it."

Nina sat down on the sofa, looking at her friend who'd transformed into a person she didn't recognize—not because of the battle wounds she carried now on the outside, but from what she was sure was lurking within

Vonetta. It both frightened and hurt her to see those demons revealed.

"So, she does want the truth." Vonetta chuckled sadly into her glass as Nina sat and didn't move. "You have no idea."

Nina just stared at Vonetta as pain wound itself around their friendship and strangled it before her eyes.

"You have never, ever, *ever* appreciated what you've had."

A self-defense fought its way to Nina's lips, but she swallowed it down, choosing information over the ego satisfaction of having her own say. Patience, she told herself as she summoned it. The facts were paramount.

"You have two loving parents, as opposed to the lot I got stuck with. Your mom, as eccentric as she is, was at every recital, and art gala, pushing you forward, had your back and stood there, taking pictures from the porch, even as you went to your prom—and danced at your wedding! What did I have? Some drunken bitch that found her way onto every bar stool, with her sole occupation being how she worked men and my father for money. Well," she said with bitterness. "I learned from the best."

Tears filled Nina's eyes as she absorbed how far back Vonetta's envy of her went. It was unfathomable as she saw it unfurl like she was watching a horror movie.

"You've got a dear doting father who has never laid a hand on you. My father did more to me than beat me when he was frustrated by my trifling mother. Trust me, you don't want that part of my truth."

"Oh, Vonetta," she found herself whispering, watching her friend go from vamp to battered child to battered woman to molested child right before her eyes.

"Then you have an education, paid for by these loving people. I have to take out a lifetime of student loans just to keep up in this wicked, old bitch of a world. But I did it," Vonetta said with confidence, raising her glass in a toast to herself. "You get to pursue your dreams—art. I get to work like a yard dog in some hole-in-the-wall, dead-end insurance job—investigating the slime of the city, but through the right people, the right connections, I move up—on my back and on my feet, which are the only things I've ever been able to depend on. I know how to work a deal."

Vonetta stood and went over to the coffee table, got another cigarette, flipped the lighter, and paced back to the living room bar, trailing smoke behind her.

"Where was I?" Vonetta mumbled after exhaling. "Oh yes, I needed another drink." She poured herself another round and sat down, taking great care with how she did so. "Then comes the men. All of them wanted to marry you, but just to screw me. Funny how life works. Well, that's the end of my story."

"Vonetta," Nina began quietly and stood, "I'm sorry that all of these things happened to you. Go to the hospital. I'm going home." What else was there to say? What would screaming invectives at Vonetta, and calling this already battered soul out, do? It was pitiful. The sight of it broke her heart.

"Oh, wait. You didn't ask me what you came here for," Vonetta taunted. "Don't you wanna know if and when your husband slept with me? Isn't that what drove you across town this morning to get in my face?"

"No," Nina whispered. "I know you didn't sleep with Anthony." Nina turned and walked toward the door.

"Why? 'Cause you think he wouldn't? That I'm not good enough?" Vonetta screamed. Her body rose from the stool in a shot, and she crossed the room and stopped a few feet away from Nina. "What do you know about him anyway? You have never taken an interest in his business, or understood the kind of pressure he was under, or the types of slimy people he kept out of your purview. I did. And what's more," she railed, "you never knew when he'd had enough, could never just give him a break, until they damned near broke his back! You didn't know what you had."

"You're right," Nina murmured. "I didn't, and I do now."

Her placid but firm comment seemed to momentarily leave Vonetta at a loss for words. But the decision to remain calm bubbled up something dreadful within her insides, and Nina let the question out on a whisper. "Did you shoot Cecil?"

"No," Vonetta scoffed. "Maybe I should have, but I didn't. I don't even know where my gun is."

Nina kept her gaze on Vonetta and didn't move. "When did you lose it?"

"Last night, when I got back from being with Tony." Vonetta chuckled, obviously trying to bait her again.

"And?"

"And," Vonetta said with a shrug, "Manuel flipped. He'd been hanging in his car across the street and saw Tony walk me out and kiss me good night."

"And?" Nina said in a controlled tone, refusing to have her questions derailed by innuendo.

"He came home, used the key, and came in . . . and went into some jealous bull about who else I was seeing, and the fact that he'd followed me to Cecil's and waited all night, and now I was doing the brother too. So I told him to kiss my ass and went to bed. No man tells me what to do, especially one that I have an arrangement with."

"Which is?" Nina could feel her heart pounding hard enough to tear the soft tissue around it away from her chest cavity.

"He gets a hefty commission on the deals I throw his sorry-ass way. I take my cut on his commissions, and he gets to get something else—when, where, and how I say so. Period."

Nina shook her head. "And I suppose you got beat up when he no longer liked that arrangement?"

"I got beat up because Manuel was talking crazy 'I love you' crap, and I didn't want to hear it. OK? Then he told me not to go to the hospital, and said he didn't want the insurance policy off the club—even though I'd worked hard to get it. Stupid bastard. It was worth a mint. And when I came back, he was in an interesting frame of mind, shall we say."

"You didn't need to try to sleep with Tony to get a policy, Vonetta." Her girlfriend's twisted logic made her move toward the door for fresh air.

"First of all, the policy wasn't the reason I wanted to sleep with your husband. That I could have gotten from him through you, easy enough. Tell me what woman wouldn't want a tall, fine man who's nice, supportive, and doing well financially? What's not to like about Anthony Williams? He is good people, Nina. You just could never see it. But what makes me so curious is that, even though I slept with him, you're still qualifying the facts with phrases like *might have* and *try*. You know everything I do is absolute."

Nina turned slowly and looked at the pathetic image that she'd once held so dear, and with so much admiration. She let out her breath slowly and put her hand on the doorknob. "Vonetta," she said in a firm whisper, "everything my husband does is absolute, too. He loves absolutely. He gives absolutely. And his friendship is absolute. And I absolutely know that he wouldn't take advantage of someone as absolutely twisted in understanding these things as you." With that said, Nina moved through the door and shut it hard behind her. It was over.

Soft sobs followed Nina down the hall, and she covered her ears as she paced across the plush salmon carpet and

waited for the elevator to carry her out of Vonetta's hell-
ish gilded cage and into the bright sun.

"Bobby Lester?" DeShields said with a wide smile as
the door in the southwest Philly project opened. "Let's
go downtown so you can tell me all about your sister,
Jackie."

The muffled cries of a woman made him stop for a
moment as he adjusted the gun in his holster. Tapping
on the door twice, Collins stepped back and waited for
the knob to turn. When he knocked louder, he heard a
rustle of movement.

"Go to hell, Nina," a female voice screamed through
the wood. "Leave me alone!"

"Police, ma'am. Open up." Collins stood back and
waited as the sound of locks turning rolled a hundred
questions around in his brain. How many damned suspects were there to this thing?

"Vonetta Winston?" Collins said without formality, then
waited.

"I ain't got nothing to say about my sister!" Bobby
yelled as DeShields cuffed him and led him down the
steps.

"You need to think real hard about her whereabouts
yesterday afternoon, and be real accurate with the times,
'cause a wrong memory could land her in prison for attempted murder and arson."

Bobby Lester yanked DeShields' pace to a sudden stop.
"Ronell came over around three, and they got into a big
argument about his side hustle, which my sister never
went along with, on account of her son. Then around

quarter to four, after he left out, we took Daekwon to his karate lessons at the YMCA. I've got fifty witnesses over there to say where we was. You can't hold me, and you can't pin no bull on my sister!''

Twenty

When the door to Vonetta Winston's apartment swung open, a very angry but very beautiful woman stood before him.

"Yeah. Took you long enough," she said, acknowledging her identity by the flippant response.

Collins looked at her and drew a deep breath to steady his nerves. No matter how long he'd been on the force, he could never get used to seeing a woman's face destroyed like this. It reminded him too much of his mother's and sister's faces—the very sight which had driven him into law enforcement in the first place.

"Well," Vonetta said, filled with disgust. "Arrest me." She turned and left the door open and went to the bar and poured another drink. "I'll give you the name of my attorney, and I'll need to put on some clothes first." She turned around abruptly and stared at the tall figure in the dark suit before her. "I can put on some clothes, can't I? And I trust you don't think I'm the suicidal type who would take a leap from the twenty-fourth floor out of a bedroom window?"

Collins appraised the fragile but voluptuous curves that defined the red robe, and shook his head. Her voice had sliced through to his memory bank. He'd seen her type too many times before: beautiful, self destructive, and without any self-esteem, wearing sarcasm and cockiness as body armor.

"Something tells me that your girlfriend who just left didn't have it in her to do this to you," he stated plainly, taking a seat on the white leather sofa adjacent to the bar where his suspect stood. "A man did this. Wanna tell me which one, and when?"

"No," she retorted. "So this is your cue to say, 'Lady, you have the right to remain silent, everything you say at this point can be held against you in the court of law.' I do this for a living myself, or used to. I just don't get to read people the Miranda. Maybe I've said it wrong, but you get my point."

"Tell me this," he said in a steady voice. "Why do women protect the men who do these types of things to them? It has always been a curiosity of mine."

Vonetta looked at the expression on the man who'd spoken. He had taken off his aviator sunglasses as he'd made the comment, and now intense dark-brown eyes were boring a hole in her. His six-foot-plus athletic form sat facing her, and she stared at the way the muscle system in his arms and chest filled out his white shirt and black suit. She let her gaze rove over his expression again in an attempt to detect fraud, noting a few scars that he'd probably received from his profession on his clean-shaven, dark chocolate, ruggedly handsome face, also noting a few traces of diminishing evidence of them. Then she laughed.

Vonetta walked over to the man on her sofa and sat down beside him. "Your name?"

"Collins. Detective Collins," he said without emotion.

"Ah . . . your mother named you Detective. Has a nice ring."

This time he smiled. "We don't know each other that well yet. Try Collins for now."

"OK, Collins," Vonetta said as she took a long drag off

her cigarette. "You want to know who beat me up?" When Collins didn't move or blink, she laughed as tears blurred her eyes. "I did."

She watched him lean forward on his knees, using his forearms to support himself as he cocked his head and turned his face in her direction.

"And, why would you beat yourself up," he asked quietly, "when from the looks of things, you have everything in the world going for you?"

"Do I?" she whispered. Something pulled at the last anchor of hostility within her. Fatigue tore at her burden, unfastening it from her shoulder harness and letting the heavy chip of granite drop to the floor in front of her. Vonetta cast her gaze to the Oriental rug pattern as it turned into a blurry kaleidoscope of color. Anthony used to look at her like that when they'd talk—nonjudgmental, firm, but with understanding, not pity.

The expression on Collins' face made her feel every bruise on her body and within her soul, as though each one were just newly inflicted. She'd lost the one thing that she and Tony had been allowed to share—friendship. No one could understand that he was like her father or brother, while also being just out of reach as an admiring male and potential lover all safely wrapped up into one. He'd advised her, protected her, cared about her, and laughed with her, not at her, and he'd done all of this while never laying a hand on her. Most of all, he'd respected her, encouraged her, believed in her like no one ever had in her life. Why was that so unattainable elsewhere, when all she'd ever wanted was to be safe? Why had that been a crime?

And in trying to get more from Anthony Williams than that, she knew that now she'd also lost the one person who had been her sister, and who forgave her any outrageous thing she did: Nina. The soft mother she never had, had been Nina. She was the sister she never had, the one who thought she was trustworthy and decent and smart and good, underneath it all. She'd lost the love and admiration in Nina's eyes, which had turned hard and reflected her mother back at her just before Nina had slipped out of her life.

Oh yes, she'd definitely done this herself, and kicked her own natural ass. That's why every blow Manuel had issued had felt like a deserved purging of guilt. She'd allowed him to throw his fists at her without a struggle, and to wrap his arms around her neck, silently hoping that he'd finish the job that her father had begun. It could have been over—all the pain, all the memories, just blackness. But, like with everything, he, like her father, was so inept.

Vonetta's hands found her face, and a deep wail of pain dragged its way up from her belly, past her throat, and out into the room.

He could only stare at the woman who had only moments ago tried to come off as a street-hardened broad. Her sobs cut right through him, as he'd heard that desolate cry for help too many times from his sister—before he had to bury her.

While his professional training kept his body immobile, his mind continued to fire commands to his arm to shield the slender shoulders that shook with unrepressed sobs. "What is the name of the son of a bitch that did this to you, baby?" he found himself whispering. "I'll find him and hunt him down in the street like a dog. Trust me."

To avoid touching her, he stood. She looked up at his movement, and her face contained more than ugly bruises of abuse. It was in her eyes. They gave him a window into her years of hoping and wishing and wanting what was always out of reach, and the glistening reflection had turned into defeat.

"Why do you care?" she murmured, wiping at her tears angrily.

He watched her armor try to cover the vulnerability in her fortress, and he sat down again quickly and grabbed her hand before the drawbridge could close. "I don't know," he said in earnest. "I'm not even supposed to, but I do. I guess I'm just tired of seeing people go through this kinda mess."

She nodded and seemed to let her drawbridge stay cracked open just slightly enough for him to enter.

"You can't protect me," she whispered. "He's well-connected with all the politicians in the city. May even run for city council himself," she added. "It'll be your job on the line, so let it rest. I got my ass kicked, what else is new? Keep your job. I'll get some meds, lie low here at home, and figure out how to make a living in a day or so."

"Why don't you let me worry about me?" he murmured, still holding her hand firmly and trying to send a signal of trust. No suspect had ever cared what happened to him before. He abruptly dropped her hand. *It isn't about going there,* he warned himself. *Ever.* "What set him off?"

Vonetta Winston looked at him hard, and she smiled through her tears as she stamped out her cigarette and appraised the hand that he'd suddenly abandoned. "Almost got in too deep for a second, didn't you?"

Her question made him uncomfortable, and he stood and paced.

"It's scary, isn't it?" she whispered in a nonsarcastic tone that he hadn't expected. "To see someone in trouble, and be drawn to them when you know you shouldn't be. That's what happened to me," she said quietly. "You want a drink?"

"I'm on duty," he murmured. "But I'll take a cup of coffee, if you've got it."

She nodded, stood, and went into the kitchen, sending a signal with a glance for him to follow her. Drawn like a magnet, he did, and he watched her prepare a pot of brew while he leaned against the frame of the kitchen entrance.

"You didn't do too bad for yourself here," he noted, looking around the upscale environment.

"Insurance detective work pays good money, if you're good at what you do, which I am," she said without innuendo in her voice. "Now I'll be lucky if I can get a job scrubbing toilets. They found out I was throwing leads his way, and he was breaking off a little commission my way. Risky, but it paid well. Wasn't illegal, but the company didn't like the potential tie to the fire, and all the possible implications. Said it was a conflict of interest— you know about that. Things that aren't illegal, but aren't necessarily ethical, either."

Collins sighed. There was no judgment in it. He was just emotionally tired.

"Yeah, I know," she said without turning around, and incorrectly taking his hard exhale as a statement. "I got involved with a married man, who had a nice society wife, who will cover for his whereabouts, and a mother-in-law who'll do the same. For years, he promised he'd leave her, and one day a few nights ago, I finally woke up and smelled the coffee." She chuckled sadly, bringing a cup of dark brew to him where he stood. "What do you take in it?"

"Nothing. Black is fine," he said quietly, then took a sip from his mug.

"Straight without a chaser," she said, chuckling again. "Just the way I like it, too." She moved to a seat at her glass kitchen dinette table, and sat down.

"When did Nina Williams find out you were dealing with her husband?"

This time his suspect looked at him strangely, and she laughed out loud.

"Tony? You think I was sleeping with Tony? In my

dreams, maybe. You aren't as good a detective as I'd given you credit for."

He felt foolish for jumping to the wrong conclusion. Somehow, he'd hoped it wasn't Anthony Williams, but he didn't know why. The jigsaw puzzle of how he felt made him take a seat across from Vonetta Winston.

"Manuel Johnson, a lead agent in my firm, is as good as I could ever get," she said sadly. "He was a placebo—married—and I knew he'd never leave his wife. It all started out as an arrangement. Both of us had issues, and needed cash, and occasionally needed a tranquilizer, which a hard roll in the hay did for both of us, from time to time. But it wasn't friendship. It wasn't a future. And it wasn't what Nina and Tony had. Out of stupidity, I tried to concoct that with his brother, Cecil, once or twice, just to get close to something like that. He wasn't the real McCoy either. But you can't manufacture the kind of foundation those Williams boys had growing up. Plus, I didn't have the bricks and mortar in me, so I settled for Manuel. He knew it and I knew it, and his wife knew that I was just something to do for him. So everybody was happy."

Although he didn't say anything, he understood what she'd just said perfectly. Collins nursed his cup of coffee and watched the woman sitting across the table nurse hers.

"Mind if I have another cigarette while we talk?" she asked, which surprised him. "I know you're not supposed to smoke during a confessional, but I figure I might as well as long as I'm talking out in the open to a priest."

The comment made him chuckle as she paced away from him, although it disturbed him. She was digging down into layers of his body armor, too.

"OK," she quipped as she sat down and extended her cigarette for him to light. "Two questions."

"Shoot," he said, striking a match and touching the flame to the end of the cigarette.

He watched her pause, then offer a sad smile. "A friend of mine used to say that to me," she whispered, then took a deep drag and seemed to shake off the memory. "Question number one. How far into Philly's finest of society are you willing to go?"

"As deep as I have to," he said in an even tone without losing eye contact with her. "And what's question number two?"

"Wanna tell me why you haven't been with another woman in months, after dealing with a married woman and getting dumped?"

Twenty-one

DeShields flipped his cell phone open and took the call from the young officer trailing Nina Williams who had been backing up Collins. "What do you mean her car went into the lot, and didn't come out after she came down into the lobby?" Panic shot through DeShields as he threw the blue light onto his car dashboard. "Let Collins know. Follow anything, any car that comes out of that lot! Stop it and search it." He listened with impatience as he was told that the only car that had exited was probably a resident—in a navy-blue Mercedes, which had left and disappeared more than a half hour ago.

Nina watched from her crouched position in the front seat of the plush vehicle, hating the stench of the expensive cologne that filled her nostrils. She kept her eye on the revolver that the driver had tucked into his belt, and panic gave way to an eerie state of calm as she heard a garage door open, then watched the light close behind her.

"Sit up," Manuel commanded. "I just want to look at you."

She obeyed and stared at him.

"I wonder what old Tony would think if I had sex with his woman?"

222 *Leslie Esdaile*

"And why would you need to do that," she said with sarcasm, "when he didn't do that to you?"

Her response drove her captor's hand across the small space to snatch her by the back of the hair, and he leered into her face as he held her close to his. "All of you bitches are so stupid," he said. "Is that what he told you?"

"No," she whispered through her teeth, "he didn't have to."

Manuel dropped his hand, and gave her a look of disgust. "Get out."

"Then what?" Nina asked. "You'll kill me for being married? For trusting my man?"

"Shut up!"

She flinched and opened the car door as the back of Manuel's hand caught her cheek and she tasted blood.

"Call him," he said evenly. "This is between men."

"I can't," she murmured, wiping at her mouth. "I have his phone in my purse. He's at the hospital with his parents, and I don't even know where to tell him to come."

Manuel began pacing, then pulled out the nine millimeter in his belt and leveled it at her. "Then call somebody who can find and get to the bastard. Now."

She froze. Who in the world was she going to call? Earl Jones' name came into her mind.

"Yo, Leonard," DeShields whispered as he stood on the landing of the law office steps glancing between Anthony Williams and Earl Jones. "We got another immediate problem. Call me back in less than five. For real, for real, man."

Collins closed his cell phone, and rang the doorbell to the lush Chestnut Hill home. When the door opened, he flashed his badge and looked at the stylish elderly woman before him. "Mrs. Cooper?"

When she nodded and bade him to step in quickly, he did. He could tell that she was more concerned with what the neighbors might think, than what he might have to tell her. Then his gaze traveled to a distinguished older man who stood in the foyer. His stare brought the man forward to extend his hand.

"Paul Carpenter," the elderly gent said as he turned to Mrs. Cooper. "I told you, honey. You needed to get in touch with the police long before it came to this."

Confusion racked Collins' brain as he looked from one senior citizen to the other. Sure, Vonetta had sent him there to find Paulette Cooper-Johnson, but who the hell was this guy? He'd assumed that the gray-haired stiff was old man Cooper.

"Then it would have all come out," the distraught lady whispered. "All of it! And it would ruin our reputations, my daughter's . . . and her husband's potential political career, all on speculation." Her face crumbled and she turned away from both men.

"Can we start at the beginning, folks?" Collins asked, rubbing his jaw.

"The beginning goes back more than twenty, maybe thirty years," Mr. Carpenter said. "How long have you got?"

Collins shook his head. "Not long, sir. Can we go back over the last forty-eight hours within the next five minutes?"

"I don't care where your partner is," Anthony yelled. "Where's my wife? I thought you guys had a tail on her!"

"Easy, man," Earl suggested.

"The message she left on my voice mail didn't give a location, and—"

"And hell! Can't you guys put a trace on the call?" Anthony hollered again, walking in a circle. "That Manuel motherfu—"

"Look," DeShields snapped, "you go running around the streets, and you'll get yourself shot, and maybe your wife hurt. He doesn't want her; he wants you. *Comprende?* As long as he thinks you haven't gotten the message yet, we have time to find him, and she stays unharmed."

"Do a star-six-nine on the freakin' phone, then," Anthony exploded.

"Can't," DeShields said with a sigh. "Too many calls came in after that, and Caller ID simply shows that she telephoned Jones' office from your cellular."

Anthony walked around in a circle for a moment. "Didn't Collins say Manuel was Vonetta's man?"

"Yeah," DeShields muttered.

"Then, if the SOB was married, and on the rise for a bid at city council—like scuttlebutt has it—then he might have had an apartment, or another house somewhere that he took Vonnie when he wasn't at her place. The hotels would be too out in the open for a man tryin' to be discreet."

DeShields rubbed his chin and flipped open his cell phone. Earl and Anthony stared at each other while the call went through.

"Vonetta Winston," DeShields said as the call connected. "Wanna ask you one more question."

"So let me get this straight," Collins said in a low tone. "Your daughter's husband was having an affair with a woman named Vonetta Winston, correct?"

He waited a moment while the elderly couple nodded their heads. His stomach churned, and he took out a

Rolaids from his jacket pocket and popped it into his mouth as he watched them. He hated this job.

"Paulette loved him so . . ." Mrs. Cooper trailed off. "I told her it would pass," she added quietly, casting her gaze in Mr. Carpenter's direction. "It always does."

"No sense in ruining that girl's life and her husband's career due to some temporary troubles that they were going through in their marriage," Mr. Carpenter said between his teeth, looking at Mrs. Cooper. "Was there?"

Collins stared at both of them, and a sudden increase in his nausea bubbled within him as he rubbed his chin again. "Wanna tell me how you two know each other?" he asked without blinking, and riding a gut hunch.

"Like Adam knew Eve," Mrs. Cooper said, folding her arms over her stylish suit front and walking away from them.

Collins tried not to allow his facial expression to change, and he drew a breath instead. "Mr. Carpenter, are you by any chance related to Nina Williams?" he asked, looking hard at the facial features of the distinguished gentleman before him.

"That's my daughter. Anthony Williams is my son-in-law."

"Call him again," Manuel hissed, flattening his body against Nina's as he pressed her against the wall. "I want him to *watch* when I do you. It was bad enough that he did Vonetta, but he crossed the line when he did my wife. So now I want him to cry, and beg me not to screw his wife, and to watch me do it to you, then cry like a baby when I put this in your mouth and pull the trigger, before I do him. I didn't get to have that same pleasure when I offed his brother."

Numbness filled her as she attempted to call Earl Jones'

number again. Tears brimmed in her eyes as the voice mail message came on. Where were they?

"Well, what was I supposed to do, other than tell you!" Mrs. Cooper shrieked, pacing toward Paul Carpenter. "Tell my ex-husband that in my care, his daughter had turned to drugs? Oh!" she scoffed as she spun and walked across the room. "That's all Wendell would need to rub in my face. Never! That, plus all the years Rose has had you at her beck and call for every silly, little imaginable thing. I don't care if you had to leave her at that luncheon! I needed you!"

"Janette," Paul Carpenter said firmly, "we've been over this a hundred times, if not once! My wife's name is Rose Carpenter, not Janette Cooper. Your daughter, Paulette, is not my Nina—even though you named her after me to drive my wife insane, and to make her never forget what I did! And even though what we had was over years ago, I still came when you called, and left Rose at that event, but you didn't call the police like I'd tried to convince you to. You have never listened when it came to the important things! Me, Rose, nor Wendell, for that matter, deserved the name you selected, Paulette!"

"When your daughter came here, Mrs. Cooper," Collins said very carefully to derail the argument between the two aged combatants, "what was her state of mind?" He held his breath for a moment and stared at the elderly woman, letting the air out of his lungs with paced control.

"She was understandably upset," Mrs. Cooper whispered. "She flew out of here around three o'clock in the afternoon, after she and Manuel had had another fight. When she didn't pick up her cell phone, I knew she was headed to harm herself."

"Harm herself?" Collins whispered, already knowing what Mrs. Cooper meant.

"Drugs," the elderly woman said quietly as she sat down on the sofa, all of the sudden looking very, very old. "I figured it out long ago that whenever she was upset, she'd run over to that guy Ronell's house, but for a while that had stopped. His girlfriend, Jackie, even called here once, yelling at me, and telling me to stop my daughter from interfering in their lives. I thought things would smooth out since Ron had a new girlfriend and a baby on the way, surely Paulette would stop seeing him then. But she temporarily took up with another fellow, a tall man was all I ever got from her, but that petered out soon, too, and she was back to calling Ronell."

"You're not implying that it was my son-in-law, or his brother, are you?" Mr. Carpenter asked quickly, reading something within Collins' expression that the detective hadn't meant to reveal. The older man stood now and walked over to a nearby chair and held on to the back of it.

"No. She wasn't dealing with either of the Williams brothers for the last few months. That I can assure you."

"How do you know?" Mrs. Cooper whispered. "Have you been following her that long? Will she go to jail for using drugs? Is that what this is all about? You don't think she shot a man for them, do you?"

He noted that Mr. Carpenter had become quiet and observant.

"No," he reassured her. "It's my job to know these things," Collins stated flatly. "If all she did was use, we can get her into a treatment program, but we'll need to find her first." That was all he was willing to say, and needed to say, and he watched the elderly couple relax as he shook his head and stood to begin pacing again as he spoke, his ears ringing from accelerated blood pressure. Guilt pulled at his insides. "Did she go to Ronell's?"

"I'm not sure," Mrs. Cooper whispered. "But, strangely, she came back here hysterical, saying something about

Ron not having her package, and he needed to go get it. That's all I got from her on the phone. Then she barged in here asking me for money, which, of course, I refused to give her. She kept lying and saying she owed it to Ron. It was a business deal she had, but you know the signs," she whispered. "Glassy-eyed, crazy-sounding . . . what other business would my daughter have with the likes of a man like that? It's all my fault."

"Where was your wife at the time?" Collins whispered, finding a chair to sit down in. Suddenly, he felt weak in the knees.

"She was at the event," the older man said, taking a seat in a chair across from Collins and looking at Janette Cooper as he spoke. "I left my wife around four, came here, and found Janette in hysterics. I stayed an hour to try to calm her down, then went back to the function, where I played the good husband at my wife's side at her event for another hour. Then I went home to argue with Rose for another three, before I finally checked our answering machine, when I got my daughter's message to come to the hospital." Mr. Carpenter hung his head and ran his fingers through his silver hair.

As Len Collins looked at the dejected expressions on the two older people's faces, he knew too well how they felt. "When did you see your daughter again, Mrs. Cooper?"

"Around five-thirty. Why?"

Paulette pulled up to the house on Greene Street and stared at it, turning off the ignition as she appraised the place she'd waited outside of for so many nights, knowing. Her hand went to her purse, and she pulled out her cell phone.

"Daddy," she whispered. "I'm going in there this time."

"Suga-lump, please don't," the old man on the other end of the line whispered. "Let Daddy do it."

"I can't," Paulette murmured. Then she hung up.

Wendell Cooper stood slowly. His brain pulled at a thousand memories as he walked over to his desk and opened it. He looked around his small apartment one last time, and closed his eyes as he reached in and felt the icy steel. He'd followed his daughter to where they fed her drugs through a bartender, The Jazz Note, and he'd done the only honorable thing a father could do—burned the damnable place of ill repute to the ground.

What did he have to lose, really, by this one last act? He'd already lived through a World War, had been decorated for valor in battle, and this was indeed war. No one had given him a medal for being able to withstand the disrespect of his wife's flings. For that, he deserved the Purple Heart—one that bled real blood. Nor had anyone acknowledged that he'd unfairly paid through the nose for years of alimony because he left, and he couldn't prove what everyone in the city knew. There was no medal for enduring that POW status.

He had already accepted living with the humiliation of having his most precious possession named after the man who had breached his household. And he'd tried to make a man out of the worthless, spoiled piece of crap that God had given him as a son-in-law. Where was the reward for pulling in every connection he had at his disposal to offer a career to Manuel Johnson on a silver platter, with one caveat? Only one: that he would care for his daughter, like he hadn't been allowed to, and he'd look after her once he was gone. That was their deal. They'd struck the agreement over a drink and a handshake—with the orders for Manuel to be discreet, if he had to wander, and never hurt his baby.

That arrangement had been breached. So now it was a matter of honor—his, and his daughter Paulette's. What did this old soldier have to lose? Wendell Cooper wondered as he found his coat and closed the door quietly behind him.

Twenty-two

Collins flipped open his phone and listened carefully as he glanced at the elderly couple before him, standing quickly as DeShields' voice poured into his ears. "On my way," he said fast as he stood. He thrust his hand in his pocket, and turned the garage door opener over and over in his hand as he spoke. "Send backup to the address."

She tiptoed quietly up the front steps, put the key in the door, and walked in. She moved toward the living room, then stopped as she heard her husband's voice coming from the basement, and a woman's voice cry out following what sounded like a slap.

They hadn't even come into the house all the way, and were probably screwing in the garage! Paulette opened her purse and pulled out a small plastic bag filled with white powder, scooped a bit in her pinky fingernail, lowered her face to her hand and took a deep sniff.

She smiled as a new wave of confidence filled her body when she swallowed. She'd kill them both, she chuckled to herself, and she pulled out the petite gun Leonard had once shown her how to use.

* * *

"If he wants me as bait," Anthony argued, "then I'm going in."

Before DeShields or Earl could stop him, he exited the unmarked sedan and bounded up the front steps. When he turned the knob, the door eerily creaked open, and he flipped an inside lock behind him to keep Earl and DeShields on the other side of it, then he followed the sound of the voices beneath him and began running when he heard the first gunshot, followed by another.

Both Earl and DeShields looked at each other, then stood back as DeShields kicked in the front door.

"Crazy bitch," Manuel yelled, inspecting his arm and walking back and forth like a trapped animal. "What was I supposed to do."

Nina's eyes were riveted to the woman heaped on the floor, and her insides screamed for air that her lungs could not take in. "You killed her . . ." she whispered. "Call an ambulance, man! What if she's alive?"

"Shut up!" Manuel screamed, all of a sudden looking up to the ceiling. "Somebody else is in here," he murmured, and he grabbed Nina, forcing a gun to her cheek. "Call him."

She shut her eyes tight and called out. "He's got a gun, let him go."

Anthony stood very still and watched DeShields and Earl from the corner of his eye from the kitchen entrance to the basement. He could see that they were advancing slowly, and he motioned with his hand for them to stop and to take cover on either side of the wall. "Manuel," he hollered down the steps. "You want me, man, not my wife. Let's do this thing man to man. Let her go."

"Screw you!" Manuel hollered back. "Come down here, you faggot, and face me like you couldn't before. I want to show you what it feels like to have somebody violate what's yours."

"I didn't take anything of yours, man," Anthony yelled back. "Let Nina go and tell me what the hell is going on."

"Bull, Williams! First your brother does Vonetta, then you do her, and, in between, you're plugging my wife, and you expect us to have a civil conversation? Are you crazy? Nobody does that foul crap to Manuel Johnson and gets away with it. Nobody!"

"You got the wrong man, brother," Anthony yelled again, feeling the blood pulse in his veins as he thought of what this deranged madman might have already done to Nina. "You got the script flipped."

"Yeah, yeah, yeah, punk. C'mon down and let's talk about it nice and slow."

Ignoring the worried glances and the fervent hand signals that Earl and DeShields were giving him, Anthony stepped onto the basement landing and began the slow descent.

He took his time, making sure that the thicket of brushes and small twigs beneath his feet didn't make a sound as he crept toward the basement window of the house. It was just like it had been when he was in the service, so many years ago. Then, Wendell Cooper waited to get a clear shot.

"You want me, dude?" Anthony taunted as he climbed down the steep staircase, slapping his chest and opening his arms wide. "Take me, but not like no punk with a gun," he said, looking at his wife's reddened, tear-streaked cheeks for a moment, then staring at the man holding the gun in his direction. "If you've hit her, I'll kill you with my bare hands," he warned.

"Brave talk from a man who's unarmed," Manuel said, shoving Nina to the side and walking toward the staircase. "But it won't be that easy," he seethed in a whisper. "I'm going to shoot out your knees, and make you watch me while I work on her . . . all afternoon."

Something fragile within Anthony snapped as his gaze went to the woman's body on the floor, then his wife's face, which fused with the mental picture of his brother's broken body in the hospital, which became his parents' faces, and Vonetta's whisper, and the burned-out shell of his club, and he felt himself leave the wooden steps as a sound of a motor entered his skull, and a gun fired, causing glass to shatter, and another shot rang out, and he came down on Manuel Johnson.

He was still yelling and punching the lifeless body that he straddled as his wife pulled at his shoulders, and Earl and DeShields bolted down the stairs, and Collins shook him and slapped him, and everybody called his name.

Then everything went silent as a labored gait was heard on the steps. The chaotic gathering stopped as they watched an elderly man slowly descend into the basement, his gaze fixed upon the woman's body on the floor, and a revolver dangling from his hands.

"He killed my baby," the old man whispered. "He'd promised me. We'd had a deal."

She held her husband around his waist as police cars and television cameras swarmed Greene Street and the ambulances carted the human carnage away from the house. Anthony's hands stroked her hair, and hers found his back. She would not let go of him as Earl Jones and Detectives DeShields and Collins approached, holding back eager reporters.

"He didn't do it." Nina wept against Anthony's chest. "None of it!"

"We know," Collins said in a solemn voice. "We got our shooter in a body bag—Manuel Johnson. We got our arsonist, Paulette Cooper-Johnson's father, Wendell Cooper. We got our safe thief, Maxine's brother Darrell—who discovered Cecil Williams lying on the floor after Manuel shot him. The safe was open because Cecil was probably going into it to replace the money he'd taken from Anthony—according to Maxine's account—and her brother Darrell called in the 911 that actually saved Cecil Williams' life. Ironic, ain't it? Your brother's woman's brother goes there to kick your brother's ass, and winds up saving the man's life. I gotta get out of police work." Collins popped another Rolaids into his mouth and let out his breath.

DeShields nodded in agreement with his partner. "The old man's gonna walk on shooting his son-in-law, but he's gonna need a good attorney to get him out of the arson charges, which ain't likely—even if Johnny Cochran represents him. He confessed in the squad car."

"He had reason enough to do what he did," Anthony said, his voice low with quiet emotion as he held Nina tighter. "I might have done the same, too, if I thought my baby girl was going to a place that was killing her."

Earl put his hand on Anthony's shoulder. "He might get a reduced sentence if someone can show that the elderly veteran was justifiably distraught when he followed his daughter to the club, after giving her money as bait to lead him to Ronell."

"Make it happen," Anthony whispered, accepting Earl's nod as a promise.

"Guess your boys weren't lying," DeShields said.

"Looks like all they did was rob you blind and run an illegal club that Johnson had his money tied to . . . not all of them will go down for drugs. Only one of 'em had a side hustle, and they didn't shoot your brother or torch the place. But they are going down," he added. "Looks like Bobby Lester, the one they call Boo, is cleared, too, along with his sister, Jackie Lester. All she did was delay Ronell getting to the club to pick up his package for Paulette—because Paulette had been desperate enough to call their place looking for Ronell. Jackie and Ron argued, like Bobby said, then split, and by the time he got to the club, it was already torched—like Lester told us."

"That means my client is cleared of all aspects of this," Earl noted. "Just make sure you guys show him and his brother as the victims when you do the press conference. I want his name totally cleared, and his insurance policy paid, without any delay."

Both detectives nodded, and Earl's body seemed to relax.

"We got a full statement. Paulette's father had seen her go to The Jazz Note, then drive away when Ronell didn't come. The old man took the opportunity to go in the already opened back door to burn down the establishment in the short time our squad cars had pulled back after the shooting. The timing on this mess was unreal," DeShields said with a heavy sigh.

"What about finding Vonetta's gun?" Anthony whispered.

"Manuel went over there the night before, took it from her purse unbeknownst to her, and that's what showed up and matched ballistics. It wasn't Paulette's gun. Then the asshole dropped it in a Dumpster, hoping we'd find it and pin the whole thing on Vonetta. It wasn't about insurance, it was about a love triangle. Manuel, his wife, and one Vonetta Winston."

"He beat her up," Nina whispered. "You should have seen her face."

"I did," Collins said quietly. "He got to her this morning, and he flipped out because she'd gone to the hospital yesterday to visit Cecil and the Williams family. He'd seen your husband talk to her last night, and put her in her car, and made an incorrect assumption about the relationship."

The men standing around one another glanced at Nina, then away. She understood. It was a code of honor among them, an odd bond of sorts that had been created by near-death they'd faced together. She watched them as they searched for the words to try to clear all of the suspicions around her husband's name, especially hers.

"I know," Nina whispered, "that he just talked to my friend and was trying to find out who was stealing from the club. She is a good investigator. It makes sense, at that hour, that he had to close up, clean up, count the registers, and he would have been gentleman enough to walk a lady to her car. Manuel was a lunatic."

She could feel Anthony's body relax in her arms, and the shoulders of the men around her seemed to drop about an inch from relief.

"Now it's just a matter of paperwork," DeShields quipped, slapping Anthony squarely on the back and shaking Earl Jones' hand. "No harm, no foul. We were just doing our job."

"And," Detective Collins murmured, looking off in the distance, "three women's lives ruined: Vonetta, beaten and out of her job, Paulette dead, and old lady Cooper left with a broken heart that will never heal."

The small group stood together quietly, absorbing what Collins had just said. Nina found words coming to her cracked lips, and she spoke to the gathering of men from a very far-off place in her mind.

"Three, six, nine," she whispered.

They stared at her.

"Three women: me, Vonetta, and Maxine. Six women: Paulette, Jackie, and Mrs. Cooper. Nine: my mother, Anthony's mother, and Vicki—all pulled into this, all swept into this nightmare by another three, six, nine . . ."

She looked at the men's faces around her. "Cecil is the monkey. Anthony is the streetcar line, and I was the goose that drank wine. Cecil pulled the back off the street-car line, and the line broke, and the monkey got choked."

"Nina," Earl Jones said in a very quiet voice. "I'm going to give you the name of a very good friend of mine. He'll write a prescription for you tonight. You've been through a lot." His gaze searched Anthony's as he dug into his pocket for a card and pen.

"Take her home, man," DeShields said with a worried look on his face. "We can get a statement tomorrow, or whatever. We know what happened."

"Yeah," Collins added. "She's been through a lot.

Nina felt a chuckle working its way from her insides, and her husband's body began to quake, which stilled her, until she heard him laugh—belly-laugh from way down in his soul.

"She ain't crazy!" Anthony said, kissing her and holding her back. "Three gave you six perps."

Both she and Anthony laughed as the small group stared at them.

"Dig it," her husband said, chuckling. "Three innocent people—my wife, my brother, and me—a goose, a monkey, and a streetcar led to three women—Maxine, Jackie, and Vonetta—which led to three more—two cooks and a bartender, who stole from the club, and almost implicated us in drug trafficking, which is six."

Earl nodded and stared at him, while DeShields and Collins remained stoic but rubbed their chins.

"Then," Anthony went on, "those three led to a shooter, a torch, and a safe job. Nine, from the six, and the three." Anthony walked around in a circle, then snapped his fingers. "I've finally figured it out," he exclaimed. "What that homeless guy meant. I couldn't have without Nina's help!"

When they all just stared at him, Anthony said the rhyme in full. "Step on a crack, and you break your mother's back, but all in time, the goose drank wine, and the monkey pulled the back off the streetcar line, but the line broke, and the monkey got choked, but they all went to heaven in a little row boat."

As Earl Jones came near him, Anthony held up his hand. "Lies to Mom nearly broke her back. All in time, this stuff stressed my poor wife so bad until she drank wine like a goose. My line snapped—the club went down when Cecil ran dumb crap through the back door of it with his women troubles. Cecil got shot, choked, but they all, the three people who were really innocent, went to heaven in a little row boat. Don't you see, a new form of transportation . . . a boat, not a streetcar, a boat, to carry the family over troubled waters? Can't you see it? I gotta do this new venture, but with a small, original crew."

"I think you both need to call my friend and set up an appointment, but let him write you a prescription for the night," Earl said in a whisper as he walked away.

"Yeah, dude. Get some rest. Take your wife home," DeShields said quietly as Nina and Anthony hugged each other and laughed.

"One of our squad cars will take you," Collins said with concern lacing every word. "The key is to let it go for the night."

As Anthony and Nina climbed into the vehicle Collins pointed out, DeShields walked up to him, the two men standing side by side.

"You all right, man?" DeShields whispered.

"Yeah," Collins murmured back. "Paulette shouldn't have gone out like that."

"I know, man. How about me and you going for a beer after we do the media thing, and get that paperwork done?"

"I'll meet you at the station," Collins said in a low tone, walking away from his partner.

"Where you goin'?" DeShields hollered as Collins crossed the yellow tape.

"Gotta go check on another victim," he yelled over his shoulder. "Make sure she's OK."

Twenty-three

He stood on the front steps of the home that he'd left not more than a couple of hours ago and rang the bell. Leonard Collins searched for the right words, but none entered his head as the small, elderly woman he might have one day known as Mom opened the door, her eyes filled with questions that he hated to have to answer.

This time, she didn't rush him in, but allowed him to follow her at the slow pace she'd assumed. He knew and understood that she walked the walk of the dying. The end was in sight, therefore why rush, her gait implied.

"Mrs. Cooper," he murmured, "have you been watching the news?"

"I don't watch television," she said quietly, then sat down. "I don't have to in order to know what I feel. Did you find my Paulette?"

Her gaze bore into him, not with contempt, but as a mother seeking the truth about her child. He'd made enough of these visits to clearly see what she really was asking. Collins glanced around the room, then allowed his gaze to meet up with Mrs. Cooper's.

"He left," she said in a quiet voice. "It's just you and me here now."

Collins' line of vision focused on the nap in the deep-pile carpet, and he began counting each strand of thread as he spoke. "Your daughter Paulette was with me for a few months. It wasn't one of the Williams boys, no matter what she may have told Manuel to get back at him. I was the one who'd tried to get her off drugs."

The elderly woman before him didn't move, nor did she blink, and she seemed to be holding her breath.

"I wanted to marry her," he admitted just above a whisper. "But she liked the lifestyle that Manuel Johnson provided, and the fact that he, at first, brought her drugs."

Mrs. Cooper's bottom lip trembled and she nodded her head, then drew a long, steadying breath. "I know what Manuel did to her," she whispered. "I know. God bless you for trying to get her away from him."

"My salary on the force couldn't compete with the revenues from the new club he'd opened underground. Nor could it compete with his sales commissions."

Again the older woman looked at him steadily while nodding, with tears filling her eyes.

"I'm so sorry," Collins whispered, "that I couldn't save her . . ."

"She's going to jail, isn't she?" The elderly lady had asked the question through a muffled sob. "You're a policeman, you can fix this, can't you?"

He stared at the eyes that held him transfixed. Within them he could see all the women like her he'd seen before, especially Paulette. And how did a man sit across from such a woman and tell her the bitter truth?

Collins drew a breath, and again let his gaze escape Mrs. Cooper's. "Ma'am, Manuel shot her this afternoon."

His ears rang with her deep wail, which began with a series of soft recants on the phrase "no," and rose and rose until her hands covered her ears and he went to her side as she rocked and screamed and screamed and rocked, and he could only pull her against him.

"Tell me," she cried, convulsing with the building tide of a new wave of tears. "What hospital? I have to call Wendell!"

"Wendell is with us," he said, holding her away from him and speaking slowly. "Wendell shot Manuel through the window, Mrs. Cooper, and identified your daughter's body. Is there anyone I can call for you?"

Paul Carpenter replaced the telephone on its base very carefully, and sat down at the kitchen table across from his wife.

"It was her, wasn't it?" his wife whispered. This time her voice was soft and had lost its familiar stridence.

"It was Detective Collins," Paul Carpenter said quietly. "He's there now and is going to call Janette's sister."

"You aren't going?" his wife asked with surprise as she stood to make herself another cup of tea.

"No," he whispered. "It's over. Sit down. I want to tell you about a long-overdue conversation I had with Nina."

"Yo, man, you sure that's a wise move?" DeShields asked as he shuffled the stack of reports on his desk and adjusted the telephone that was cocked between his shoulder and ear. "No, no . . . I don't have a problem getting the preliminary paperwork done. Call me later when you're ready for that beer. Just be careful, amigo, you sound real open right now."

Somehow his car had driven itself to the luxury apartment that overlooked the skyline. He wanted to go to the twenty-fourth floor and look out over the lights below. He needed to rise above it all—all the filth, and dirt, and mire of city life. Thankfully, the doorman recognized him and didn't require the basic visitor's drill as he flashed his badge, which allowed him not to have to pause, or think, or change his mind.

His arm reached out and knocked on the door that it had earlier in the day, and a form allowed him entry . . . now wearing a white cotton shirt. And that same female form smiled, then looked at his face, and guided him by the arm to her in-home bar.

Without words, she poured dark liquor into a short glass, and handed it to him and waited and watched, then poured another.

"You make a good bartender," he murmured halfway through the second tumbler of Scotch.

"I watch the news, and I read body language well," she said quietly. "Have you eaten at all today?"

"Don't think I have a stomach right through here."

"You wanna talk?"

"Not particularly."

"You want to sit on the sofa and just listen to some music to get your head right?"

"That's better than a conversation," he said in a low tone, downing his drink.

Without being asked, she fixed him another and brought it to the coffee table. He stood and crossed the room to join her as she turned on the stereo mercifully low. When smooth jazz filled his ears, his shoulders relaxed and he leaned his head back and closed his eyes.

"Take off your jacket," she whispered, "and turn around."

He complied, and released the strap of his shoulder holster, allowing her to guide the leather and weapon off his body to place it beside his drink on the table. Her fingers found his neck, and she worked the piano wire in it, causing his arms to hurt and his shoulder blades to burn as she pulled while he kept his eyes closed.

"Let me take off your shoes," she murmured.

He didn't respond or move, just allowed her to undo the laces and slip his wingtips off without protest. Then she returned to her knees behind him and began working the sinews of his back until his head could roll from side to side without pain. Then she left, floating away quietly as his body soaked into the white, soft leather and the music washed over him like a warm summer rain.

The smell of meat and onions brought saliva to his mouth, and it rolled over the acid base of tension in his gullet. He wasn't sure if he'd dozed off or not, but the smell of something good was now closer.

Collins sat forward and yawned as he opened his eyes. He looked down at the heaping plate of steak and mashed potatoes, then up at his benefactor.

"Thank you, baby," he whispered. "Thank you so much." Appreciation snagged the rest of what he'd wanted to say in his throat, and she seemed to understand that as she slid next to him, sipped on her drink and closed her eyes. It was her way of saying, "Take, eat, I won't bother you while you do. This is a moment of peace given to you."

"A beer goes with steak better than Scotch," she said with a soft smile after he'd taken several mouthfuls of food.

"If you bring me one, then I'll know I got shot this afternoon and have already died and gone to heaven."

She laughed. It was not the shrill laugh he'd heard before. This was tender and earthy, coming from a bruised angel from the other side of paradise.

He watched her stand up and that movement alone created a Pavlovian reaction within him, as his mouth tasted the beer before she brought it. With a nod, he accepted yet another gift of her hospitality, and he swallowed the amber liquid with the flawlessly seasoned beef she'd provided. Then he looked at her.

Vonetta Winston, who are you? He pondered the question as she sat across from him, looking into the large brown eyes and the battered face that still had the glint of a survivor's determination within it. His gaze traveled to the delicate shoulders that had been equally bruised, and his fingers almost reached out to touch the dark rings around her neck where a man's hands had encircled it in anger.

"I should have done this for you," he whispered as a pang of guilt besieged him. "Did you go to the doctor?"

She smiled and tucked one leg under her, and let her dress fall over the other one, which was slightly injured. "I went to see a private doctor. I couldn't deal with the hospital scene. They ask too many questions."

He nodded and understood. "Can I take you to dinner, I mean to buy the next round, the next time we do this?"

She shook her head no. "Let me ask you something," she said in a soft voice. "When you're hurting, do you feel like getting dressed up to go out?"

Her question made him feel worse, but he smiled, accepting her honest brand of truth.

"No," he replied with a sigh. "This is what I wanted. Sanctuary."

"Right," she murmured. "Isn't there a time in a person's life when that's all they want and need? A safe place?"

"Yeah, too many times."

"What made you come to this sanctuary, Detective Collins?"

"Leonard," he said. "Len."

"Leonard . . . Len," she repeated. "It has a nice ring to it."

He laughed with her. "Guess I kinda came off as a hard ass when we did this introduction the first time around."

"Guess I kinda came off as a hard ass when we did this get-to-know-you thing, too," she mimicked, making him chuckle harder.

"But you still didn't answer my question," she teased, picking up his empty plate and floating out of the room.

"Let me ask you this," he said with a smile as she came back and sat across from him again. "You knew I was coming back, didn't you?"

Vonetta cocked her head to the side and put her finger to her bottom lip as her gaze went toward the ceiling. "Hmmm . . . I played a hunch, detective."

Her statement made him grow serious because it told him that for the first time in too many years, someone had actually seen him as a person, had pierced his armor, and understood that he bled red blood. "What do you see when you look at me?" His question had come through that armor, leaving a gaping hole of vulnerability as his only meager gift to offer in return for her hospitality.

He watched the playfulness go out of her expression, replaced by an intense examination of him, which also held empathy.

"I see a fellow prisoner of war," she whispered. "I see a man who people don't see. I see a father inside of a man who has yet to be that, and has only been the perpetual Uncle Len. I see a person whose eyes have seen so much ugliness, but who can change lenses when he looks at the people he loves, to see only beauty. I see a man who is tired of his job, and wants to do something else, but doesn't know how. And I see a man who just lost someone he cared for but couldn't save . . . and has been a monk because of that, and because he's scared."

"What is he scared of?" he whispered, while acknowledging within himself that she was frightening him now with her undressing of his soul.

"He's afraid to try that high-wire act with no net again, having just fallen, only to crash and burn. Yet he also knows that he will never have the things he really wants unless he gets back up there again, and tries to balance over the cliffs. Ask me how I know about high wires."

Leonard Collins sat back and appraised the woman in

front of him whose beauty radiated from the inside out. Maybe he'd been wrong. If he were Anthony Williams there would have been no way he could have resisted this side of Vonetta Winston.

"Well," she said with a wide smile. "Was I right?"

"On all counts," he murmured, picking up his beer. He allowed the cool liquid to clear his throat and to buy him time.

"Manuel is still on your mind, isn't he?"

Her abrupt question startled him, even though he'd expected it sooner or later. "The bastard is going to fry where he's going," he said evenly. "I just came back from Paulette's mother's house. Her ex-husband, who she's still attached to, and her child all gone in one fell swoop. I have to believe in a higher system of justice than what we do on the streets, or what's the point?"

Vonetta shook her head. "It never was supposed to go this way . . ." Her voice trailed off and her gaze became distant. "Do you blame me?"

"No," he said immediately. "Look at what he did to you, too. This guy was off the hinge. Besides, if I blame you, I'd have to blame me. I can't even go there right now."

"You blame me for what happened between Tony and Nina temporarily?"

While he was thankful that her gaze had returned to him, he wasn't prepared for the question. "No," he said in earnest after thinking about it for a moment. "No . . . not really."

Her focus on him remained steady, and he accepted the nonverbal question for clarity. "Listen," he began again slowly. "Like you said, who doesn't hope for sanctuary? I've been there myself a time or two," he admitted. "Like you also said, we're both POWs."

His comment made her smile, but he understood that it was his acceptance of who she was, and who she'd been, that made her do so. But what she didn't realize was the effect that she had on him. Staring at Vonetta Winston was like taking truth serum.

"What do you see when you look at me?" she asked quietly. "Tell me for real, for real."

He leaned closer and looked at the woman now wearing white, who earlier wore flaming red, and smiled. "I see vast complexities and contradictions," he admitted. "I see a strong warrior queen who will slay a man, and I see an angel who will nurse him back to health after she's done so. I see an independent, feisty broad, and I see June Cleaver. I see a streetwise vamp, and a soft waif who needs protection. I see so many things that brought me back here, just to see if I was seeing right," he said.

"Look closer," she whispered, and leaned forward till she was only inches from his face. "Tell me who you saw this morning when you couldn't look at me, and you asked me why women allow this kind of treatment."

As he stared at her, his vision blurred, and he couldn't look at her any longer, so he allowed his gaze to slip away. "I see a seventeen-year-old boy who is pumping iron and trying to bench press more than two hundred to be able to one day beat his old man," he said on a hoarse whisper.

"Why?" she murmured, covering his folded hands with one of her own as she leaned closer.

"Because his dad, who's in the Marines, always hits his mom and makes her look like you did this morning, which in turn makes her drink . . . and one day, before he's old enough to be able to best him, his father has a heart attack, and the same woman his father beat for years cries herself sick at his funeral. And that boy wants to know why. And his sister, who is beautiful enough to have any man she wants, finds a man who does the same thing that their father used to do—with fists and words that cut deeper than the blows—and that now twenty-

year-old man runs to her rescue time and time again, and
begs her to never go back, but she always does. Until the
last time," he murmured, swallowing a lump in his throat,
"when he goes to find them both lying on the floor, his
sister shot and that SOB who got away by killing himself,
all before that man-child could keep it from happening."

He sat back and downed his beer, and looked toward
the door feeling too out in the open, as DeShields had
warned.

"It happened again, didn't it, with Paulette?"

"Yup," he muttered, still looking away. "I met her on
a 911 follow-up. Neighbors had called, and she'd refused
to turn him in or go to the hospital. Her mother had
pulled some strings and tried to get us to investigate. So
I saw her, and something in me flashed back. I'm a vet,"
he said, laughing self-consciously. "I can still hear certain
screams in my head at night."

"If it makes you feel any better," she said with a
chuckle, "I still have flashbacks, too."

He considered her face, this time touching the bruises
with the tips of his fingers, tracing the lines of abuse. "I
knew it was him before you told me," he whispered. "It's
like a fingerprint. Each batterer has a style, a certain way
they leave their marks, because they swing with the same
force, and land the blows in the same places every single
time."

"And here I thought that I was special," she joked self-
consciously, "and that Manuel only gave that to me."

Len shook his head. "No, baby. That's the tragedy of
it all. Two gorgeous works of human art vandalized by
someone who was too screwed up and immature to know
the priceless value. Like going into the Vatican with a can
of spray paint. I can't do this kind of work anymore."

Her hand covered his and he brought it to her cheek.
She kissed the inside of his palm. "If you could change
jobs, what would you do?"

He allowed the warmth of her breath to supplant the trepidation her question caused. "Here's a laugh for you," he said with caution. "I'd work with kids, young guys, doing some recreational sports, teaching them how to be men, trying to get them off the corners . . . I don't know. But social services doesn't pay, and I don't have a degree in teaching anything to anybody."

"Do you need that much money to live?"

The question startled him, especially coming from this unlikely source.

"I never really thought about it," he said honestly. "Guess I was trying—"

"To keep up with another man, maybe . . . like Manuel, who didn't earn an honest dollar in his life? You gotta compare apples to apples, not apples to oranges," she challenged.

His gaze swept the room, and he chuckled. "Inside a month, you'd be done with a poor camp counselor. Admit it, girl."

"At one point, you might have been right," she said, having to accept that naked truth from him. "But, ya know, Len, things have a way of happening that make you shift your perspective."

He nodded with her in agreement. "I hear you."

"When I saw them bring out my nemesis in a body bag, instead of feeling good, I thought about that poor girl's mother, and I thought about her father, and I thought about how close I came to where she is now. Then I thought about the other people who came so close to having their lives irrevocably altered. And I thought about all of the things I'd taken for granted, like good friends, and I walked around this apartment thinking about what, of any, of this can bring me joy and laughter and fulfillment—just by sitting here, being here, and sharing my space? I didn't like the answer. And I knew I'd have to call Nina one day, and look Tony in the face and apologize to atone for whatever harm I'd brought their way . . . and to give Maxine the respect she deserved. Oh, there's so much mess I have to clean up to start over on the right foot. But I'm willing to try because things can be replaced, Len. People can't."

Her quiet acceptance drew him to her, and his eyes searched her face as his lips gently brushed hers, mindful of their rips and tears. Then they found the tip of her nose, and her forehead, and the backs of her hands, and the very edge of her shoulders, and he sat back and let her lean on him the way he needed her to . . . without fear and without consummation, which could come later when they both were healed.

Twenty-four

"Thank you for not going this time, Paul," Rose Carpenter whispered to her husband as she sat down and looked at him intently. "This means a great deal."

"I couldn't go," he said in a quiet voice. "I thought of how blessed we've been and how much we almost lost when I was watching this story unfold on the news. It's made me do a lot of thinking."

His wife concurred by nodding as she sipped her hot tea. But still, talking to her felt so formal, so rigid, so cool and without intensity. The words that they exchanged were as if they were discussing the casual progress of a tennis match. But this time, after hearing how close his child had come to not being, and after seeing what he saw, he said a silent prayer for warmth, and asked for a way to break through the glacial surface between them.

"You know," she said in a very small voice, after a long while as they sat in companionable silence, "Nina came to me and we talked."

"I know," he murmured. "She and I talked, too, and our daughter asked me some very hard questions that I hadn't thought about in years. I mean really, really stopped to try to analyze."

Rose chuckled. "Some things can be analyzed to death, Paul."

"True," he replied without any hint of sarcasm. "I learned that the hard way."

"Paul," she whispered, and looked at him very softly for the first time in years, "where did we go wrong?"

"I don't know. I asked myself that question, honestly, while I was responding to Janette's call. Please hear me out, and don't get offended."

He watched her expression, which didn't change.

"I'm not," she said with a tinge of surprise in her voice. "I'm really not . . ." Then she laughed. "It's liberating to know that I'm just curious."

Her reaction confused him and he sat back and studied his wife for a moment before speaking. "You're not upset in the least that I had this epiphany while driving to Janette Cooper's home to help her with a problem with her daughter?"

"No," Rose said. "Because it finally dawned on me when I saw your face after Janette called your cellular that you weren't enjoying this any longer. You had been having a good time at the function, were steeped in great conversation with some of your friends. I was off floating and chatting with mine, and all of a sudden, you receive this needy call. But for once in my life, I didn't feel like the nagging wife," she said. "I wasn't the one on the other end of the line in hysterics. I wasn't the one who had to wait on my man's assistance. And I realized that I had a life. Most importantly, I was no longer the victim of your actions, you were."

Her statement stung, but he'd requested the truth, so he had no choice but to take it like a man.

"You know what I realized?" he whispered, becoming awestruck by her new perspective. "I realized how foolish I felt for being tethered to this secondary life, and that no matter who I left you to go see, it would eventually unravel into this messy ball of yarn. Then I wanted to drive my car off the expressway ramp for wasting the better part of our lives on this game of hide and seek."

"Water under the bridge," she murmured, and became suddenly distant.

"Can we speak to each other truthfully tonight?" His question was more of a plea than a coarse request. They had swept their problems under the rug for so long that he was now unsure if they even knew how to tell each other the truth any longer. He pushed himself back in his chair and he waited, his gaze holding hers with steadiness. His wife became silent and her eyes filled with tears, but there was no sign of resentment in her expression.

"I wish we could have talked so many years ago, Paul."

"So do I," he admitted in a quiet whisper. "Think of how much pain we could have spared this household."

"I saw that, too, when our daughter came to me asking how to save her marriage, and I was so afraid for her. It was like it was happening all over again as I tried to explain what now didn't make sense." Rose Carpenter dabbed at the corners of her eyes and began to stand, but her husband held her hands fast.

"This time, don't get up and end it when it's getting to the heart of the matter. Let's not do that anymore."

He waited for her acceptance, and as she relaxed enough to sit back down slowly, he relaxed. "What could I tell that bright, passionate young woman of ours? I wonder what she sees now when she looks at me, her father, and other men?" He had asked the questions so quietly that his wife had to strain to hear him.

In that moment, Rose Carpenter decided to tell him the truth.

"She sees a knight in shining armor, and the evil queen who didn't understand him and thus drove him to his demise, or out of the house—the same thing I saw in my own mother until I finally understood," Rose said in a distant voice. "That's why we mothers tread a very fine line between divulging the truth about our situations, or covering them up for years. It's a delicate balancing act that requires diplomatic aplomb and a lot of sacrifice."

"That seems so unfair, Rose. Are you sure that this is the real perception she has, or your own view of yourself?"

She could tell that he had not meant the question as a dig. It was in the way his eyes held the furtive quality of a student trying to learn something new, something complex, and just beyond his grasp.

"No," Rose said simply. "The mother is always the one who is blamed. If she speaks ill of the father, no matter how terribly he has behaved, she is blamed for the condition of her child's mental state. If she disciplines them too much, she is blamed. If she does not discipline them enough, she is blamed. If she holds them too tightly to her apron strings, she is blamed, and if she loosens their ties so that they can fly, she is blamed for not being caring, or nurturing, or warm enough. We are always blamed, Paul."

She watched her husband sit back to wrestle with the bare facts as she had stated them, and as her comment seemed to seep into his mind, she felt a measure of satisfaction that she hadn't been able to claim for years—the knowledge that her voice was heard.

"Paul, it's very simple. If a mother takes away the hero, she is charged in her child's mind with manslaughter. Do you understand? And that was too big a price to pay, by any stretch of the imagination. I couldn't bear to see indifference from you reflected from your eyes, and resentment from the depths of hers, all at the same time. So I sacrificed my need for being the quote unquote apple of your eye, to at least retain some measure of respect from my daughter, whom I love without question."

"Rose," he whispered, "what kind of choice was that?"

"A very hard one," she stated plainly without anger.

"But it had to also be so hollow, and you didn't seek this admiration elsewhere for all of these years?"

"It was a bitter pill," she admitted, gathering her arms about herself as though in protection. "But women of my era did it every day. I was no exception. And to answer your question about seeking those glances elsewhere, yes, I sought them, but not from the source you would imagine."

The look of pure confusion on his face annoyed her. She didn't want to discuss what was so basic, and so painful. But the crisis with their child pulled at the nether regions within her, and made her fearless to expose that vulnerability. Her mind formulated a response, and she sat before the perpetrator of crimes against her soul, her mind screaming, "Take me, not my child," just as any mother would fearlessly give her life for her own child.

"I sought admiration from my girlfriends," she whispered. "I sought it from my coworkers, and church groups, and felt worthy, and whole, and good about the things they patted me on my back for . . . and I converted desire for my husband into desire to achieve, and I allowed my little awards and plaques to be my culmination, my orgasms, if you must know."

The stricken expression on his face drew hot tears of rage to her eyes, and she wiped at them bitterly, becoming angry with herself as she thrust her chin up with dignity. But her trembling bottom lip betrayed her.

"My mother lived through this nightmare," she spat, her voice quavering with emotions that were now too explosive to control. "Who was I to whine about my lot in life?"

He watched her fold away her feelings and neatly tuck them back where they had come from. But this time, he couldn't allow her to store them in the vacuum-sealed protection like her wedding gown in the attic. Through all their arguments, and all of their cutting remarks, she had never once referenced her own mother this way, and he could not let the subject die on this fragile note.

"You said your own mother had lived through this nightmare," he repeated. "Do you want Nina to go through this too?"

"Of course not," she fired back with a shocked expression. "My heart broke for that child when she told me it was beginning to happen to her."

"Did your mother ever talk to you, I mean tell you about her nightmare in a way that could help you not live one out too?"

For the first time since they'd opened Pandora's box, his wife sat back and seemed to truly hear his question in a way that made her lower her defenses. Her shoulders relaxed, and her gaze softened, and this time he could tell that the tears, which now filled her eyes, were born of hurt, not rage. And her expression pulled at a very far region within his soul as he watched the damage that he'd inflicted unfurl, and truly saw it for the very first time.

"My mother never told me," Rose whispered. "But children see damage—whether it's a punch or a cutting word."

"Your father beat your mother, Rose?" He was so aghast that he almost stood to rush to her side. But as she shook her head slowly, he committed himself to his chair.

"My father was a deacon in his church, a pillar of the community, and a very prominent attorney. My mother was a schoolteacher, which was an honorable and high position for a woman in that day."

"I know, but Rose, people of any socioeconomic status can be batterers, and, I am well aware of your parents' pedigree."

"I just rattled off their résumés, Paul," she said in a soft voice. "He didn't hit her with his fists. He beat my mother's self-esteem to death with his words and his ex-tramarital activities."

They both stared at each other for a while, and her gaze caught the edge of the windowsill and the light made the moisture within her eyes sparkle.

"I received my erudite command of the English language from my father, whom I admired with all of my heart. I also tested out my abilities on my mother from time to time, with cruel remarks and cutting responses, just the way I had seen him speak to her. I applauded his career accomplishments and wanted to be just like him when I grew up. I found her accomplishments to be subpar to his, and I watched that woman wither on the vine with so little compassion . . ."

His wife's voice trailed off and she covered her mouth with her fingers to stop a sob, and when he reached for her, she pulled back and held up her hand.

"No, let me tell the truth that you asked for, Paul. It's high time."

He nodded and his wife drew a deep breath, breathing him into herself as she did so. Her image blurred due to his own unshed tears as he witnessed her transform and become a young woman right before his eyes.

"I watched my mother say little, and arrogantly felt that she did so because she had no drive, no ambition . . . and I assumed that my charismatic father spoke to her the way he did because she was not his equal and he thus had a right to be bored with her trivial conversation. Then I found out why my mother had so few words to say and why she functioned in a daze and clothed herself in activities beyond the church and within the safe haven of her schoolteacher friends. On her bad days, Mom would have *episodes,* as she called them, and need to se-quester herself in her room, which I later came to find out were crying jags."

Paul Carpenter sat very, very still. Even his lungs were

having difficulty pulling in air from the room as they filled themselves with the pain that had been released within the confines of the kitchen walls.

"It was the day my mother held a lace garment in her hand, and I walked into her bedroom. Tears had ravaged her face, and she held up the nightgown to me and asked, 'Do you think this is pretty?' I was confused and sat down next to her on the bed, and I told her yes, then she began to cry, and I couldn't get her to stop."

Rose stood and paced and leaned against the sink with her back to her husband. "Then my mother began to wail, and she threw the gown across the room, and swept away all of her perfume bottles on her vanity, and she cried some more. Then she screamed, 'Then why doesn't your father think so?' I stared at her for a long time, and she stood in the middle of a room looking like a lost child, and in that instant our roles reversed, and I tried to comfort her, and coo to her, and my heart shattered because even at twenty I knew he'd done something unspeakable to the woman we loved but had all taken for granted."

Rose turned and folded her arms over her chest. "In my mother's defense, I went to my father, just as Nina had come to you."

He watched in fear as his wife drew a breath and summoned strength into her body in a way that straightened her carriage. Her chin then lifted to tell the rest of her truth.

"And he tried to make me an accomplice," she said firmly. "He gave me pat phrases like, 'You know how your mother is,' on and on and on and tried to remain the white knight in my eyes, but this time I would not be moved. So I asked him point blank, 'What would dissolve a woman so thoroughly, if not another woman?' And he could not look at me, Paul. Then I asked the million-dollar question, 'How many?' Again, my father could not look at me, and the eloquent spokesman mumbled, yes, mumbled something about grown folks' business. And I went up close to his face and I slapped him for my mother, and received a slap back. And for the first time in my life I knew fear—the fear of being abused, of feeling the awesome difference in strength between a man and a woman."

Her chest was heaving now, and he wanted to make her stop, but her eyes burned with a memory so far away that he knew he couldn't reach her even if he tried.

"But still I held my ground as I held the side of my face. And I told him that I would never, ever marry a man like him. That I would always have my own bank account, always have my own friends, always have my own life, and would never set foot in the church where he was deacon—and probably sourced for his concubines . . . and I told him that with such ferocity that I made my hero cry. For the first time in my life I felt so alone, and so ashamed, and so conflicted, because I had just lost my father to the realization that he was just a spoiled child."

A hard sob broke free from her throat, and she covered her mouth again with her hand, but she didn't shield her eyes from him, and she stared at him as though she were having that long-ago battle again.

"Paul," her voice quavered, "when I went to my mother about you, she held me in her arms and cried like a baby for me and she apologized to me, for what was happening to me. Until Nina came to me for help, I didn't understand how we as women take on the burdens of those we love, as though everything is our fault. And I never came to my mother again after that. I lied to her because as I lived through your first affair in her kitchen, I witnessed her reliving all of my father's transgressions, and I didn't want to put her through that again."

His wife's newfound calm unnerved him, and he

watched her cross the room and take a seat at the table, then dab away the tear streaks on her face as though she were erasing the entire discussion.

"So. You have the truth," she said in a matter-of-fact tone that belied just how deeply she'd dredged her memory to carve out her pain. "And I married my father, even though the man I married was in a different profession and is physically different in coloring. The little girl in me that first admired her father found an orator, an intellectual, a prominent social figure, and a charming, charismatic philanderer, while the mother in me stood by and watched as her own little girl, Nina, chose a tall, handsome, well-respected businessman from humble beginnings—just like her father—and this mother prayed on her child's behalf to everlasting God that her mistakes had skipped a generation."

He felt very, very small as his wife's confession bore down into him. Tears fell from his eyes and coursed down his cheeks, and landed with big splotches on the table-cloth. He did not wipe them away. He didn't feel he had the right to. Suddenly years truncated into moments, and he saw her pain as a driving force.

"What would you have wanted your father to do," he asked quietly, "if you could go back and have that conversation with him today?"

"I would want him to atone," she replied immediately. "I would want him to hold my mother's hands and admit that his failures as a husband were not her fault alone, not because she wasn't smart enough, or pretty enough, or had stressed him, or had not said the right key words and phrases he needed to hear at some ambiguous moment."

Her response had come so quickly and so clearly that it took him a moment to absorb it all, and while he paused to collect himself, she pressed on, flowing through the floodgate that he'd opened.

"I used to hold you up to my father's face as a weapon," she admitted, then released a bitter chuckle.

Her statement made him look up and cock his head. "You held me up to your father?" It was absurd. Her father had been the Olympic bar that he could never achieve in her sight.

"Of course I did," she said with confidence. "Always. And it cut him to the bone."

She'd made the comment so earnestly as she leaned forward and stared at him directly that he reached across the table and held her hand—in that moment, more to steady himself than her.

"I would parade your accomplishments in your field of psychological study before him like badges of honor," she whispered. "I would tell him how *wonderful* my husband was, and how doting, and how proud I was of him for the type of work he did, all the while minimizing anything my father wanted to tell me about his. In my mind, when he'd try to receive a glimmer of my admiration, I would send him the signal, 'Go tell it to your wife, you son of a bitch, make her eyes sparkle, take your drink from her cup, not mine. I have a husband.' It was my slap in his face, for me, and especially for my mother, whose eyes seemed to shine brighter each time she watched me deliver a punch. It was a while before I even found out that she'd always speak so highly of you, especially in earshot of him—and tortured him vicariously through you."

He was speechless, and she smiled.

"Haven't you learned yet that women fight with words, because our fists are not strong enough to match a man blow for blow—but in that arena, we are heavyweight contenders?"

Rose sat back and placed her hands over his, and sighed. "You got swept up in our war, I suppose. I take responsibility for that part of it. But I wanted you to beat him, Paul," she said plaintively as new tears filled her eyes. "I wanted you to best him, and show him how a man was supposed to treat his wife."

He could not breathe. All the years of thinking that she pushed him because she felt that he wasn't good enough, all of the cool transactions between Rose and her father had not been because she was so spoiled that she had taken his achievements with blasé entitlement, but rather because she had lost respect for the man. And he, as her husband, had disappointed her so by his own lack of understanding. He was running the wrong race, using the wrong unit of measure, and had cast away his wife's faith in all men by becoming just like her worst nemesis.

"Oh, my God, Rose, why didn't you ever tell me? I thought I could never live up to your standards, or those set by your father. I thought he disliked me so much because I wasn't good enough for your family. . . ."

"All you had to do was love me, Paul . . . to honor and cherish me, and you would have beaten him by a mile, by demonstrating that it's not the profession that makes the man."

"And what answers can I ever give our own daughter now . . . ?" His voice trailed off as he searched his wife's eyes for solutions. "I am so, so sorry, more than I will ever be able to make up to you in this lifetime," he whispered.

"I didn't have the answers for her, either," his wife admitted. "Don't feel bad, for whatever you might have said. I found myself babbling. Me, at a loss for words? Oh, think of it," she said, laughing in self-deprecation. "I've been telling her what to do for years, then all of the sudden, she grows up and brings this huge problem home that I haven't lived long enough yet myself to find the answers to. It was totally unnerving. Until you and I just talked, I didn't know what was buried within me. So how could I begin to tell her?"

"Rose, listen to me," he pleaded. "I had to tell her that I was not a knight in shining armor to you, therefore I could not be that for her. I had to recant all my sins before the eyes of innocence, and yet I could not lash out at a man, her husband, who at the time I thought might do, or be doing, to her what I did to you. And in that moment, I understood your parents' pain, and their careful consideration of a suitor for you, and I saw their heartbreak through the way I felt about Nina, and how deeply, deeply disappointed they must have been in me. Then, dear lady, I saw you," he admitted, now unable to speak.

"You saw me?"

He watched his wife's throat move with a hard swallow, and her gaze shifted from him again to escape out of the window.

"Indeed, I saw you—full of laughter and light, and then made sad and insecure, but beautiful nonetheless. *I had no right, Rose.* No right." Hot moisture filled his eyes and spilled down his face.

For the first time in a long while, she saw her husband as a young man. Although his cheeks were now leathery to the touch, her fingertips remembered how they used to feel as she wiped his tears of honesty away. And when he clasped them gently between his own and closed his eyes to kiss them, something inside of her stirred that had withered with time. The ecstasy on his face from her acceptance of such close physical proximity echoed through her as he held her fingers more tightly now and pressed them harder to his mouth with his eyes still closed.

"They hadn't slept with each other for four months," she admitted, "and I was stricken."

"Tell me why," he whispered, praying that she would answer with a truth he needed to hear.

"Because I remembered what it was like to want a

man . . . to want to be touched, and to ache for that fulfillment, and here my child was asking me how to recapture that gift that was being taken away from her, and all I could point her to was a prescription drug." Rose tried to remove her hand from within his, but he held it and wouldn't let it go. "I can't discuss this part of it, Paul," her voice quavered. "I don't want to cry anymore about this."

"I don't want you to cry," he said, trying to soothe her. "Ever, about anything again, unless it's from joy. What can I do, now, today, to make this right?"

Their gaze met each other's halfway, and he watched his wife take in a deep breath.

"Frankly, I don't know."

"Do you want to be with someone else, to have your own space? I owe you, Rose, and more importantly, I never stopped loving you, as hard as that may be to understand."

"That's *all* I ever wanted, and your friendship, and your respect, and for you to hear me. Moving away and divorcing at our late stage in life makes no sense."

He could feel her old shield of self-protection beginning to raise itself against him, and he fought with it this time, instead of running away behind platitudes.

"No," he said, looking at her intently. "I don't want to be housemates anymore, and I don't want you taking anything to make you not want to be touched. I'd rather have you declare that you were traipsing away to the islands somewhere to be in love, than to just passively slip away during our golden years. No."

"What if I did suddenly stop taking medication?" Rose looked at her husband and laughed. "Do you think I would have been able to deal with the way we've lived, and keep scandal from our door at the same time if I had?"

He smiled. "Not the Rose I once knew. No."

His response somehow made her face immediately
cloud over, and just as abruptly, she slapped him.

"Again," he whispered, "for every time I was unfaith-
ful." He did not shield himself as his wife hauled off
again, struck him, then lowered her head to the table
and sobbed. He didn't move.

"Why are you so intent on raising this dead subject?"
she yelled, her eyes searching his face in the process. "It
was fine the way it was. Calm."

"No, it wasn't fine," he murmured, leaning forward.
"Not for you, not for me."

"I was so passionate when I was younger," she whim-
pered. Then she bit down hard on her bottom lip.

"And you probably should have created some scandal
to get my foolish ass to wake up, or left me for another
man. Why didn't you?"

"Because I loved you, and wanted to be here!" she
shrieked. "And I wanted to slap you without fear of being
slapped back. And I didn't want an excuse, but wanted
an apology, a deep-down-to-Georgia apology, and the
knowledge that if I forgave you, vampires would never be
allowed to cross the threshold of my home again, Paul.
And I wanted my passion for you to come back. I didn't
realize how much I wanted any of those things until I
watched my own daughter being stripped of them. It was
a violation that I had to sit at this very kitchen table and
watch as she told me, in absolute, heart-rending detail,
then she reached out and said, 'Mommy, make it stop
hurting.' And for the first time in my life, I couldn't help
her. Do you understand what that feels like?"

They fell quiet after her outburst and sat staring at each
other. His wife's small bosom heaved with spent fury,
hurt, and God only knew what else. And her question
lingered in his mind like the humidity that makes clothing cling after a summer storm, and he wondered what
else about her had he squandered . . . her eyes. He had

wasted those beautiful, fire-filled eyes that could drive a hole through the chest of any man. And he had taken the razor-sharp mind before him for granted, and most assuredly wasted the lot of her heart, which was a deep well beyond measure, and for the life of him, as he stared at her, he couldn't remember why.

"I know," he finally whispered. "I know what that meant to witness her pain. She sat across from me on the sofa, her eyes like a doe caught in the headlights, and she asked, 'Daddy, how can this be fixed?' And, Rose, I swear to you, for the first time in my life, I was looking at you when looking at her, and thinking at the same time, what you must have asked your father, and what demons he tried to slay within himself on your behalf. What tears did I make you cry, all for a weak man's ego? And my child, whom I kissed before she was even born through the skin of your belly, was at the mercy of another man, and when she left, Rose, I fell to my knees and begged the Father to not let the sins of this man be visited upon his daughter. *Do not let her pick one like me,* I prayed, and when I sat at Janette's and heard her tale of woe, and I came to understand that Paulette had found a replica of her father in the world and married him, that's when I came to know a fear like I have never known, dear Rose. You must understand what I have just learned." A sob tore through him and he released her hand, and he covered his face and lowered his head to the kitchen table to finally weep hard without shame before his wife.

He heard her move, yet he was too bereft to stop her this time. How could one turn back the clock, and make things whole once they'd been split asunder by his own hand? The very question itself drew a new wave of sobs up and out of his lungs, and it took a while before he realized that someone was stroking his hair.

The sensation created an unbearable ache within him

to be held. His telepathic plea was answered by an embrace, which scorched his spine as it wrapped itself around him and the chair as though they were one. Through the new awareness of her being, his skin greedily soaked up the surrounding warmth of his wife, and his ears drank in her soft whispers to "Hush now."

But instead of exacting calm, her voice threaded its way through his nervous system and set off land-mined memories of how much he'd missed her, while her hands gliding down his arms and her gentle kiss at the nape of his neck made him sob and shudder with want all in the same breath, till he found himself turning to place his hands on either side of her face, finding an eager mouth searching for his amid the tears.

And as he pushed himself up to stand, and the chair fell backward to the floor, he remembered feeling twenty, when she slid perfectly into the place that he had saved for her. Just as his hands remembered her back, the way it arched for him in youth, he knew that she remembered too when her spine flexed under his hold. There, in the kitchen, his hands remembered his wife as she had been, but now their memory was made crystal by the deep appreciation of finally understanding who she was.

Twenty-five

"I don't care," Maxine said to her brother as she put on her sneakers. "I'm going."

"After all he did to you, and almost landed us in the slammer, you're what?"

"I'm going," she said without looking at him.

"No, you're not," Darrell hollered. "Oh, no you're not!"

"Stand aside," she threatened quietly, then stared at him.

"No."

"Do I have to remind you," she whispered, "who gave you a second chance, who forgave you when you had to go away for dumb bull? Me," she said plainly. "Me."

"That ain't got nothin'—"

"It has everything to do with it," she said even more quietly than before. "You had a wake-up call, and you had somebody to look you in the eyes and believe you when you said you'd changed." Maxine accepted her brother's silence as an acknowledgement as she walked across the room to grab her purse.

"And if he burns you again, sis, what then?"

"Then," she said just above a whisper, "he'll never see me again."

"Sure," he said in disgust. "That's what they all say, Max."

She walked over to her brother and touched his anger-filled face. "Am I a liar, now?"

"No, but you love that fool."

"I do," she whispered. "I also love you."

"But why you let him treat you like that . . . and get away with just dogging you out?"

"I don't honestly know," she admitted. "But this time is a little different."

"Yeah, how?"

She watched the young man before her who had just recently left his teens. He folded his arms over his chest and sighed, making her follow suit.

"I want you to remember this, Darrell," she replied, pecking his cheek. "Every woman is some man's sister, or mother, or woman."

He blinked as he stared at her and she smiled.

"So while you're out playing and breaking hearts, I want you to think of me, and to see my face. Remember for me that you're hurting somebody's dear sister, and when those girls you stop, drop, and roll, then disappear on start calling the house, I don't want you to have me lie for you anymore, or to tell them you'll call, when you've sat in the kitchen and laughed with me about how stupid they are. They have feelings, Darrell."

"See, you trying to change the subject on me," he argued, but this time not looking her in the eyes.

"No, I'm not. This is all about the same thing. I'm going because the man I love was asking for me, and his sister called to tell me so. And I'm going out on a limb to believe that after seeing death real up-close and personal, maybe he's had a wake-up call. But, I also know that, Darrell, I've changed, too, and if there's any yang with his game, I'm gone. Won't be no drama, no theatrics, I'll just get ghost on him without discussion. Is that fair enough?"

"Only if you promise that, if he burns you, you'll leave it alone this time, Max."

"Deal," she said with a smile and extended her hand to her brother's folded arms.

Begrudgingly he took her hand and shook it, then dragged her against him in a bear hug. "I love you, you ole crazy thang," he whispered against her hair. "You'd better not let him hurt you no more, Maxie. Honest to God, my heart can't take it."

"Whatchu gonna do now, Jack?" Bobby said quietly as he rubbed his sister's shoulders in the cool evening air. "Ron's prob'ly gonna have to go away for a long time."

"I know," Jackie whispered as she sat at the Septa stop, cradling her son in her lap. "I might have to let Cecil take this one for a while." She cast her gaze at her brother's stricken face and quickly added something to help him understand. "Just for a little while, till I get myself together. He seems like he's got a nice family."

"More 'n we got," Bobby said with defeat. "You sure you wanna do that, baby? Plus, how's Daekwon gonna take it?"

"He's young, still. He'll adjust. But I need to go back to school and be able to take care of this next baby, him, and me—*by myself.*"

"I don't know . . ." her brother sighed.

"Boo, I can't drag this child up to prison to see his brother's father in the joint. I just can't do it," she whispered, swallowing hard as she spoke. "I might not have done much with my life, but this isn't how I ever saw it. Sometimes I just wish I could turn back the clock. Haven't you ever felt like that?"

Her brother's eyes contained a haunting look filled with understanding. "I hear you, Jack," he said quietly as they waited for the trolley. "I just wish I could do that for you now."

"It ain't your fault—ain't nobody's fault. Sometimes, it's just the way things go," she said to reassure him. "Then again, sometimes, you've just gotta take the weight for what was your fault. Am I making sense?"

Bobby Lester let his breath out as he took the last drag on his cigarette. "Too much sense. Let's squash it. We gotta do what we gotta do, is all. If you decide to give the kid a fighting chance with them Williamses while you go back to school, then I stand behind you. If you decide to try to make it on your own, well, that's cool, too. Either way, I gotchure back."

They let silence fall between them and be their comfort. Jackie leaned into the soft curls that pressed against her breast as her son slept hard and carefree against her, and she kissed him while saying a quiet prayer. Even at five, her son was almost too big for her lap, and the more pregnant she became, the less room she'd have for him, so she held on to the last thread of time that she'd be able to hold her son like this. And where she lived, she knew too well that boy children grew up fast and died young. By the time she got out of school, and made something of her life, the streets would already have him. Her lips found the tiny ringlets beneath her nose again and she kissed them hard as hot tears fell into them. Maybe this one would have a fighting chance—if she could just let go and let God . . .

Anthony squeezed his wife's hand tighter as they entered the hospital and went to the intensive care unit. When there was no sign of his family, he could feel her hand leave his and her arm wrap around his waist.

"Let's ask the nurse at the desk before we assume the worst," she whispered, and guided their bodies forward.

"My brother, Cecil Williams, isn't in the room I left him in," Anthony said with a swallow. That was all he could say.

The nurse smiled unexpectedly and stood to walk over to a clipboard on the far end of the desk. "We upgraded his condition to guarded, then stable, and moved him to room three-sixty-nine about an hour ago."

Nina and Anthony stared at each other, and then both laughed, as the nurse looked puzzled.

"Me and the family been watchin' all this stuff on the news, boy!" Anthony's father exclaimed as he and Nina approached. "I just came from callin' you—everybody's in there with Cecil now. C'mon!"

Half-hopping and half-dragging them both, his father added them to the crowd of family around Cecil's bed.

"They been threatening to put us all out, and we told them to go ahead and call the police—we wasn't leaving Cecil's side till you got here."

"Yo, Uncle Tony!" his nieces and nephews hollered in unison, only to quickly receive a round of female hisses to be quiet.

His sisters simply bundled around the couple, kissing them, petting them, and squeezing them too tightly.

"Maxine's on her way here with Darrell," Vicki said quietly to Cecil, but loud enough so that Anthony could hear. "He's been asking for her since he woke up," she added with a wink.

"You just missed Rev," his father exclaimed, "and boy, y'all missed a doozy!"

"Rev made a lot of sense," Vicki argued, "He was talking about geese."

Nina and Anthony stared at each other, and Mrs. Williams chuckled.

"It was deep. You know how Rev weaves and winds a

sermon till you're ready to fall out, but this made sense. He said the geese from behind honk to encourage the ones out in front," their quiet sister Darla said.

"Yeah," Mr. Williams noted. "They ain't like crabs in a barrel."

"No, Pop," Rhonda said. "They're birds."

"If you gonna quote a man of the cloth, get it right," Mrs. Williams commanded. "Rev said we have to be like geese—fly *together* in formation. When the geese fly, they form a V, and it helps their whatchacall?"

"It makes it easier for them 'cause the wind pulls with them, not against them," Vicki clarified.

"Unison flight improves their wind coefficient," Pebbles said. "And when one drops out, the whole flock feels it."

"That's the point I was coming to, Miss Smartie," Mrs. Williams said with mock indignation that made them all laugh. "But they do a curious thing for animals," she murmured, becoming serious and making the group go quiet to hear her. "If one drops formation, two fly down and wait with the injured one until it dies or can fly again. Then, the three fly up together, making haste because they have a small formation of their own, and when they catch up, they fall in, and they go on their merry way. Don't that sound like our family?" Her face shone with pride as her smile beamed.

"It does, Mom," Anthony said in a whisper, casting his gaze toward Nina who had been compared to the goose. "Rev's reference to the goose means a lot to me." He wondered if he'd ever be able to comprehend how his wife had summoned the patience and strength to come down to the ground to endure the wait by his side until he'd healed enough to fly again. So many forces behind the scenes had been at work, and he suddenly understood his mother's belief system and her guiding light of living by faith.

"Come here, son, come close so I can hug you," his mother exclaimed, throwing her arms around him and Nina as they did. "Get close to Cecil, too. He can't talk much with the tubes in him, but he's awake and understands everything. Tell us in your own words what happened."

Nina stood back and watched her husband as he held court at his brother's bedside, and she folded her arms around herself and sat down in a chair that an eager youngster had abandoned. A simplistic peace washed over her as her husband spoke, and she found herself yawning and hungry, and needing to lay her head down on the side arm of the chair.

"I want to put this out here in front of everybody," Anthony said in a tone that made all the questions, side commentary, laughter, and squeals cease.

The sudden quiet made her sit up in her chair and stare at him too.

"What if there were a place," Anthony said, casting his gaze from his brother to Nina, "where my brother could work out every day, and learn how to walk again as part of his job and his therapy? And what if this place served only wholesome foods and juice at the bar, but needed a solid restaurant manager, like Maxine, and her backup, Darrell—who can be trusted with a man's life? And what if this same place also had a day-care center where three women could work and bring their own children, and there were internships for young teenage coaches and mentors to work with their peers in the after-school program?"

Nina watched him use his hands, painting the wide mural that had been sketched in pencil in their kitchen together, but Anthony had added colors and oils and layered it with wide strokes with enough room to include everyone. He was truly an artist, and only now was she beginning to see the full range of his gift. She would have to point that out to him later and tell him how proud she was of him.

"And what if there were a six-bedroom house available that was only twenty minutes away from said place, that had enough room for three day-care and after-school teachers and their children, near a good school, that could bus them all to their mothers' place of employment, and those mothers could give their support system a break, and finally let the original pair travel and live and love without worry? What if there were such a place?"

His sisters were crying, and his parents stood up, side by side in awe. Nina stood, too, and walked over to her husband who was still painting, and kissed him.

"And, what if this place had classes, and art, and culture, and beauty, and green all around it and took care of everyone's dreams who worked there. Would you come with me to this place?"

"I would call that place heaven," his sister Vicki whispered.

"And," his mother added through her tears, "I would say that this family was finally flying in formation, up high, and close to God."

"But son, how're you gonna afford something like that?" his father asked through a furrowed brow. "I don't mean to throw no water on all these grandiose ideas, or ground no geese that's trying to fly, but your place done burned down, and we gotta help you rebuild it first. That could take years until—"

"Insurance," Anthony quipped, looking down at his brother as he spoke. "The club was well-insured, and the fire was a way out. I had my mind to selling it and splitting the proceeds with Cecil, but I couldn't figure out a way to make the numbers work."

"God's way," his mother whispered, "is all in this stew. In His time, and in His way, not ours. The silver lining to every cloud. . . ."

Cecil reached for his brother's hand, and Anthony grabbed it and stooped down. "I know what you're thinking, but don't talk," Anthony whispered. "Your disability coverage will carry what you send Jackie until you get on your feet and come work with me at the center. And I know you were putting what you took back into the safe when you got hit."

Two large tears rolled from the corners of Cecil's eyes as he shut them.

"You just gotta promise me you'll take care of the boy, and not keep him a secret," Anthony murmured, glancing at his mother as she covered her mouth and sought his father's shoulder. "We can make room in this family for Daekwon. Don't you want him to see how a man should live his life? You're his father, and you have to own up to him, and give Jackie her due, regardless of whether you guys have split."

Cecil nodded with effort, and the gurgling sounds in his throat made everyone go still.

"Tell Maxine I'ma marry her," Cecil rasped. "Soon as I get on my feet. I ain't forgot about Jackie neither. Will do what I'm supposed to. She's good people. Got a lot to make up for all way 'round."

"Comin' that close to meetin' yo' maker will change a man," their father said quietly, touching Anthony and Cecil's arms at the same time. "Ask me how I know, one day."

A murmur of agreement swept the room and Nina found herself in the chair again, but needing to vomit.

"Get her some water," Vicki commanded to one of the youngsters standing closest to the door.

"Bring her that trash can," Anthony's sister Pebbles ordered to another child, while Rhonda and Darla each took one of Nina's hands.

"It's been too much excitement on that po' chile," his

father announced, heading for the door in a flurry of motion. "I'ma get one of them white coats in here."

"Jus' hold on now, everybody," Mrs. Williams said with a smile as she approached Nina and lifted her chin. "When's the last time you ate, baby?"

Nina couldn't remember as she looked up into the tender eyes that had asked the question, and she could see worry etched across Anthony's face.

"Make her agree to lie down," Anthony whispered. "She doesn't listen to me, Mom," he stammered. He noticed that everyone had stopped moving and fussing about to look at the wise center of their universe.

"Yes, this chile do need to lie down," the eldest woman in the room proclaimed, "after you feed her a little something and she calls her momma."

"I'm fine," Nina protested. "It's just been a rough forty-eight hours, and my parents have been through enough. I'll call Mom—"

"Now," Mrs. Williams ordered, turning Nina's face from side to side, inspecting it for fullness with arthritic hands and motioning toward the telephone next to Cecil with her head. "You gonna let your momma's mind rest easy, right this very minute. Then, with her and your daddy on the line, we all gonna pray and say thank ya, Jesus."

"You can't argue with Mom," Anthony said. "I'd say a prayer is in order, after all of this."

"You ain't said a mumblin' word, boy," his father added, coming back into the room and standing next to Anthony as Nina proceeded to dial her parents' house.

"You thinkin' what I'm thinkin'?" Vicki asked the group of sisters.

"You know Mom be on it," Pebbles said as Nina connected and began speaking to her mother.

"Called mine every time," Darla laughed.

"You?" Rhonda chuckled with a hand on her hip. "I was cold busted. How you do it, Mom?"

"That comes with age," their mother said, then turned to her elder son with a wide grin. "Tell your wife to give her mother the good news."

"Oh yeah, Nina," Anthony yelled across the bed. "Tell Rose about the family business we're all going into."

Nina turned her head as she held the receiver and looked at Mrs. Williams, who'd begun to laugh.

"No, son, that's not the good news I'm talking about."

When both Nina and Anthony exchanged a shrug, Mrs. Williams sat down.

"Pass the phone over to me, honey. Let me break it to Rose that she's gonna have to enter a new phase in life— one that ain't easy, but that brings a lot of joy. Tell her I want to talk to her, so I can let her know she can call me anytime. She's gotta lot to learn about being a grand-mom."

"What?" Nina whispered, hearing her mother's shriek trail off as she nearly dropped the phone.

"Mom, don't get our hopes up like that," Anthony murmured as he kissed his mother's forehead. "It's—"

"Don't question how they know, son," his father said. "All *I* know is Natalie done dreamed about fish again, and that's more accurate than any doctor's appointment I've seen over the years. Told you not to kill the goose that laid the golden egg, since we on the subject."

Anthony found himself crossing the room as his wife slowly reached out, stunned, handing the phone to a sister, who then passed it to another sister, who squealed as she passed it over to their mother. The harmony of excited women's voices brought a distressed nurse to the door, who was ignored as the vocal celebration commenced. Anthony wrapped his arms around Nina as his brother smiled past the tubes in his throat, and his father scratched his head, and children giggled and whispered, and he knew that his mother was right.

And the crowd of family in the room began to seem far, far away as his mouth found the lips of the woman he loved more than life itself, and he understood about hearing what a woman was trying to tell a man for the first time—how there was no such thing as logic when a man talked to such a woman because her guesses and hunches, and dreams and sixth sense of unveiling life through parable and riddle were real enough to forecast life and death, and it was more real than any business, and more sophisticated than jazz, and no less eloquent a form of complex expression that he so deeply respected now as his hand found Nina's belly, and his knees bent so that he could kiss and pay homage to the vessel of her womb. And he wept against her without shame as she laughed and cried, too, and her fingers twisted themselves through his hair as he nuzzled the source of all creation. How foolish he'd been not to hear her before when she'd spoken to him with her own insistent melody of love's purest note.

Epilogue

Six months later . . .

"Hey, Vonetta!" Nina yelled as she passed the book-store portion of the center on her way in.

"Hey, gurl," Vonetta said, coming around the counter to touch Nina's stomach by ritual. "How's it feel to have the baby move around a lot?" she asked excitedly, then turned sideways. "Can you see a change yet?"

"No," Nina said, "but you wait. Then you'll be complaining like me about being kicked awake all night."

"He's got his daddy's old schedule, huh?" Vonetta quipped, making them both giggle.

"Well, the poor chile was made in a club," Nina said in a conspiratorial tone, "but don't let Mom Williams know, she'd pass out. Anyway, where's that fine husband of yours?"

"Gone to pick up the after-school kids, then to a local basketball game—thank God," her girlfriend said. "He is under me twenty-four seven, Nina, and made me quit smoking. I can't even have a beer. I'm in total lockdown."

"I know whatchumean," Nina said. "Tony doesn't even want me to lift my sketch pads for class. We'll have to work around those guys."

"Yeah," Vonetta whispered. "I'm tired of health food,

truth be told. I could go for a big, juicy Quarter Pounder with cheese."

"No! You know what my weakness is?" Nina confided. "Reese's Peanut Butter Cups, but they give me gas so bad, I have to keep the window open at night."

They slapped a high-five, and put their arms over each other's shoulders.

"What y'all concocting now?" Maxine yelled through the juice bar pass-through, then hollered for Darrell to bring up some more ice.

"Just misbehavin' is all, and trying to get some real food," Vonetta said as her customers browsed. Then she caught herself. "Oops, my bad . . . I meant high-fat, impure foods that will clog your arteries and kill you," she corrected.

"You sound like Cecil and Daekwon," Maxine said, laughing. "Both of them try to sneak cheese steaks when the boss ain't lookin', but Tony smells it on their breath every time."

"Shhh!" Nina whispered, putting her finger to her lips and making Maxine giggle as a few die-hard customers gave a disapproving glance from their juice bar stools. Then she winked at Maxine. "That's because Tony is salivating for one himself." Nina laughed quietly into Maxine's ear after she waddled back to the juice bar and Vonetta took a break from the bookstore to sit beside her. "But he's been on a mission about this new healthy lifestyle, and trying really hard."

"I know our brother misses his Johnny Walker," Maxine chuckled in a whisper. "First week in here was the worst! And poor Cecil . . . Lord have mercy, when the hospital put him on a diet to help his breathing and digestive tract and to take the weight off that hip, I thought Darrell and I were going to have to strap him to the bed to keep him from hopping around the corner to order a hoagie."

"Which one of us y'all talking bad about now?" Tony said, dropping a load of ice and coming up behind Nina to rub her belly with both hands. "You're not feeding my child any junk food, are you?"

"No, honey," she said, batting her eyes in a way that made them all laugh. "I'm as innocent as the driven snow."

"Hey, Nina," Vicki hollered, coming in for her shift. "Your dad teaching tonight?"

"Not this week," Nina said in a happy tone. "They're in Aruba."

"Shut up!" Darla yelled into the fray as she dumped a load of fresh fruit into the bar hoppers. "These old folks are just getting out of hand."

"When are Mom and Pop due back?" Tony called out to Rhonda, who was in the kitchen.

"I don't know. All I do know is we done lost all our baby-sitters with your grand plan of sending folks off on cruises and whatnot. When the geese on the ground gonna get to fly?" Rhonda said, sighing.

"Girl, be quiet," Vicki argued good-naturedly as she delivered an order to the kitchen pass-through. "We're going to Disney World after Nina drops. What else you want?"

"Disney World is for the kids," Pebbles said, adjusting the rows of vitamins near the juice bar area. "I think Rhonda was talking about a romantic getaway with her new man."

"Stop telling my business all through the center, dag, Pebs!"

"If you and Vonnie know like I know," Vicki said, nodding in Anthony and Nina's direction, "y'all better get it all in now before these babies come. Ain't that right?"

"Word!" Maxine hollered from the back.

"You ain't told nothin' but the truth, sis," Darla hollered.

"That's *all* I was saying," Rhonda laughed.

"We just have to take turns, and put nookie on the calendar—make a schedule," Pebbles said.

"Oh, pulleese," Vonetta said. "Really, y'all?"

"For real, for real?" Anthony murmured, feeling his wife's belly through her sweater.

"Seriously?" Nina stuttered, "It's that hard to make time for just the two of you?"

"Yes!" The veterans of child rearing yelled in unison, then burst out in peals of laughter, causing customers to join them.

"The first year, after they've sucked all the nutrients out of your body, then kept you awake twenty-four seven, then they want to sleep in bed with you all night. Ain't that right, Dar?" Vicki said, holding her sides as she slapped a high-five with her sister Pebbles.

"Oh yeah, Tony, get ready," Pebbles warned, "for the bad dreams that send them into your bed unexpectedly in the middle of the night—and midstroke, brother! And I'm not talking about the stroke of midnight, either."

Nina looked at her husband's expression as he blanched, and it made her laugh as she dabbed her eyes.

"Not, midstroke . . ." he trailed off, which only seemed to make the gathering of women laugh even harder.

"Cecil almost got a hernia like that one night, tryin' to pull out too fast," Maxine chortled, then leaned down on the counter to roar with laughter at the memory.

"Girl, stop!" Rhonda begged, wiping her eyes. "Can't you see that tall, fine Leonard up in Vonetta-vamp's face when a little bird runs, jumps in the sack full throttle, then pees the bed? He might go back to being a detective and book the child for criminal trespassing!"

"Y'all just trying to make me and Nina scared, that's all," Vonetta argued with waning confidence. "Tell the truth."

"You wanna be scared, then you and Nina keep goin' to those natural childbirth classes. Scared is sixteen hours of labor, and your epidural runs out!" Vicki laughed hard as she accepted another run of high-fives.

"Mom Williams and my mother never said anything about that," she whispered, looking at Vonetta, then glancing at Tony.

" 'Cause they wanted grandchildren, gurl," Rhonda quipped. "They don't tell you the whole deal till it's too late."

"It's better not to know until you need to know," Pebbles said, and went to wait on a customer to help Vicki out.

"Yup, y'all too late," Darla said.

"Gotta take it like a woman," Maxine added.

"It goes by fast . . ." Vicki said, sighing. "Eighteen to twenty years of not getting none steady will go by before you know it," she added with a belly laugh as she slapped her brother on the back.

Vonetta, Nina, and Anthony just looked at one another as peals of laughter surrounded them.

"It's a rude awakening," a customer added from her perch.

"Yeah," another joined in. "It's wonderful being a mom, but it's work."

"It ain't no day at the beach all the time for us dads, ya know," a fitness center client stated as he collected his slushie.

"Word," another male customer called out from the bookstore, as he signaled to Vonetta that he was ready to make his purchase.

"And, where were all you folks with this wonderful advice before we did this?" Vonetta said as she strolled across the center. "That's what I wanna know. Tampering with evidence. I've been hoodwinked . . . bamboozled . . . scam-a-lammed . . . It just ain't right!"

"We were too busy raising all our kids," Vicki yelled and laughed. "Where were you latecomers?"

Anthony and Nina looked at each other and then hugged as they were overcome with a case of the giggles.

"We were pumping iron and listening to smooth jazz, and drinking Chardonnay . . . and trying to be smooth . . . and Lord have mercy," he exclaimed, making everyone laugh.

"Tell you what," Nina whispered into Anthony's ear. "We've got full coverage in here today, and the kids won't be back with Leonard for an hour or so. Wanna sneak home and put a dent in that eighteen- to twenty-year sentence?"

He glanced around the center and felt a little self-conscious as a few male customers winked at him, and his sisters nodded and giggled. Then he looked at his wife's happy, upturned face and hustled her to the door.

ARABESQUE

The Soul of Romance

Arabesque and BET.com
celebrate
ROMANCE WEEK
February 12 — 16, 2001

Join book lovers from across
the country in chats with
your favorite authors,
including:
- Donna Hill
- Rochelle Alers
- Marcia King-Gamble
- and other African-American
  best-selling authors!

Be sure to log on
www.BET.com
Pass the word and
create a buzz for
Romance Week on-line.